Broken Wand
....
A Novel
Denise Tyler

Copyright © 2020 Denise Tyler
All rights reserved.

Frontispiece

'No one entering this world can ever escape sadness. Each in turn must bear burdens, both rich and poor, and in turn, bid loved ones farewell. Each one must suffer that sad goodbye when loved ones come to that final moment, that each in turn must face. But for those who make this life a pledge to the human spirit, there comes the assurance of a memory that made life worth living.'

Extract from the Broken Wand memorial ceremony, conducted at the funeral of a magician in which a wand is broken to symbolise the loss of magical power, the first of which was conducted by the Society of American Magicians at Houdini's memorial service in 1926.

Broken Wand

Prologue

I try to raise my heavy head and struggle to open my eyes, slowly becoming aware that I'm on the floor of the stage in a crumpled heap; something's gone very wrong.

I press a hand to my clammy forehead and blink in an attempt to clear the blurriness. The heat from the stage lights feels intense and when I try to look up, they just become star shapes that fill my vision; I flinch away from them. Rubbing my eyes, I see a black smear on the heel of my hand which confuses me until I remember the eyeliner.

My breath is coming in short gasps and I fumble with my bow tie, trying to loosen it, frustration making its way to my trembling fingers that in desperation I wedge between collar and skin, trying to drive a space between them. I try to speak but my mouth is parched; my tongue sticking to the roof of my mouth, clinging to the ridges there.

I try to put my weight on one leg to push myself up but there are hands holding my arms with gentle pressure and a disembodied voice saying, 'Just stay put for a minute, just take it easy.' It's coming back to me in pieces: I remember walking out onto the stage, as if it was slow motion, feeling so tense, feeling angry, hot, sweating, but nothing after that. If I could just stop this buzzing in my head I could probably remember.

I only ever wanted to be a magician on the telly. I just wanted to feel that admiration, that respect, that belief people have in you that you really can do the things you're doing, that you're not just conning them; see childish awe on their faces because of me. I wanted to show them things that never should be possible by any other means than magic.

As the seconds pass the stage in front of me starts to come back into focus and the details are emerging, slowly, bit by bit, like a reel of film inside my head.

We'd walked out onto the stage together, she was next to me, full beam smile on, charm dialled right up. It was all going according to plan: the entry, her hand lightly on mine. Now, with a

Broken Wand

dreadful lucidity, all I can picture is Angelique, locked in a coffin, helpless.

The memory crystalises; looking down at her at that moment it was as though everything else faded away – no noise, no lights, no audience – just pure, white anger and her, looking back at me from the coffin. I saw in her eyes that she was trying desperately to work out what I was doing, what I was thinking. I saw her mouth moving as I swung the chainsaw in front of me and started it up, but I couldn't hear her through the fizzing in my head like interference, never mind the mechanical scream of the chainsaw as it kicked into life. Even the roar of my own pulse was deafening.

I moan as I remember gripping the chainsaw tightly, wielding it too close to Angelique's head. I remember the sudden shock of being out of control, but it was too late; I was leaning too far forwards, the weight of the chainsaw pulling me down and before I could stop it, I fell.

The last thing I remember are her wide blue eyes, locked on to mine, full to the brim with terror.

Broken Wand

1

Seven months earlier. Friday.

I'm out the back of the shop, having a quiet fag, enjoying the rare feeling of spring sunshine on my face, even if it has bounced off two slabs of office block to get to me. I can forget myself, for a few precious moments, my head tilted back to greet the warmth.

The management trainee comes out to find me, breaking the spell. I look sideways at her, saying nothing, one eye creased shut against the sting of smoke in it. I don't offer her a cigarette; I already know she disapproves just by the way she's looked down at my hand and pursed her lips. She's on the fast track this one, a graduate doing her three months here at this branch in the City because she'll end up working at HQ down the road with the kind of dicks we serve in here. I hope she knows they'll treat her like a lady (and not in a good way).

'Sorry to interrupt,' she says curtly, 'but there's a customer who wants his money back. Not sure I can authorise a refund?' I know she's hating having to ask me, the nearly forty-year-old with the straining shirt, the one who never really got past go, at least in her eyes. She probably assumes I didn't go to university and she'd be right. It's never been the rite of passage in our family that it most likely has been in hers.

'OK,' I sigh, 'be there in a sec.' As she turns back to the shop a breath of fresh air from the river reaches me having made its way along the corridors between the buildings, more of an exhausted wheeze by the time it gets here but welcome nonetheless. I never actually see the river when I'm at work; the Tube station is the other way and I just want to get here at the start of my shift then out again at the end of the day.

I look down at the almost finished cigarette pinched between my fingers and wish it could last longer. I keep meaning to give up the fags but well, you know. Luckily by the end of the day I reek of coffee and it just about drowns out the smell of the smoke; I only have a couple a day so it's not too bad. People still notice on the train though; I can tell. Half a minute in and they glance up from their phones to find the source and as I don't bother to change before I leave the shop, it usually doesn't take them too long. The City people next to me sniff and look away but that might not be because of the strong aroma of coffee and cigs. I still have my name badge on half the time, letting the combined commuters on their way back to Romford and beyond know that I am Mike Forester and I'm a branch manager in a high street coffee chain called Java Hut so probably not worthy of their attention.

What the badge doesn't say is that Mike couldn't give a shit about Java Hut and only planned to work there until his career as a TV magician took off. But it's been years. I'm still plugging away at the pub and club circuit with the magic act, the odd black tie do, but repeat bookings are getting thin on the ground and I'm wondering if I should just jack it in, make some proper money doing something else. It makes me sad to think of it, the time I've put into the act, but what choice do I have? If it was going to happen, it would have by now.

I'm thinking this as I take a last long, lung-warming drag on the fag. It's near the filter now and bonfire acrid. You know you're smoking when you squeeze that last bit out. You don't get that with vaping. I press my lips together and force the smoke down my nose, enjoying the familiar way it smarts. Feeling a chill, I glance up at the building opposite but instead of the sun I see clouds, big rolling grey ones reflected in the top few floors.

When you walk around here all you see are big glass buildings, the kind that stand with their legs apart, hands on hips, saying 'I'm a bloody great bank, come in if you think you're hard enough'. There's nothing subtle about this place. It's cold, soulless, money making.

I look across the alley at my reflection in the black mirror of the building opposite, but I can't hold my own stare for long. I drop my fag butt, grinding it into the concrete and go back into the shop, kicking at the box that's propping the heavy fire door open and letting it swing shut behind me, noticing that the last delivery hasn't been sorted out yet as I go past more boxes, stacked at a high lean. I'll have to get Carlos onto it after this.

A few steps and I'm behind the counter. The management trainee is already talking to some customers in Spanish. Of course. I muster a smile while she finishes and say:

'You speak Spanish?'

'There's a few countries on the bean belt where it'll come in handy,' she replies, 'not that I knew that when I started learning it at GCSE of course.'

'Of course,' I say with a quick smile. I can see she's trying to work out if I'm taking the piss. I'm actually wondering whether to ask her what the bean belt is. I take the plunge. She glances at me curiously, still trying to work out if I'm serious or not. She decides I am but judging by the way she gives her answer she can't quite believe that I don't know it's a belt of countries around the equator where most of the world's coffee beans come from. How did I not know that? Had they told me when I trained and I'd just forgotten, not thinking I'd be needing to know it for very long, if at all? Maybe they just bleated on about it now to graduate trainees to make them think they were playing fair with the planet and appeal to their greener natures.

I catch Cathy's amused eye over the trainee's shoulder. Cathy's one of my best employees, been here a few years now and made the staff board of glory more than a few times. One of those naff HR things where you stick a photo up with a gold star next to it where everyone can see it. The first time I took her photo for it she flicked a V-sign at me and stuck her pierced tongue out to make me laugh, then dared me to use it. 'Go on,' she'd said, 'let the inner Mike out.' Her expression now tells me all I need to know about her opinion of the trainee.

'So, who needs a refund?' I ask quickly, turning my attention back to the trainee.

'Gentleman at the end of the counter,' she says, inclining her sleek, blonde, high-ponytailed head towards him, all but dismissing me as she turns to the next customer. I glance over and of course it's a young City bloke in an expensive suit with the confidence to match and a similar looking mate in tow. He's looking fired up and glancing round the café to see who's noticed him. I immediately get the feeling that would clutch at me if I found myself perilously alone with the older boys at school in the nooks and crannies of the old 1950s building; my stomach tensing up, holding my breath and looking for a way out rather than facing them, like a trapped mouse in a roomful of cats, the odds always stacked against me. Sometimes they planned it, hunting in packs, sometimes just dumb luck they came across me; either way, it never ended well. I discreetly wipe my instantly warm palms on my trousers, swallowing the feeling down as far as it will go, reminding myself as I go over that company policy is a no-quibble refund.

'Can I help?' I ask briskly.

'Are you the manager?' he asks in an entitled voice, automatically assertive. He's a few inches taller than me and not afraid to stare me down.

'Yes, how can I help?' I repeat, being as civil as I can and resisting the urge to point at the name badge. I'm aware that the trainee is watching while she serves, as are Cathy and Carlos. We don't often get asked for refunds so there's a passing interest from them; anything to break the monotony of soya milk frothy coffee and packets of kale crisps.

'This is disgusting,' he says, 'I want my money back.' His eyes have hardened, he's challenging me silently to refuse. I see a muscle tense in his cheek, aware his friend is smirking next to him and from the corner of my eye I see Cathy look up at him briefly as she uses the till beside me, clocking his manner for later discussion no doubt. It feels like some kind of power kick, aimed at me. It's a young pup vs alpha male thing though I hardly think I'm an alpha male, just older. He's probably earning more than me already working round here. Despite thinking he's a wanker I quietly agree to refund him and process it at the till as quickly as I can, just wanting the situation to end.

The swaggering continues while I do the refund and his friend smirks some more, looking round to make sure people are still watching. Most of the customers are just looking away, pretending they haven't heard anything, embarrassed. It's not until they've left, laughing and puffed up, that I see he's drunk most of it. I throw the cup in the sink and head to my office. By office I mean a desk in a corner out the back but it's somewhere I can go to look at the orders and, in this case, try to put the humiliation to the back of my mind. I can feel the trainee's eyes on me as I walk through the door behind the counter. I wonder what she's thinking about this place now.

I stay in my office for the rest of the afternoon, coming out once to check the chiller cabinet shelves and fill in some orders. Cathy pops her head round as she finishes her shift to say she's off.

'You OK?' she asks, 'you look tired.'

'Yeah, I'm fine. Just – you know,' and I gesture with a nod of my head towards the shop.

'Yeah, I know,' she replies, and I know she means it. We have an understanding that we're both just here for the money so we do what we can to not take it too seriously. Without her, this place would be unbearable. 'But you did the right thing,' she goes on, 'and he was an epic prat so don't worry about it.' She cocks her head to one side and smiles broadly; I return it. It does take the sting out a bit, her saying that. 'Better go, school waits for no mum, especially the single ones,' she adds, flashing me another smile and a wave as she leaves.

A few hours later and it's my turn to leave, on the Tube again heading to lovely Romford and thanking whatever wants to be thanked that it's Friday. I'm not working this weekend. Carlos, my deputy, is on cover. I've got a show to get ready for tonight and I can forget all about coffee and idiots for a few hours. Thank God.

2

I turn up early at the pub in the heart of Romford and nod hello to Dave the landlord standing behind the time-worn dark-wood bar that spans the width of the room. It's still a bit light outside now the days are getting longer; the lowering sun hitting the old-fashioned engraved mirrors lining the wall behind the optics, which have been there so long they're fashionably retro. Bar stools with fraying tapestry seats cluster at odd intervals, some with people on them, alone with their thoughts and early evening pints. The pub missed out on the gastro movement and clings on to its ageing clientele with tar-stained fingernails, banking on them to fill the cavernous Victorian bar and drink more than one or two pints of warm beer a night.

I walk the length of the room, passing Dave whose expression never changes from vague as he wipes smoky-grey glasses with a grey tea towel. I can smell the bleach that has been sloshed about in the gents that afternoon as I make my way past them to the stairs, the lino treads tacky from decades of spilt drinks.

I go up and glance round the function room; the burgundy carpet worn shiny in places and the small bar with its shutter down, padlocked against thieves. Function chairs are stacked precariously against the wall, gold paint chipped and flaking, red velvet seats patchy at best with years of use. Weirdly, apart from the loos, it doesn't smell as bad as it should. Pub rooms used to smell sweet and sickly, musty and kicked, the scars of far too many chaotic nights evident in fading good looks. Now there's no smoky blue haze when the lights are dimmed, nothing to make it feel like a wannabe cabaret club and not just a tacky room above a pub in a time warp.

I put my suitcase of props on a dark wood table covered in white rings from an absence of beer mats. I can't bring myself to get warmed up yet or even go to the loo; I'll wait until the ammonia has died down a bit. So I sit on the edge of the table, hands folded in my lap, wondering how many will come this evening; wondering how many will nip out for a smoke halfway through, how many will check their phones and how often. Those little white screens are like a pin in my dreams. There are too many distractions now, it's hard to keep people's attention, no matter how hard I try.

My mind meanders back to the beginning of the dream when I was nine years old and wanted a Paul Daniels magic set for Christmas. It had been in the window of the toy shop in the high street for ages and I saw it when I walked to school and back, stopping whatever the weather to stare at it, the longing to own it almost more than I could bear. It had Paul Daniels, the magic man himself, on the front and all these yellow and pink stars round his smiling little face and a speech bubble that had 'Now that's magic!' in it. Pretty naff, now I think back on it, but I loved it. I wanted it, my own little bit of TV sparkle.

I loved the way Paul Daniels would explain the tricks on his show, I watched them closely and made notes because we couldn't afford a video recorder so I only had the one shot. I felt like he was talking to me alone, that his explanations were showing me the way. I practised the tricks with makeshift things in the house – ping pong balls, egg cups, hand towels, anything I could get my hands on.

And then one day I was walking to school in the rain just before the Christmas holidays and it wasn't in the shop window anymore. I was so gutted. I scanned the entire window, wishing and hoping it had just been moved. I went in on the way home and searched the shelves, but it had gone. And so, I thought, had my dreams.

Christmas Day came round and with it came Grandad. Under his arm was a box wrapped up in silvery paper with cartoon Santas all over it. I knew it was for me the second he came through the door, but Mum made me wait until he had his coat off and was sitting down with a pale ale before I could open it. It was taped but it came open easily and I got my first glimpse of it, a bright yellow 'P' on the corner of the box. My mouth dropped open and I tore at the rest of the paper. There it was – my very own magic set, my very own bit of awe. Grandad asked if I liked it and I mimicked Paul

Broken Wand

Daniels' high little voice and said, 'Not a lot – loads!' and laughed, hugging it to me, making everyone else laugh as well. I got up and thanked him, stepping on my dressing gown cord and nearly tripping in my excitement. I'd got a Southend United gloves and scarf set, which I'd put straight on with my pyjamas, but this, this was something else. Mum got up to go to the kitchen and Dad sat in his armchair, reading a book he had been given by Mum. Something to do with gardening organically, whatever that meant.

    I sat on the floor and cleared a space on the rug to get everything out of the box and showed each one to Grandad in turn. Playing cards, a length of rope, plastic balls, plastic cups and quite a few new things I didn't recognise. And a wand. An actual, bona fide wand. I tried it out, tapping the hearth, tapping the baubles on the tree, tapping my Dad's head which made Grandad laugh. I would have to practise, I thought to myself. Before school, after school – practise my socks off.

    And I did, I really did, but all it's come to is this – a ropey pub up the road in Romford. Other people who were around when I started out have moved on, done different things, created new acts or just given up but it seems I'm stuck here, in the twilight zone. Maybe it's time, last orders on this dream. Maybe it's time to put the suitcase in my parents' garage. Or sell what's in it. I could have a holiday. Maybe.

3

'I still can't believe this is your local,' Joanna had said to Angelique as they made their way to one end of the bar, Joanna carrying the drinks. Angelique had spotted a small, round table in the corner and sat down on the low stool, arranging her bag on the floor beside her, noticing with an inward grimace the patches of dark grey gum that were so trodden in they were part of the carpet, interspersed with the odd ancient cigarette burn.

'Yes, well,' she'd muttered for Joanna's ears only, 'as soon as I upgrade to a consultant's salary I'll be able to live in Shoreditch as well as work there. Until then, Romford it is.' She'd raised an eyebrow along with her drink to clink with Joanna's and taken a much appreciated first sip, glancing quickly round to see how many people were staring. Not too many and they'd looked away when she caught their eye, the usual pattern. She'd resigned herself to the never-ending curiosity years ago, accepting it had made it less intrusive, even if every glance was a reminder of her difference.

'I feel like someone's about to step to the piano and tinkle the ivories for a good old sing-song,' Joanna had commented sarcastically as she cast her eyes round the long bar. The barman idly twisted a glass in a grubby tea towel while he watched the TV on the wall in the opposite corner as it noiselessly showed a football match. The door at the other end of the pub had swung open, the frosted glass dully reflecting the bar lights before it closed with a well sprung thud behind a man in a suit carrying a suitcase. He'd nodded in recognition to the barman with a forced smile.

'Look,' Joanna said, 'looks like they do B&B. Not sure I'd take the chance personally, must have been a fair few murders round here in the past, you know, in the good old days.'

'I think you're getting a bit carried away there Joanna,' Angelique had cautioned, 'he looks like the magician on that poster over there; must be doing a show tonight.'

Joanna's face had instantly lit up.

'Oh, let's go. That has to be seen if only as a sociological study. Him, the audience, modern society and its urban gatherings.'

The magician had made his way past them and opened the door to the stairwell, lost in his own thoughts, the large suitcase banging into the door frame as he swung round to the stairs.

Angelique had watched him over Joanna's shoulder as he went past and she was struck by something about him that seemed familiar; maybe it was the way he walked, trying not to be seen, or maybe it was the way that his thoughts were so overbearing he didn't seem to be there at all, he was so lost in them. Angelique had not only sensed it as he made his way past but recognised it as clearly as if it was her walking down that long bar, trying not to attract attention out of habit, used to hugging the sides of rooms and avoiding eye contact, never quite off guard but hoping to pass by unseen. She knew all of this; it was part of her too.

'What's that look?' Joanna had asked as she watched Angelique's face.

'What look?' Angelique had snapped back to the present, aware of her friend's scrutiny.

'That one just then when he walked past,' Joanna said, nodding her head towards the stairs, 'seen him before?'

'No, I – no I don't think so. Maybe around, you know.' Joanna had glanced at her again and Angelique had avoided making eye contact as she took a deliberate sip of her drink, aware that even though it was fleeting, something deep in him had chimed with something in her.

More people had started to come into the bar, more pints were poured and conversations started. One or two glances had come their way, but the football and their mates were more important. Eventually, people had started to make their way up the stairs and Angelique and Joanna joined them, finding a space at the back of the room where they could sit together, though it hadn't been exactly packed. The barman had switched the room lights off, nodding at the magician over the audience's heads as he went back down the stairs.

'Showtime…' Joanna had stage whispered as she gave a little

Broken Wand

jazz hands wave in front of them.

Angelique had become thoughtful as she watched the show. She scrutinised the tricks and saw that they were performed with care and skill as she'd tried to work them out, delighted when she couldn't. But still something had nagged at her, something more that she couldn't quite put her finger on. Whenever his gaze had rested on the audience, it was as if he didn't really want a reaction, like he didn't really care if they applauded or not. He wanted their attention but not to the point of personal contact; something stopped him just short of that. He had given the audience cues when he produced the card someone had chosen, so they clapped in the right place, or when something disappeared into thin air and reappeared from under someone's chair. But it quickly became clear there was an absence, that he wasn't giving it his all and the audience had been confused by him, almost as much as he seemed to be by himself.

She'd found herself wondering what had happened to make him fall out of love with it or if he had simply given in to boredom. Slowly an idea had formed in her mind.

Broken Wand

4

Twenty minutes into the act and I'm not winning them over. I can't quite see to the back where the room lights are off, but I think it's about two-thirds full. There are two lights on me on this tiny stage, just a couple of black blocks all of twelve inches high. I can see enough to tell they're not bored yet, but it won't be long; I know the signs by now. They've gone from a general feeling of expectation to applauding when I give them the obvious open arms 'ta-da' type of cue, glancing at each other and clapping a few times anyway because they can see I'm dying on my feet and they feel sorry for me. It's the pity claps that sting the most.

I've given up trying harder these days, it just makes it that little bit more desperate. So, I go through the motions, asking someone to sign that day's newspaper across the front page before folding and tearing it up in front of them, making sure it rips nice and loudly, scrunching the pages. I ask someone in the front row to agree it's destroyed before I unfold it, shaking it out like twisted laundry, complete again with the signature verified by the man who wrote it. A ripple of applause follows as I hold the paper up triumphantly in front of my face so they can't see me not smiling.

I place a small table in the middle of the stage and borrow four coins from a lady in the front row. I lay out a handkerchief on the table and put the coins on the corners before taking two squares of card, one red and one yellow, and start covering the coins and hiding them and moving them around, at one point making it seem as if they were coming through the handkerchief from underneath to appear beneath the cards. I ask the lady to point out where her money is and of course, she's wrong each time. Eventually I make them all disappear and while they're amused, they're underwhelmed, and I wish that I could make myself disappear; anything but have to go through the agony of finishing the act.

There's a guy watching at the front who has his legs stuck out in front of him, crossed at the ankles, slouching down a bit with his arms folded across his chest; one of that breed that's determined

Broken Wand

not to be impressed. He never claps and just smirks at each trick I do. I can see his phone sticking out of the top of his back pocket and think briefly about asking to borrow it, wrapping it in a hanky and then smashing it with a hammer, just so I can see his face when he understands that's all I'm going to do. Instead, I borrow a £20 note off him and turn it into a fiver just by folding it into a tiny square and then unfolding it. People are impressed by that and when I offer it back to him, he waves me away and asks for his £20. I tell him deadpan that I haven't learnt that bit yet and for a second I'm tempted to stick to it, but I smile and of course I turn it back to a £20 and even he's forced to applaud a bit.

I do a few more of the close-up 'spot me doing it if you can' tricks and ask a guy further along the front row to pick a card that I make appear unexpectedly in his shirt pocket at the end of the trick. His girlfriend is ecstatic, possibly pissed, and laughs like a drain, totally out of proportion with how impressive the trick is, even I can see that.

Then I try something bigger to finish on, hoping they'll appreciate the effort. I ask for a volunteer who's with a friend that can phone them and while she's standing next to me, I ask her to inspect a black bin bag, which I turn inside out to show the rest of the audience that it's empty. I ask for her phone and place it in the bag before blowing it up like a balloon, asking her to tie the neck of the bag tightly with string. Putting it on the small table, it lolls to one side and I ask her friend to phone her, so everyone knows her phone is still in there. When it finishes ringing, she confirms it's her phone. So far so good. I walk past her to fetch a pair of scissors which I brandish above my head before handing them to her and ask her to cut the top of the bag off, just below the string, and take her phone out. Her face falls when she sees it's not there; she giggles at me and shakes her head. There's a ripple of interest from the audience. I ask her friend to phone her again and this time the ringtone comes from the back pocket of her jeans, where her phone is now.

'Is that your phone?' I ask triumphantly and she laughs as she confirms it is. I usher her back to her seat, motioning for the audience to applaud her. She giggles with her friend as they inspect her phone, checking for the missed call, and I take a bow and thank them for coming.

I've barely finished speaking when they start to gather themselves to leave. The room empties pretty quickly as some of the blokes nearer the back have sidled off downstairs to watch the footy anyway. I pack up and head downstairs to pick up my takings from Dave. It's smaller than last time.

'See you in a month then,' I say as I turn to leave.

'Yeah, about that,' Dave begins, a hesitant tone to his voice telling me this isn't going to be an easy conversation. 'We're just not getting the people in for you Mike,' he continues, almost apologetically, as though it's his fault no one is coming. 'I think it's best if we give it a rest for a bit and see about doing something later in the year, round Christmas maybe. I've got to shake things up a bit according to the brewery, get my figures up. Sorry mate, it's not easy.' He doesn't make it clear if it's not easy letting me go or if it's not easy getting his figures up. Either way I'm toast.

'Right. Yeah, no problem,' I say, smiling and waving a hand in front of me as if shooing the rejection away like a fly, trying to hide my embarrassment by making it easier for him. 'I get it, really. I know it's hard. I'll stay in touch then,' I say, though we both know I won't. He offers me a pint as a friendly gesture, but I'd rather get home.

5

As soon as the show finished, Joanna and Angelique shuffled with everyone else down the narrow staircase to the bar where they'd left by the closest door, not keen to take up the offer of last orders.

'Well, that was fun,' Joanna had said as she pulled her jacket on against the chilly night, before adding sarcastically, 'let's do it again, really REALLY soon. Going to the Tube?' When Angelique didn't respond, she'd glanced down at her, saying: 'You've gone a bit thoughtful.'

'Oh, sorry no, just a bit tired, that's all,' Angelique answered, pulling her bag straps higher on to her shoulder.

'You sure?' Joanna pushed, 'I know that look. What are you hatching?' she'd asked as they started to walk away from the pub.

'I've got an idea, that's all. About magic.'

'Magic? What about it? New hobby?' Joanna had suggested.

'Wondering how easy it would be to create a new star,' Angelique had replied, causing Joanna to stop and turn to her.

'With him?' she'd said, pointing back to the pub, incredulous. 'Are you serious? You've had some good ideas in your time but that? That isn't one of them,' she'd added emphatically.

'But don't you see?' Angelique had countered, 'that's where the challenge would be, the challenge and the reward. If I could do that, get him noticed, I'd get myself noticed.' They'd walked on again, pulling their coats around them against the evening chill, each staring at the pavement for a few steps.

'And if we don't get him noticed – which is more likely,' Joanna had eventually said, carefully, 'complete waste of time and energy. Not too sure what you think you see in him but why don't you sleep on it. I think you'll see things differently in the morning. That's probably just the gin and the bright lights of Romford talking.'

'Yes, OK,' Angelique had replied, noting the 'we' Joanna had just dropped in but choosing to ignore it for now. 'I'll see.'

Angelique knew better than to go into too much detail with Joanna too soon, certainly not to talk about what she thought she saw, or saw was missing, in the magician. She had seen Joanna hijack projects before, worm her way in until no one dared breathe let alone make a decision without checking with her first. She'd wait until things moved on, if they did, before she discussed it too much with her.

She wanted to keep it to herself, to formulate a plan of her own. Something felt different about this and there was, after all, plenty of time to involve Joanna later, if at all.

6

The cash from the pub isn't in my pocket for long; I pick up a curry, exchanging a few words with the guy behind the counter as I sit on the chair by the door.

Glancing round the restaurant, I catch the eye of a woman who was at the pub. She's looking at me and whispers something conspiratorially to her friends, who turn to look at me before turning back to the table and giggling. I'm grateful that the curry arrives as quickly as it does.

Standing outside the front door of my flat I put the suitcase and the curry down to forage about for my key. The light on the landing is really bright and I'm glad to get inside, wedging the door with my foot while I retrieve the bags. The strip light in the kitchen flickers and makes a noise like something small trapped inside is tapping on the tube to get my attention. I really should update the place and put spotlights in but well, money, and it's only rented. I eat in silence and twenty minutes later the remains of the curry are congealing in front of me. And that's it. The meal is finished and I have nothing to do now except leave the plate in the sink because there's no one to mind if I do.

I sit back in my chair and look down the hall to the front door; I can see the suitcase sitting there. Odd to think that everything I ever really wanted is contained in it and all I can think to do right now is toss it in a skip. If I'd had more time, if I hadn't become bogged down in the coffee shop, if if if if if.

I stand up quickly, scraping the chair on the floor, hoping that the suddenness of it will jolt me out of my thoughts. I toss the plate in the sink and run the tap over it too fast and it sprays me, making me swear and jump back a little. The cartons I press down into the bin upside down so I can force another day out of it. 'Right,' I mutter, leaving the kitchen and its sprayed worktop to fend for itself. I grab my laptop and flop onto the sofa, impatiently putting in passwords to get online. The Wi-Fi is frustratingly slow. But I'm soon checking out magic props for sale on a couple of the marketplace sites and I make my way round them, wondering how to disable all the bloody ads that pop up everywhere. Most of the props I see are pretty tacky and basic. My stuff would fetch good money; I've built it up carefully over the years. Some of them were second hand when I bought them so they've seen better days but I've looked after them and anyway, a prop is only as good as the magician using it. I try and work out what you have to do to sell stuff: take pictures, put them on your laptop, upload them onto this site, create a profile… and it all seems like too much trouble. I think I'll stick an ad in the local paper after the weekend.

I pause, staring at the screen, and my inactivity lets my mind wander aimlessly back to self-pity. A familiar, well-worn thought circles me like a bird of prey, biding its time, knowing it has me firmly in its sights: maybe I would have made it by now if Jenny was still around. She always encouraged me, came to my shows and led the applause and I always wanted to do it for her; she made it worthwhile, she was proud of me.

I glance at the picture of me and her on the shelf above the TV and I feel a familiar ache begin to flex its muscles. When she died it was like everything shifted slightly sideways, that I'd lost a compass point somewhere inside me and I have never yet been able to find my way back. No amount of magic was going to help heal that wound but I carried on, treading magic water and hoping that somehow the spark would come back if I just gave it time. No one has ever come along to replace her so who am I doing it for?

Stopping the magic act feels like giving up but for the first time it feels like a relief as well. My mind's made up; it's time for a fresh start.

7

I sit at the small kitchen table and wallow in the thought that I don't have to get on the Tube; that I can sit like this all day if I want to, enjoying not going to work on a Saturday. I can just sit here in a t-shirt and boxers, drinking tea and trying to wake up, though I do regret last night's late curry which is still making its presence felt.

I rub my eyes and head, slowly feeling the sleepiness lifting as the tea and white-blue spring daylight begin to pick me up. Saturday morning is always a bit drained after a show but it's worse when I have to work. It's just past nine and I haven't moved yet, the silence in the flat being gentle with me, when the landline rings; its tinny version of something classical shredding the peace. I wince and turn my head in annoyance but make no move to answer it. I'll have to get it cut off when I sell my stuff, no point paying for it even if it is in with the TV package.

I turn my head away and drink more tea until it rings out and I listen to the message being left, expecting it to be my parents, the only other people who still call it. But it isn't.

'Hi, my name's Angelique and I saw your magic show last night at the Lion. Hope you don't mind but the landlord gave me this number. I wonder if we could meet up as I have an idea to run by you that you might be interested in.' She left her number and rang off. I'd forgotten Dave the landlord has this number; I've only ever given it out for bookings and it was on my original business cards years ago. I wasn't expecting this and I remember that I made a decision last night, that this isn't supposed to be happening anymore.

I replay the message and it's clearer this time round. It doesn't sound like a booking; 'an idea to run by you', she said. A flicker of interest registers in me.

I'm mulling this over and staring out of the window when the deciding thought pops into my head. You need the money, it says, and you have an empty calendar. I decide it wouldn't hurt to find out what she wants, so I call her back. We arrange to meet in a coffee shop in the high street at two.

Wandering into the bedroom I glance in the mirror at the paunch filling out my t-shirt, my unshaven face and my thinning hair. Nearly forty. I'm gripped with a sensation of doubt as I look at myself: who rings people out of the blue like that? More to the point, who rings me? It can't be anything serious – I think about cancelling but still something won't let me; I can't be rude like that even if I don't know her and I'm overtaken by the need to make an effort, to get ready, to at least show her that I'm professional off stage as well as on and underneath it all, glad for something to do. One last time. Then I'll quit.

By half past one things have been improved with a shower, a shirt, a shave and toast and I feel a bit more confident, maybe even a little bit hopeful that it wasn't a booking at all but something more personal. My mind flicks back to the pub last night; there had been a good-looking redhead at the bar downstairs, tight dress and high heels, who glanced at me when I came out; maybe it's her.

The thought grows on me and I glance at the photo on the shelves of me and Jenny, wondering if she knows what I'm thinking, trying not to feel guilty. Maybe things are looking up but it won't change my mind; I'm still selling my stuff.

Broken Wand

8

I get to the café five minutes early and order tea because the thought of coffee on my day off just doesn't work for me. I'm glad I put a coat on as the spring weather is all blue skies and sunshine but colder for it; it's helped to clear my head at least.

Sitting at a table in the window, I stare out at the grinding traffic and shopping-weary pedestrians while absently fiddling with my teaspoon. When I lose interest I note things around the café; a couple of tables uncleared, sugar and napkin dispensers untidy, staff unwilling to interrupt their chat to sort it out. Still a few tables busy though and there are teens hanging out on the sofas, probably been there a few hours already. I check my watch; she should be here soon. Nerves – or is it excitement? – flash through me like a static shock and I take a deep breath, rubbing my hands together above my tea.

The door opens, letting the noise of the traffic in, and I glance over. A young woman walks in, trendily dressed in black trousers, a jumper and a denim jacket, her hair a really light blonde, poker straight; she looks confident as she goes to the counter, seemingly oblivious to the curious stares that follow her, mine included. Is it 'dwarf' or 'little people' now? I'm sure I've heard both. I look away and think back to Java Hut company policy, idly trying to remember the last minorities advisory from HR as I stare out the window but I can't even remember when that was, let alone the details. I make a mental note to check on Monday.

The teens are nudging each other and smirking, not trying too hard to hide their amusement. One even sneaks a picture of her on their phone, not quite masking it. I don't bother saying anything but look out the window again and back at the door; she should be here soon. I'll pay for her coffee, that should make a good first impression. I'm thinking about this when a voice says:

'It's Mike, right?' I look round, surprised as I've been here a while and no one new has come in. I find myself looking at the palest blue eyes I've ever seen and it's her, the small blonde lady.

Broken Wand

I'm caught out, surprised and then try not to be. As I sit there mute, she introduces herself.

'It's Angelique, we spoke on the phone this morning,' she says, holding out a hand which I briefly shake but hardly feel, 'mind if I sit down?' I nod and mutter 'yeah of course', indicating the chair opposite and shuffling in my seat a bit, trying hard not to catch anyone's eye, conscious that we've got everyone's attention now.

I know what this must look like because it ticks all the boxes – a blind date, a blind date that couldn't have been more blind. What the hell, why didn't she say? Don't be stupid, I berate myself, what would she say? "You'll know it's me, I'm the dwarf." Oh God, we really don't say that, do we? But it's OK, I'm only thinking it, is that still bad? I glance round the room and try to claw the situation back.

'So, hi,' I say, 'you wanted to talk about the act. How can I help?' I'm instantly aware that I'm talking with a louder than usual voice, instantly feeling like an idiot. I lace my fingers together in front of me and start tapping my thumbs together. She gives me a half smile full of recognition.

'You don't have to shout,' she says patiently, 'but then you know that.' She says this so definitely that it takes me off guard but at the same time, puts me at ease. I smile by way of an apology. 'They don't,' she goes on, indicating the girls behind the counter, 'bless them. They can't quite get to grips with the fact that I'm short, not deaf or even stupid. Unless they think I can't hear them way up there on their ridiculous high heels. They can cause quite nasty injuries, high heels. Surely not practical for café work. Not to mention recent studies which suggest they may actually alter the muscle structure in and around the ankle. And that's got to hurt eventually. I don't bother with them myself.' I'm conscious of my eyebrows rising. She says all this so casually, almost as if she's a bit bored by having to explain it again. Then she looks me straight in the eye and says, 'Are you going to walk out? Only you looked like you might want to just now so here's your chance to do so, though I would add that you'll miss my proposal and I think that would be a shame.'

Broken Wand

'Er, no, I'm not going anywhere,' is all I can muster, hands spread and smiling like an idiot in an attempt to reassure her that I'm not the idiot I may have at first seemed.

Just then the waitress comes over and puts Angelique's drink down in front of her, herbal tea by the smell of it. The waitress looks down at her and then me before unsubtly spending a bit of time at the table right beside us, noisily stacking cups on plates before glancing at us again as she heads back to the counter. We both wait for her to leave. Angelique picks up where she left off.

'I'll try and be brief. I saw your show at the pub last night – I was at the back with a friend in case you're wondering how you missed me – and while you looked like you couldn't wait to get off the stage, I was impressed with your magic set. Basic, but skilful.' I do a sort of snort laugh at this in my surprise and draw breath to speak but she cuts me off with a raised hand. 'Let me finish. I would like to work with you.'

'With me?' I ask, my eyes widening in surprise. 'How? I mean, in what way?' I hadn't expected this; at best I'd hoped for a final gig to do, certainly not this.

'I looked you up online, or tried to,' she goes on, 'and was pretty surprised to find you don't have a web presence at all. Why is that?'

'Well, I...' I stumble, blinking rapidly while I try to think of a plausible answer, 'I never really had time to, I mean, there's the day job and –'

'No excuse,' she cuts in, 'super-easy and quick to build, you can get an off-the-shelf version up in minutes. I can do that for you – create a presence that gets you out there.' Now it's my turn to hesitate.

'Did you see how few people were in the pub last night?' I ask. I don't doubt she can do what she says she can, but I'm not sure she can do it with me. 'Nobody's interested in this kind of magic anymore. It's all about making cards appear out of people's backsides and getting people to believe they can teleport.' I'm beginning to feel that I may be wasting my time. 'Is this a piss-take?' I demand, 'are you being filmed?' I look quickly round the café but no one is paying us any attention.

'No,' she says calmly, unruffled by my outburst, 'I'm serious. I think it just needs the right audience and tweaks. I had a scoot round the internet and you're right, all the current big stuff is young, big, attention seeking. I think if we do it the right way, people would welcome a bit of warmth and charm. With an update, of course.' She stops talking and waits for me to reply but I can't for the life of me decide what to think. I've gone blank; I'm just staring.

She leans forward, palms down on the table. 'Look, I understand social media; I know how to harness it, I know how to give people what they want and what they don't yet know they want. It's what I do for a living. Trust me, if you decide that you're willing to give it a go we can start with tweaking some of your tricks, make them quirky, unique to you, work out the best way to film them, build a new act and go from there.' She's warming to her theme and her enthusiasm glints in her eyes. 'We'll go straight to internet, build our audience and make sure we're noticed by mainstream online channels as soon as we have a substantial following, which won't be long with me doing it.' I'm still staring. I still don't know what to think.

She fixes me with an intense look and I notice again how blue her eyes are. Really light blue, almost white-blue, like the pale spring sky outside. 'Don't take this the wrong way,' she says, 'but I can't see that you've a lot to lose if you really feel no one wants to use you anymore.' I lower my eyes in a confusion of embarrassment and self-recognition. She's right, of course. Just last night I was going to put my gear up for sale; I really don't have anything to lose. And there's something about the way she speaks, so confident, so self-assured, that makes me think she knows exactly what she's doing. I can't help thinking that she feels familiar to me – not in a physical sense, I know I've never met her – but like something just out of reach, a sense of a dream that's faded on waking.

'Look,' I begin, calmer now, 'it sounds interesting but I don't know much about the internet and I don't have a lot of money to go spending on something like this. How would we film it? How would you go about getting it online?'

'I'll take care of all of that. The company I work for in Shoreditch has access to all the latest market reports on platforms and trends.'

'But I can't afford that.'

'You won't have to pay, they won't know anything about it. I'd be doing this in my own time, to prove a point in a way. Just taking a bit of knowledge home with me, that's all.'

'To prove a point?' I echo, feeling a bit uneasy about where this is going. 'Is this some sort of bet with someone?'

'No, no; nothing like that,' she says, dismissing the idea with a wave of her hand, 'I just want to start doing things in my own way and this would be a good opportunity to do that. Look, I'll send you the company's details so you can have a look and see the kind of thing we do currently. I'd be taking you above and beyond that. In a nutshell, we specialise in optimising brands on the internet via social media, increasing visibility by utilising web platforms, that sort of thing.'

'Oh,' I nod, trying to keep up, 'well, it sounds good. But what about television? Would that be an option?'

'Not sure why you'd want to do telly in this day and age; internet stars make way more money and online streaming channels have much bigger audiences in a lot more territories.' I smile at her and she half smiles back. She knows I don't have a clue. She adds: 'You'd be the lead of course, I'd have a steep learning curve into the world of magic.' She sips her tea, while all this information settles into my brain like leaves falling on the surface of a still pond. 'So what do you think?' she asks eventually, 'will you at least give it some thought?' I shrug and say yes, I'll think about it, like I would say anything else. 'Great!' she says, 'You've got my number so you can give me a call when you decide you want to be famous.' She smiles properly now, like she means it and before I can stop myself I smile back like I mean it too.

At home there's a message on the answering machine from my

Broken Wand

parents, reminding me about Sunday lunch at theirs tomorrow. As if I could forget. As if I would have other plans.

9

Angelique and Joanna walked along a row of converted red brick railway arches, their destination a small gathering of people clustered in a puddle of light that spilled from an art gallery; animated chatter carrying across the early evening chill.

'Remind me again,' Angelique asked, 'who the artist is?'

'Dougie Neville. Made a big splash with his grad show at Glasgow Art School last summer,' Joanna said off-handedly, 'a 'buy now before the prices go through the roof' sort of splash, you know, innovative stuff like upside down cash tills nailed to the ceiling with receipts hanging down out of them like streamers, that sort of thing,' she explained.

'Ah,' Angelique replied, smiling to herself as she caught Joanna's unimpressed, sarcastic tone, 'and how do we know him?'

'We don't. We know Angie who knows Terry who got us on the list through his current boyfriend.'

They joined the short queue and gave their names to a young woman dressed entirely in black with wide trousers that skimmed her ankles, silver grey hair contrasting beautifully with her dark complexion. She scanned her iPad and ticked their names with a touch, crouching down briefly to Angelique to murmur a welcome and indicate a table of drinks with a waft of her hand before turning to the next people in the queue.

The gallery wasn't too full yet and the white, high-arched brick ceiling made it feel spacious, naked fluorescent tubes hanging obliquely from taut wires giving a stark, bright light. They strolled in silence for the first few pieces, taking them in and moving in shoal like coordination with the other guests.

'Deliberate statement or just skint - what do you reckon?' Joanna asked, indicating the old and battered torches and camping lamps hung from wall brackets to illuminate the art. Angelique didn't feel the need to reply. Joanna rarely went to an event involving art or literature without having to make at least one overly loud and potentially controversial comment and she justified it by saying she would never be taken in by pretentiousness. Angelique had learnt over time not to bite; act nonchalant and keep a straight face and hopefully people wouldn't think you shared the opinion.

It didn't take long to look at everything at the show and after Joanna had helped herself to another drink they moved to the front of the space to chat and let other people move round.

'No chairs,' Joanna pointed out as she sat on the floor near the wall while Angelique stayed standing, drawing a few glances. They were silent for a few moments, watching the other guests mingle and chat, some more than others were looking around the gallery to see who they should meet next. The atmosphere grew as the volume of the conversations increased and people greeted each other like long lost relatives.

'So I met the magician for a coffee today,' Angelique said, as offhandedly as she could, 'you know, from the pub last night?'

'Oh?' Joanna replied, as much a question as a statement of surprise. 'Quick work; you didn't tell me you were meeting him?'

'Telling you now. Anyway, spur of the moment really; I called him this morning.'

'And he turned up?'

'Of course he did,' Angelique said with a hint of impatience in her voice. Joanna raised her eyebrows. 'Oh come on, I knew he'd come,' Angelique responded, 'he had a look about him at the pub that said 'someone get me out of this'. I knew if I said I had a proposition for him he'd bite.'

'Maybe he did. Personally I just thought he looked a bit dull, but if you want to read more into it, that's up to you,' Joanna replied, taking a large mouthful of her wine. 'So how did it go today then? What exactly did you two find to chat about?'

'Well when I got in last night after seeing him at the pub I tried to find him online. Nothing, not a scrap of info. So the question bubbling away in my brain was how easily could something so raw be transformed into a trend in its own right? I mean you do it with ideas and think tank stuff all the time so how hard can it be?' she added, slyly.

Broken Wand

'Not entirely sure you can directly compare the two,' Joanna began, choosing to ignore the barb. 'I manipulate carefully targeted individual minds to make sure they swallow a particular way of thinking, usually sweetened with something for their own gain so we get a PR'able result for the greater good; you manipulate minds to make people buy in to stuff they don't really need but 'discover' they can't do without and then remain loyal to. I mean, look at this room. Full of people who have been led down a shiny new trendy alleyway into thinking they're being different until they all look and think the same,' Joanna said as she waved a vague arm at the gathering. Angelique paused to take in the room, pondering this.

'So my challenge then,' Angelique said eventually, 'is to make sure I create a unique individual that goes against the flow. Self-made social media stars are everywhere, literally globally, far outreaching anything television could do for them in the same time span. That's a market I want to explore.'

'And how do you plan to do that with a pub magician, my far sighted friend?'

'Forget what he does for a minute,' Angelique said, warming to her theme. 'I'm planning to take a normal person and make them into a solid online phenomenon from a standing start. And what if I make it really hard for myself and pick a person doing something that needs a reboot in its own right; something that with a bit of life breathed into it could be reinvented for a new audience today by tapping in to the way it used to be.' She pointed away to her right to emphasise her point before carrying on. ' I could create a slow magic movement; analogue magic in a digital world. If I can cut through all the online noise with that, I can do anything.' She spread her arms wide, her wine dangerously close to swirling out of its glass.

'And you seriously think that's doable?' Joanna replied, less convinced.

'Yes. I think so. Things move so fast in the online world, you just have to be faster. You're always looking for the next opportunity to get your client in front of the right audience, be aware of the next apps and software before they're even launched and when they do, get a bigger following than Ed Sheeran in as short a space of time as possible. I mean Christ, if he can do it I know I can. And if I can do it with this guy, people will sit up and take notice.'

'Yes, I expect they will,' said Joanna, 'one way or another. But I thought you liked it where you're working; haven't you got them eating out of your hand?'

'I wouldn't put it quite like that,' Angelique bristled. 'I like working in this field, I like being one of the people to predict and create the future online but you know I've got my eye on consultancy in a couple of years.' Angelique paused for a moment, taking in the room again, the way people were discussing the art and gesticulating to make their points before commenting: 'People think all this stuff is fresh and new and organic but it isn't. It's people like me making them think that it is, putting ever more tempting morsels on the already groaning internet buffet. They don't know if they're getting Harrods food hall or Iceland but they swallow it anyway.'

'Nice,' Joanna said, with a small snort of laughter. 'Anyway, what do you think your Mum will think? I mean, she's always advocated a steady job with a stable income; it was bad enough when you decided to go in to the wonderful world of online marketing with your Oxford first, I can't see her backing plans to be a consultant. Bit dicey on the steady income front, especially when you're setting up.'

'You don't have to hide behind my mother to make your point, Joanna,' Angelique replied carefully, a hint of a warning in her voice, 'I know perfectly well what she'll think. I'll tell her when I'm ready.' Joanna played with her wine glass, spinning it gently by the stem, enjoying having made her point.

'Well, if it's what you want, good luck with it. Are you going to tell work?'

'No, not yet. Strictly personal. Bit of fun in my own time. For me.' She added, hoping Joanna took the point that it was her project and hers alone. 'If it doesn't work, it doesn't work but you don't know 'til you try.' Angelique said, as lightly as she could.

'True,' Joanna agreed. 'So what's next then with this .. What's his name again?'

'Mike.'

'Mike the magic man from Romford. Dreamy.' Joanna rolled her eyes and took another large sip of wine so she wouldn't have to make eye contact with Angelique.

'He's thinking my proposal over, going to give me a call if he thinks it would work.'

'Do you think he will?' Joanna asked.

'Pretty sure I can guarantee it's the shiniest piece of silver to cross his palm in years so yes, I expect he will,' Angelique said, looking intently at Joanna to let her know the subject was closed.

'OK, Madame Angelique, I'll take your word for it. I look forward to seeing this take off.' And she raised her glass to Angelique before draining it.

10

I quickly enter Mum and Dad's hallway, shaking the rain off my jacket as I do. It's a heavy enough shower to have got me wet just coming from the road to the house. I can hear voices and stand still for a second or two while I figure out who it is. I'm not much of a one for parties but it's Sunday lunch in my honour so I can't really make excuses.

I find a coat hook to hang mine on and sit on the stairs to put on the slippers Mum keeps for me under the hall stand. The living room is bright as all the lights are on and music softly spills from the record player, notes from a jazz clarinet drifting around. Dad resolutely refuses to give up his record player and keeps his vinyl in mint condition in the mistaken belief it'll be worth a fortune one day.

'Here he is!' says Dad. 'The birthday boy.' He stands and extends an arm to usher me in to the middle of the room. The neighbours from across the street, Ian and Kath Peterson, are arranged on the sofa. I went to school with their daughter, Amanda. No doubt I am in for several minutes of having to enthuse about what she's up to and how many kids she's managed to produce since I last saw them. She'd seemed hell bent on having a barn full of children and when she was 15 said to anyone that would listen that she didn't see the point of school when she really wanted to live on a farm, be a housewife and raise kids. She'd married a farmer that she'd met at an agricultural show so who knows, maybe she actually has filled a barn by now.

'Look Mike, the Petersons brought you a balloon.' Dad has that unique holiday camp entertainer expression on his face that is overly gleeful and at the same time embarrassed at having to enthuse about something that clearly makes him uncomfortable. We look at the dining table set for five people at the other end of the knocked through living room where a large, gently swaying foil balloon with a holographic 40 emblazoned on it is tied to the back of the chair at the head of the table. 'Had to tie it to the chair, kept getting muddled up in the light fitting,' Dad explains. I glance up at the round ceramic light fitting that looks like an upturned pasta bowl with flowers painted on it.

'Well at least I know where I'm sitting for tea unless any of you is a time traveller,' I say, by way of a witty reply. Dad laughs a bit too loudly.

I'd been trying to avoid this, being forty. It's actually not until Tuesday and this was just supposed to be Sunday lunch to celebrate with my parents but they might have got a bit carried away and mentioned it to the Petersons. Or they invited themselves because they'd always known when my birthday is, which is more likely.

'Drink son?'

'Yes, thanks, I'll have a beer. Where's Mum?'

'Out in the kitchen, you know, getting things ready. I'll get your beer.'

I sit down in an armchair opposite the Petersons, smiling at them and helping myself to a few peanuts from the dish on the coffee table.

Mum appears in the kitchen doorway, a big smile on her face and the most flower covered dress I have ever seen on the rest of her. She sees me look at it and self-consciously explains that it isn't every day your son is forty so a new dress was hardly an extravagance. Dad inches round her and hands me my beer, poured in to a glass; we're going to be posh today.

'I remember spending weeks looking for something special when Amanda got married,' Mrs Peterson chimes in again, 'but then weddings are quite special, aren't they,' she adds, smiling brightly at Mum before turning to me. 'When are you going to find that special someone Mike? Don't keep your Mum and Dad waiting too much longer or they'll give up hope!' and she laughs a high tinkling laugh and rocks forwards on the sofa. Mum laughs too but I can see the barb has hit its' target and I can think of nothing to say to take the sting away because basically Mrs Peterson has hit the nail on the head and she knows it. I smile at Mum and tell her how lovely she looks.

Broken Wand

'Yes, Ruth, you do; you look lovely,' Mr Peterson says and he smiles at her, raising his glass an inch or so in salute. Mum blushes ever so lightly, smooths her skirt and deftly changes the subject.

'Lunch is almost ready so I'll just go and start getting things together,' she says, turning away quickly as I ask if she needs a hand.

'Don't worry, it's your birthday, your Dad will help,' she calls over her shoulder and Dad follows her in to the kitchen where Mum starts clattering crockery and giving instructions.

'Hope you don't mind the balloon only we thought, you know, forty only happens once,' says Mrs Peterson, 'it'll be Amanda next month.'

Here we go.

'Of course,' I say, as if I knew this all along, 'how is Amanda, doing OK?'

'Oh yes, she's doing really well,' she gushes, 'now the youngest two are at secondary school she's started a little business from home, selling natural dyed wools from their sheep. It's going rather well, seems there's quite a market nowadays for anything British and natural. Cottage industry they call it.'

'License to print money, from what I can see,' Mr. Peterson says. 'Still, if people are prepared to pay it..' He leaves the sentence unfinished and rolls his eyes with a smile on his face. Amanda always did have a knack for getting people to do what she wanted. 'Look, let me show you her website,' he goes on, 'we've got a minute.' Before I can protest, Mr Peterson is whipping out his phone and fiddling about with it, angling it away from the light and holding it at arm's length so he can see it clearly, tapping away at the screen. 'Got it. There's a video that shows you the farm and what they do. Here.' He hands it over and I find myself looking at a film about Amanda's farm; it looks idyllic. Beautiful Kent countryside filmed in sunlight, flocks of sheep and children all over the place, well-built tan-faced farmer in a check shirt deftly shearing a ewe and then Amanda's voice over all of it, explaining the farm, the family traditions, the natural goods they produce. And then there she is and I have to suppress a smile. She's got a

Broken Wand

purple blazer on; it's a wool, tweedy looking one over a light blue shirt but her hair's swept up like Princess bloody Anne and on top of that, a tweedy flat cap. She really is taking this seriously. Mr and Mrs Peterson are quietly beaming. I make all the right noises about it, how proud they must be etc. and then Mum walks in with a steaming dish of veg, Dad following her with a leg of lamb so I quickly suggest we all sit down to eat. Dad goes to sit in the chair next to Mr Peterson.

'You should sit here Dad.'

'No, birthday privileges, you take head of the table.'

'Smells amazing Ruth, as ever,' Mr. Peterson smiles across at Mum and winks, as though it's a private joke. Mum tucks her hair behind her ear and invites everyone to help themselves.

'Ooh!' squeals Mrs Peterson suddenly, 'Forty - imagine it, our babies Ruth, forty! Doesn't seem like five minutes ago they were out there on that street racing around on tiny bikes. Remember how Amanda always used to win the races Mike?' and then that bloody laugh again. She looks round at Mr. Peterson. 'Remember Ian?' and I can tell by the way her upper arm twists that she's slipped her hand over to his thigh under the table, maybe to give it a little squeeze. He just sits up a tiny bit straighter and manages a thin, sideways smile at her before shifting in his seat to dislodge her.

The ever bubbly Mrs Peterson keeps things going, bringing up bits of gossip about Rainham and the people in it, the worn down suburb of Romford we live in, and of course the saintly Amanda.

I watch Mum while she eats. She always paces herself, watching everyone's plates so she doesn't finish too soon or too late. Her eyes flicker about the table, making sure people have what they need, checking if they want more of what they've just finished. I've watched her do this for forty years but it's like I'm seeing it for the first time, how her mouth purses while she checks, stopping just short of cocking her head to one side like a watchful bird. The lines around her eyes have become more creased and she's jowly now, her neck less visible under her chin. She has those brown age marks on the back of her hands like Grandad did but her hair is still the same colour, even if it's not real anymore. I wonder if I'll be sitting at a table with my grown up kids in years to come wondering where that time went. But I'm not married, there isn't even a girlfriend now. I stop chewing and for a moment their voices fade. What if I don't even have this to look forward to?

'Mike?' Mum breaks in to my thoughts.

'Sorry, what?'

'I said do you want some more carrots?'

'Uh, no, thanks Mum.' She smiles tightly at me. There's a brief lull in conversation as everyone seems to have stopped to look at me in unison. I swallow hard and blurt out:

'I'm going to be starting a new magic act. I've got a partner.'

'Oh?' says Mrs Peterson, her interest piqued, sensing news.

'Yes,' I reply, realising too late that I'm going to have to carry on. 'We're going to start working on it next week in fact, harness the power of the internet to take it out to a wider audience.' I'm emphasising all this with widespread hands; it was about all I could remember of what Angelique had told me but it had the desired effect. Well, it had an effect. They were all looking at me more intently now, Mum with an even tighter, surprised smile on her face and cutlery hovering over the plate; Dad with the biggest question mark in his eyes. Mrs Peterson speaks first.

'Oh, well that's nice Mike. Everyone should have a hobby, makes the working day seem lighter, I always say.' What would she know? Never worked a day in her life. Housewife through and through, Mr. Peterson earning all the money and getting promotions so they had a cosy retirement. She still ran around after him.

'It's not a hobby.' I say. 'Angelique is very knowledgeable about the internet and she's keen to learn the ropes so we decided to go for it. We start next week.' A slight pause while I smile at everyone.

'Angelique?' says Mum.

'Yes.' I am beginning to think I shouldn't have laid this on them over lunch with neighbours. It was clearly a surprise to them and Mrs Peterson will be loving it. I glance at Dad who is looking at his plate now.

Broken Wand

I'd mentioned the M word, the thing that frustrated them the most about me; my belief that I would make it someday in magic. I offer to help Mum clear the plates and she readily agrees while everyone else starts saying how lovely it has all been.

'How long?' she asks once we're in the kitchen.

'How long what?'

'How long has this Angelique been hanging around for then?'

'Since Friday.'

'Friday?' she stares at me. 'You've known her since Friday and you think that she's going to be your business partner and make you some sort of star?'

'Well, technically I've known her since yesterday, that's when we met but she saw the act on Friday. She's really switched on. I think it could really be something.' I hadn't thought that at all until that moment when I had to justify myself to Mum. 'She's clever and she's got ideas.'

'Oh well that's all right then if she's got ideas,' she hisses, glancing at the open kitchen door. She plunges some plates into the dishwasher. 'Michael, it's not that we don't think you should do magic as a hobby, you know that, but you have a steady job and soon you might have a wife and responsibilities. Why don't you just stick to what brings the money in? See if you can get promoted.' She lays her hand lightly on my arm and tries to smile. I know she speaks for both of them.

'Mum, I'm forty.' I say, just a hint of exasperation making threading through my voice.

'I know dear. I was there.'

'And I'm currently single so where has this married with kids idea come from?'

'We live in hope,' she says drily and as she does so, grimaces slightly and puts a hand to her chest.

'You alright Mum?' She lifts her chin and takes a sharp breath, reaching in to a drawer for a packet of indigestion tablets, popping one out and quickly chewing it, breathing out as she does so.

'I'm fine, just a bit of indigestion,' she says and heads back out to the table.

Broken Wand

I don't stay long after lunch using work the next day as my excuse. I ask the Petersons to give my best to Amanda and leave them with Mum and Dad, no doubt ready with the questions as soon as I'm gone.

11

I make my way back to the flat, sit on the sofa and flick the TV on. There's a choice of football or a western and I can't be bothered to look through all the other channels. I leave it on the football so I can just let it wash over me.

After a few listless minutes I go and grab a tin of beer from the fridge, glancing at the pitifully small amount of food in there before slamming the door and turning my back on it. Staring at the pizza leaflet that lives on the kitchen table I wonder if I'm hungry but Mum's second helpings of steamed pudding ('go on, it's your birthday!') are still making their leaden way through my stomach. I take a long swig of my beer hoping it will help to ease its path and look down at the car park behind my block, the large wheeled dumpsters that stand in their own shelter at the back are crooked and their corners stick out, no doubt shoved in quickly by the bin men.

The rain's stopped but there are still pools of water everywhere, including in the dented bin lids. Beyond that are identical rows of roofs and the tops of fences that section up the gardens, more roofs beyond that and a grey-washed sky above. All the same. All small except the sky and even that can't be bothered to throw in a bit of blue today.

Football commentary buzzes away in the background pulling me back to the sofa where I sit, twanging the tab on the beer can with my thumb over and over. I'd been thinking about what Mum said as I made my way home and it niggled away at me now. Maybe she had a point. It had all been a bit quick, after all. I mean, someone just walks up to you and says all this stuff and you're dazzled and you think it must be a good idea. But is it? Telling Mum and Dad, saying it out loud has made it all a bit real. Two days ago I was giving it all up. I think back to how I'd felt that night in the pub and know that I don't want to go back there again. I don't want any more kicks in the teeth, I don't know how much longer I can brush them away for. I know they're right; I should stick to the day job, go for promotion maybe. I reach for my phone to call Angelique. No point leaving it. She answers on the second ring.

'Hi Angelique, it's Mike.' There's a pause and I can tell she's wondering who the hell Mike is so I add. 'The magician?'

'Oh God yes, hi. Sorry, I'll save this number to my phone so I'll know next time. I was going to call you actually so you beat me to it.'

'You were?' I hadn't expected that and my heart sinks a bit. Had she already had second thoughts?

'Just wanted to say Thursday would suit me best so we'll go for that. I can be back from work by 7 so shall we say 7.30 then? I'm really excited to get started. I've been watching some stuff on YouTube and I have some suggestions but I expect you'll have some ideas as well so we can compare notes. OK?'

'Er, yes, sounds good,' I hear myself saying.

'Good. Well, as you have all the stuff, I'll come to you but if you don't mind I'll bring a friend. Can you text me the address?'

'Yes, but –'

'Great! Although hang on, how do I know you won't murder us?' she asks. Before I can answer she laughs and adds: 'Only kidding, you don't look the type and you haven't met Joanna yet! Well I'll see you then.'

I'll tell her on Thursday. Probably better to do it face to face anyway.

12

Angelique found Joanna in the foyer of the small independent cinema, pondering the snacks that were laid out in wooden veg crates propped up on the counter.

'Which do you think, vegan butterscotch popcorn or organic dark chocolate covered brazils?' Joanna asked immediately, taking a packet of each down from the shelf and showing them to Angelique.

'Ah, depends,' Angelique replied, shaking her head briefly, trying to focus on the packets being waved in front of her, 'are we sharing?'

'Might do.'

'Then one of each I suppose,' Angelique said, tapping each packet in turn, conscious of the people in the queue behind Joanna and smiling up at the man behind the counter. Joanna turned to pay while Angelique looked at the posters on the front of the kiosk. 1960's thrillers, Hitchcock mostly, and a couple of new European indie films that were coming up once the main festivals were over. She found herself looking at a poster for a Polish film; a tall, handsome man standing behind a beautiful younger blonde with his arms wrapped round her, nuzzling the top of her head as she leant back on him, her eyes closed and a luxurious smile on her face, both clearly lost in each other and their thoughts. It looked like they were oblivious to the world around them and Angelique made a mental note of the film's name; she would watch it to see if the happiness lasted. They moved over to the usher who was checking tickets; Joanna handed him theirs and he ripped them slightly.

'Where are your boosters please?' Joanna asked as he did this. He glanced up at her with a query on his face. 'Booster seat,' She added, looking briefly down at Angelique. He looked flustered.

'Ah, we only have those for kids so -' he stuttered, glancing over at the kiosk for help. 'What I mean is, will that do? They've got Buzz Lightyear or Princesses on,' he asked Joanna.

Broken Wand

'It's fine, I'll take a Buzz Lightyear.' Angelique interrupted, 'never did hold much truck with the princess type.' She smiled at the usher and shot Joanna a look. They moved aside while the usher ducked behind the counter to find a booster seat and returned with it, sheepishly handing it to Angelique with a smile before turning to the next people in the queue.

'You shouldn't let them get away with it,' Joanna said as she helped Angelique up in to her seat, 'you shouldn't have to put up with Buzz bloody Lightyear.'

'Joanna,' Angelique began with a note of irritation in her voice, 'I don't mind and you don't need to mind for me. I can ask my own questions.' Joanna held both hands in front of her, palms forward, and bowed her head slightly.

'OK, OK,' Joanna said, in a conciliatory tone, looking sideways at Angelique. 'You seem tetchy - long day?'

'Oh you know, long meetings listening to the creative team waffle on about the future impact of digital connectivity on business and society, like they know anything about it.' Angelique helped herself to some popcorn while she spoke and they both chewed while they watched a trailer. 'Remember that magician I had a coffee with?' she said, quickly sucking the sticky bits off her fingers as the trailers went on.

'Ah yes, Mike the magician; star of the Romford pub circuit. What about him?' Joanna asked before turning to Angelique in mock surprise. 'Don't tell me he blew you out?'

'Quite the opposite,' Angelique replied, tartly. 'Well, I think he was going to but I didn't give him much leeway.'

'You surprise me,' Joanna said sarcastically.

'Whatever,' Angelique replied, dismissive of Joanna's teasing. 'Look, I've said I'll go to his flat on Thursday to get things kicked off; it's easier there because he has all the props and stuff. Will you come with me?'

'To a pub magician's flat in Romford? Try stopping me. Should be fun.'

'You have to behave Joanna.'

'Why?'

'Because there's something about him that I can work with. He seems a bit lost and I think I could genuinely help him. I don't want you to scare him off.'

'Careful there Angelique, don't go letting emotion get in the way of things. Establish what you want, achieve it and move on. You know the rules.' Joanna said as she tilted the popcorn bag in Angelique's direction; she helped herself.

'Those are your rules Joanna; I'm not a political lobbyist, thankfully.'

'Don't knock it 'til you've tried it; I made a kill today, two months in the making. Cross party agreement; still glowing,' Joanna said, nudging Angelique gently with her elbow and snorting a small laugh through her popcorn. 'Two months of coercion, conversations in corridors, conversations in meetings, white papers, submissions, pretending to care.'

'Why do you do it if you're so cynical about it?'

'I'm good at it and I like the end result. I like it even more if I happen to agree with it. All the preamble, the buttering up, it's worth it to see the pay off.'

'Then you'll understand why I'm going to have to know Mike better before I can help him; I'm going to need to know what I'm working with to make sure I can do it. No point finding out he's a no hoper in two months time.'

'True, and you'll need my assessment, naturally. Of course I'll come.' Angelique felt a stab of annoyance at this automatic assumption that she would need her help.

'Not so much that,' she countered, 'but I don't know him yet; more a safety thing.'

'Sure. Can't have you going to strange men's houses on your lonesome now can we? I'll bring some pepper spray just in case.' The lights went down in the cinema and the opening credits of the film came up. Angelique lowered her voice to a whisper.

'I think your personality will be enough to keep him at bay; it usually is. Anyway, I think he's pretty harmless.'

'Recognition at last,' Joanna said, throwing her head back and slumping down in her chair so her head was resting on the back of the seat. She flashed a quick grin at Angelique before turning her full attention to the film.

13

I'm on my way to the bathroom with a new loo roll in my hand when the doorbell goes. It makes me start and for some reason I check my hair in the bathroom mirror, running a hand over it. When I open the door I look down at Angelique then straight back up again at another woman with her.

'Mike, this is Joanna, Joanna, this is Mike.'

'Bad moment?' Joanna asks with a straight face as she glances down at the loo roll I'm still holding.

'Ah – no,' I say, and I wave the loo roll around before wedging it onto the top of the radiator in the hall, glancing quickly round to make sure nothing else embarrassing is lying about after I tidied the flat in a rush after work. I know I'm going to blow her out but still polite to make the place presentable. It's a sixties block so the rooms are a decent size and the windows are big but that's more for the light than the view. I've been here fifteen years and other than paint the walls when I moved in, I haven't changed anything. It's still got those ridged glass doors between rooms that make a million slices of you and a couple of the cupboards in the kitchen are original too. Big floor to ceiling ones. It's got another big cupboard at the end of the corridor so space to keep my stuff, not that there's a lot of it. I look back down at Angelique and am struck by how the black eyeliner she's put on makes her eyes stand out even more. It suits her.

'Come in, please.' I stand aside to let them in making an exaggerated arm wave to try and cover my embarrassment about the loo roll but making it so much worse. I quickly shove it in the bathroom cupboard on the way past while showing them in to the lounge and offering beer but they both ask for tea so I go and try to find three matching mugs that are clean.

I bring the tea in and sit opposite them. Joanna is still stony-faced but behind her eyes it's as if she's doing sums, glancing round the room and adding things to different columns; I smile at her but she doesn't return it. Her short bob of thin, jet black hair has a high, severe fringe straight across her forehead which does nothing to soften her sharp features. She too is wearing a lot of eyeliner but it's the nose stud that catches my eye. It's quite big, designed to draw attention. I catch myself staring and quickly smile again.

'So, Angelique,' I begin, 'what do you, I mean, how do you want to do this?' I'm planning on saying something at the end of the chat, some way of letting her down gently but I may as well hear her out first so it looks like I've thought about it.

'Well, I thought we could start with a bit of getting to know each other? I'll go first,' she says, and without seeming to draw breath carries on. 'I'm 27, and as I said before, I work for a new media company in Shoreditch and head up their project management but I can't afford to live there yet so that's why I'm in Romford, but not for long if I can help it. I'm an Oxford graduate, originally from much further into Essex which is not like it seems on the telly.' I like her directness, it's challenging but not in a bad way like some women. She indicates it's my turn and I decide to try a bit of personal info to lighten the mood.

'Well, I turned forty last Sunday,' I say with a smile that neither of them return. Nor did either of them say happy birthday or anything so I carry on. 'I grew up down the road in Rainham. I manage a coffee outlet in the City which pays the rent and as you know I work as a magician in the evenings, when I can.' When I can? What did I mean by that, that my life was so packed with social engagements I could barely move for them? I wince inwardly and hope they don't pick up on it. I draw breath to carry on but though I search my thoughts for something interesting, I don't have anything to say.

'What made you want to be a magician?' Angelique asks, mercifully. I think about this for a moment, and decide to go with the truth.

'Well, when I was a boy, my Grandad gave me his wand. He'd been a magician in pubs and clubs when he was a young man, before the war, but then he went off to fight. He was a P.O.W and did shows for people in the camp with whatever he could find and

Broken Wand

he made the wand.' She looks quite interested in this, which encourages me. 'Hang on and I'll get it.' I nip down the corridor to the big cupboard and dig the wand out. I don't keep it in the suitcase and in fact never use it; too worried I'd lose it if I did and it doesn't look very professional – just a painted stick really. Now that I've told them about it, it looks very stick-like indeed and for a split second I consider saying I can't find it. I go back less excited about it, standing in the doorway with the wand pinched between the fingers of one hand. 'This is it,' I say, waving it about a bit. Joanna holds out her hand and I give it to her. I have the unnerving feeling that she might snap it. Then, when she's examined it, she says:

'Nice piece of history, that.'

'Thanks.' She hands it to Angelique and while she's looking at it I carry on. 'They had playing cards as well that were sent to them and when you peeled the numbers off, there were sections of maps underneath. A whole pack made up a map of the country they were in and they could put them together and use them to escape. Clever, really.'

'So did he carry on, when he got back?' Angelique asks.

'No. He couldn't do it without thinking of what happened after that. He said to me once that he would wish he really could make people disappear and sometimes, when it got really bad, he'd try to concentrate so hard on doing it that his brain hurt. He never told me anything else, I don't think he really wanted to talk about it. He was prone to quiet moods apparently, not that I really knew him before, obviously, but that's what Mum says.' I can hear myself talking nervously and going on without thinking what I am really saying.

I haven't really told anyone much of this before; maybe because I knew this was the last time I might actually be able to so it doesn't matter what I say. 'And then he got me a Paul Daniels magic set when I was nine and that was that.' I feel like Angelique is really listening, that she's genuinely interested. I'm about to ask if she has any experience of magic when Joanna asks:

'So which coffee company do you work for?'

'It's a Java Hut, over near Liverpool Street.'
'Oh they're the worst.'
'Sorry?'
'Taxes. They don't pay them.' I really don't want to discuss it or have a row so I spread my hands and say:
'Look, I just work there.'
'But that makes you a key player. You could change it from within, start a petition of employees or something. You can't ignore it. Mind you, they're not the only ones, but that doesn't let them off the hook.' I look over at Angelique who offers a smile and asks for more tea.

I silently thank her for getting me out of the conversation and head to the kitchen. I've seen the newspaper reports of course and yes, they had sent us information about it in case people asked and I have to admit I do feel uneasy about it. But like Joanna said, they're not the only ones and they pay my wages. I bring the tea in and set it down on the smoked glass; I don't have coasters and they clink as they land, spilling a little. I've tucked a packet of biscuits under my arm and smile apologetically.

'Forgot I had these – would you like one?' I ask as I unwrap them. They are chocolate digestives which I bought specially. I don't usually eat biscuits; my takeaway habit feeds my middle-aged waistline well enough. My Mum would have put some on a plate, I think, as I put the open pack down on the table, feeling like things are still a bit formal, not being helped by Joanna looking at the biscuits like they've just crawled in by themselves.

'Think I'll just go to the loo,' she announces.
'Down the corridor, on the right,' I say and for some reason add 'spare loo roll in the cupboard if you need it,' with a smile on my face. She looks at me briefly before glancing back at Angelique and stalking out of the room. 'So, what did you have in mind for the magic act?' I ask as soon as she's gone. I find myself hoping that she'll see it all as a bit of a gamble and back out to save me having to. I'll protest a bit if she does and then agree it won't work as quickly as possible. At least then I won't have to let her down and she does seem nice. She sits at the front of the sofa and leans in

intently, emphasising her words with spread hands.

'I've got an idea to film us doing a show that we put on the internet, after rehearsals and a bit of planning obviously. Short ones at first, ten minutes, short enough to watch on a lunch break, long enough to hook people in. I know how to get it seen on the right platforms and we'll go from there. But first I need to learn a bit about magic so we can tweak it, update it, give it an edge. I've got the same idea of the basics as everyone else but I need to build on that – can't push it if I don't know what 'it' is.' As she speaks, she begins to get more animated, maybe she was waiting until we were alone. 'Obviously, it would have to be in our spare time to begin with but that's OK. So many people get spotted on social media channels now, it's like a massive audition platform, you never know what might happen.' Once again I'm trying to take it all in.

'But I can't do all that fancy stuff they do now,' I say, grabbing the chance to get my apologies in. 'I can't make Tower Bridge disappear or sparks come out of people's eyeballs.'

'I'm aware of that,' she says bluntly, 'but I'm also a firm believer in it's not what you do but how you do it that counts. When we actually do solid, clever old school magic that we add creative twists to they'll see we're more than meets the eye. It's down to how we package you, how we put on a show, you see? We need to layer you up a bit, provide some depth.' I'm starting to see what she's getting at.

'So would someone film us at a gig then? Is that it?'

'No, we'll do closed set to start with.' She sees my blank look. 'Which means we just film ourselves, no one else is allowed in and the less like a grotty pub the better. It might look good if we were in an abandoned warehouse or something, you know, use stuff we find lying around. They won't expect that from you.' The idea is growing on me. I pinch my lip like I do when I'm thinking or nervous. I picture the warehouse and me in black tie. It could be quite cool. Maybe I'd just give it a few weeks, just to see. It couldn't hurt and there's something about her enthusiasm and confidence that makes me easier about it.

'Well, like you said before, I don't have anything to lose so why not?'

'Exactly; if it doesn't work out, so be it but you don't know 'til you try.

'And you know how to get it on to the internet and how to promote it?'

'Yes, like I said, it's what I do,' she said deliberately. If she's getting impatient, it doesn't show all that much but I suspect she's just good at covering it. Just then Joanna comes back into the room with a small smile on her face, plonking her bag down beside her with a flourish.

'How are you two getting along then?' she asks, almost friendly, 'sorted out who's going to wear the skimpy dress and fishnets yet? Personally, I think they'd suit Mike better.' Her eyes glinted.

I see Angelique throw her a glance but Joanna just raises her eyebrows and smiles brightly back at her. Suddenly Angelique is all bustle, picking up her coat and bag, standing as if to go.

'Look, we've got a thing to go to but let's get started next week, yes?' Angelique says, briskly. 'We can sort a time out over the weekend.' She smiles a smile that reaches her eyes this time. It catches me off guard and I smile back, nodding my agreement.

'Great. I'll be in touch,' she adds as she ushers Joanna out of the door.

'Bye Mike, it was lovely to meet you!' Joanna flings over her shoulder and then they're gone.

Once I've chucked the mugs in the sink, I try to remember the last time I've been involved in something like this or even felt as nervous about something but actually, I like it. I like that maybe there is a last chance after all. I'm glad I decided to go with it.

14

Joanna and Angelique found a free table at the back of a tapas bar where Joanna ordered a bottle of red and a plate of olives while they were still taking their coats off.

'I couldn't believe it when he got that old wand out,' she began, adding her folded coat to Angelique's on the chair and helping her up before sitting herself. 'I mean, God, he's like a throwback to Dad's Army. Are you sure you want to play with him? He's no match for you, there won't be a challenge in it.' The waiter showed her the bottle of wine and she hastily waved permission at him to fill the goblet shaped wine glasses without breaking the conversation.

'I think he's got potential actually,' Angelique replied, more firmly than she felt. 'I mean, I know he's no intellectual genius but he knows magic and he's willing to help pull this together and take a chance.'

'Jesus, don't go soft on me. You know the objective here - no chances taken, no quarter given.'

'Yes, but you're a man-hating uber bitch,' Angelique replied matter of factly as she tasted the wine.

'Don't go complimenting me,' Joanna said as she deftly speared an olive with a cocktail stick and bit down on it.

'Seriously though,' Angelique continued, 'I think I'm going to enjoy this. It's actually got potential.'

'And what about your Mum? What does she think about all this? Spoken to her yet?' Angelique paused before answering, taking a large sip of wine and fiddling with her cocktail stick.

'Actually Joanna,' she said carefully but still looking at her wine glass, 'I'm seeing her on Saturday.'

'Ah, the mother lunch looms large,' Joanna replied, annoying Angelique with her lack of seriousness as she manoeuvred the olive stone to the corner of her mouth before putting it on her folded napkin. 'Going out this time or over to her?' she continued.

'Over to her,' Angelique replied, hoping that would be the end of it.

'Are you going to tell her? I expect she'll have a fair bit to say about it.' Joanna persisted, enjoying seeing Angelique trying not to answer.

'I expect so too,' Angelique said, breathing deeply as Joanna kept on looking at her, expectantly. 'I'll explain it's a social experiment that will further my career.'

'If it works,' Joanna said, a finger raised in Angelique's direction.

'It will work. I will make it work.' Angelique said firmly, with more belief than she was actually feeling.

'OK,' Joanna replied, 'if you say so. But how exactly are you going to sort his act out? I mean, that's a pretty big idea and I don't remember the last time we had an in-depth discussion about how to do magic.' She refilled her glass almost to the brim before tilting the bottle towards Angelique with raised eyebrows who nodded her agreement to a top up.

'It can't be that difficult,' Angelique began, 'performance analysis, in-depth research of a variety of acts, pull some ideas for changes together and utilise as many platforms as possible. Magic is everywhere if you don't understand science, said somebody clever.'

'Ha. That may well be so Confucius but I don't think GCSE physics will cut it given your plans.'

'It's called research, Joanna.' She picked up the menu and studied it, cutting the conversation dead until Joanna turned the menu over for her to the English side. Angelique took advantage of the moment to change the subject.

'Speaking of science, when did you start dabbling in the chemicals again?' she asked Joanna, rubbing beneath the tip of her nose and sniffing to make her point clearer. Joanna's eyes narrowed for a split second.

'You spotted that,' she asked quietly, without changing her expression.

'Well yes. You came back from the toilet at Mike's as happy as Pinocchio with a very full nose, no strings and very chatty.' Joanna didn't comment but fiddled with a corner of the napkin holding her

Broken Wand

cutlery. 'How much are you doing?' Angelique asked.

'Not much, it's just occasionally when I feel the life ebbing out of a situation like with marvellous Mike there. Political lobbying is extremely dull sometimes and really stressful the rest. It gets me through.'

'You're doing it at work?' Angelique asked, incredulous. Joanna glanced round quickly to see if anyone was close enough to hear. Angelique lowered her voice and asked: 'How do you get it past security?'

'Christ, I don't do it in the corridors of power. I do it before I go then I can cope with the corridors of power.'

'Bloody hell Joanna, be careful. You did say you wouldn't go back there.'

'I'm not back there. I'm just taking the edge off. You've no idea how stressful it can be, trying to convince people how to behave politically when all they want to do is whatever secures them the most votes in the short term.'

'Are you saying our friends in power are self-interested and cynically motivated? That's not exactly new. You've never been quite so honest about it before though.'

'I thought I could still change things when I was on the way up but now I'm fully integrated in to the ways of political compromise, I'm not so sure. The system's not for turning.'

'Can't you make change from the inside?'

'The kinds of policy I'm lobbying on, all the corporate legal jargon and nit-picking, it's amazing anything is ever changed. Unless someone's brother-in-law is involved of course, then you'd be surprised how quickly wheels turn,' she raised a knowing eyebrow at Angelique as she lifted her glass to her lips. 'And anyway,' she continued, 'you're about to experience your first proper dose of making people do what you want then dropping them and moving on so then we can swap notes.' Angelique didn't comment immediately but looked at Joanna impassively. Eventually, she said:

'Is your opinion of me really that low?'

'Oh come on; that's not a low opinion in my book and you know it.' Joanna replied.

'I've had to fight harder than most to make headway,' Angelique began, 'but that doesn't mean I have to be fighting all the time. This isn't about that. This is about adding a few things to the CV that will boost my chances later on if I need to pull something out of the bag.'

'Or the hat,' Joanna quipped with a snort, satisfied with her own joke.

'Hilarious. Call it a productive hobby if it makes you feel any better.'

'Don't you think he's taking it a bit more seriously than that? You've sold it to him pretty hard.' Angelique was silent for a moment, pondering her now empty glass.

'Well, I just had to convince him to give it a go,' she replied, 'it's not like there's a contract or anything, he doesn't have to hang around if he doesn't like it.'

'True. And nor do you.'

'Exactly. So we're all good. Let's order - I'm starving.'

15

Angelique felt the same sense of pressure she always did when she pulled up in a taxi outside her mother's terraced house; re-living the sensation she was about to receive exam results, that she'd get an A for being punctual and then have to navigate her way round the meal to keep her grades up.

Plant pots on each side of the four steps up to the front door were well tended and had a bright show of spring flowers in them, bulbs her mother would have planted with precision spacing in autumn and chosen to give continual colour. Their plucky show did little to settle Angelique's nerves. She climbed the steps between glossed black railings that stood to attention and gleamed in the late morning sun, knocked on the door and waited.

'Angelique,' her mother said as she opened the door, her coordinated trousers, shirt and cardigan in shades of blue immediately giving her an air of neatness and practical elegance. 'Forgot your key again?' she asked rhetorically as she bent down to give her a kiss on the cheek. 'Come on, don't let the cold in,' she urged, ushering Angelique through the door. The truth was, Angelique hadn't forgotten her key, it was in her bag but sometimes, especially the last few years, she felt that really it was only for emergencies.

'Smells good,' Angelique said as she laid her coat over the hall stand, her mother closing the door behind her.

'It's just a chicken,' she replied, walking purposefully down the hallway to the kitchen. Angelique's eyes fell on some post propped up on the hall stand addressed to Ms. L. Watson and it briefly reminded her of the time she had taken to calling her mother by her christian name, Linda, as a child. It didn't last long. 'I am your mother, Angelique, kindly refer to me as such. After all, nobody else can' had soon put a stop to it.

The table was already set and the kitchen pristine. Linda always liked to do as much of the clearing away and washing up as possible before a meal so all that was left to do was put serving dishes and plates into the dishwasher. Even the roasting tin had been washed and put away, the chicken covered and keeping warm under foil on a serving plate on the hob. This and a covered dish of vegetables were soon transferred to the table where warmed plates were waiting. Last to arrive was a gravy boat.

'Ah!' Linda exclaimed, 'serving spoons.' With everything ready on the table the tin foil lids were removed and piled neatly by the sink, ready for washing and folding away neatly for re-use.

'So, how are things with you?' Linda asked expectantly as she nudged the vegetables towards Angelique. Angelique knew from a lifetime's experience that 'fine' would only lead to interrogation so she gave a breakdown of her current work situation, keeping to the salient facts, Linda not being interested in workplace gossip - her own or anyone else's.

When Angelique had answered her mother's few questions they talked briefly about life for Linda in the teaching profession. Angelique had finished her food while Linda described the pros and cons of SATS tests, after which conversation had lulled to a deafening silence, punctuated only by the clinking of cutlery. Angelique looked over at Linda who was concentrating on spearing a small piece of everything on to her fork; it was usually difficult to gauge Linda's mood and today was no exception. Angelique had decided to test the water while Linda was still eating.

'Actually, there's something else I wanted to tell you,' she'd begun, keeping her voice as neutral as possible.

'Oh?' Linda responded, glancing up from her plate.

'I've started a new project, something to help push my career on.'

'At work?'

'No, in my own time.'

'Does your employer approve of moonlighting?'

'It's not moonlighting Mum and it's not competitive to their client base anyway. That's why I'm doing it actually, to demonstrate my versatility across the field in non-competitive markets.'

'I see. So what does this new project entail exactly?'

Broken Wand

'Well,' Angelique began, thinking back to her pre-prepared speech, 'I'm going to be implementing a social media strategy on an act in a specific strand of entertainment to ensure a future for it in a fast evolving market place.' She paused for a few moments to let this sink in.

'Sounds very technical,' her mother commented. 'What particular strand of entertainment is it you are talking about?' Angelique had hoped her mother wouldn't ask too many question, that this would be one of those times when she accepted what was said but clearly, it had sparked curiosity instead.

'It's a magic act actually,' Angelique replied with as much confidence as she could muster. Her mother didn't comment but laid her knife and fork neatly next to each other on her plate and rested her forearms on the table either side of it.

'Oh?' was all she said. Angelique felt the full impact of the 'oh' as it landed on her side of the table, demanding a full explanation as it did so, backed up by her mother's unflinching gaze.

'I'm going to work with a magician who performs in and around London,' she began carefully, 'pubs mostly, sometimes restaurants and he needs a reboot. The act's got a bit tired so I'm going to apply some modern marketing skills and help to modernise it.' Her mother's expression didn't change and she didn't comment. 'And then I'm going to turn him into an internet sensation,' Angelique added.

'I see,' was the eventual measured response from her mother.

'I'm actually really interested in the magic,' Angelique continued, 'the psychology of it, the way the mind wants to be tricked, wants it to be real.'

'Yes, well,' her mother said as she stood and reached for Angelique's plate across the table, 'I can see how that aspect of it might be interesting.'

'Maybe it was in my Dad's blood,' Angelique said, lightly. Her mother looked at her, with one eyebrow slightly raised before turning to the sink and taking her time to reply. Angelique had learned, over the years, not to squirm under Linda's classic teacher's intensity and she quickly tried to sit up straighter while her back was turned. She didn't know where that comment had come from, she had said it as soon as she had thought it and felt slightly light headed at having done so.

'Why would you think it has to be an inherited thing?' Linda asked as she turned to face her, leaning back against the sink and folding her arms.

'Just wondering where this interest might have come from, that's all.' Angelique raised her eyebrows and looked questioningly at her mother, knowing she was taking this point as far as she would dare to but still hoping it might lead to some information about her father.

'Your interest stems from your own intellectual curiosity I expect. A mind as strong as yours is always going to want to explore new avenues, no matter how ridiculous.'

'Ridiculous?'

'Yes. Well, surely you must see that this isn't a viable route for someone with academic integrity to follow. I mean, it's nice you want to help this - what's his name?' She tailed off, waving a hand vaguely.

'Mike,' Angelique supplied.

'Mike,' she continued, 'but it's hardly an impressive subject when you work with such well known international companies.' Angelique took a deep breath, tapping the kitchen table with one nail before replying.

'I'm doing this to show my versatility and flexibility. To show that I can take anything and make it work, that if I can do that with Mike, I can do it for a company or a specific strand within one. It will demonstrate a whole different skill set and break me in to new areas.'

'Well I suppose if you can justify it as career advancement then it will be worth it. But do keep the bigger picture in mind Angelique. You have career goals.'

'Yes Mother, I'm aware of that.' The two women exchanged a glance.

'Will you stay for a cup of tea?' Linda asked her without unfolding her arms or moving away from the sink.

Broken Wand

'No, thanks, I need to do some shopping on the way home.' Angelique made her way back to the hall table and gathered up her coat and bag.

'No taxi?' Linda queried.

'No, I think I'll walk for a bit; still quite full. Thanks for lunch.'

'Right, well, safe journey home then,' Linda said as she stooped to peck her on the cheek before closing the door behind her.

16

I meet Angelique by the entrance to Shoreditch High Street Tube and we make tracks to her friend's office space. We're not using her company's offices as she doesn't want them knowing just yet. Probably best until we have a solid plan. She's still in her work gear and looking smart, older somehow but that's probably just the clothes making her look more business-like, though she does have a less relaxed air about her than usual.

'Good day?' I ask, to break the ice.

'Yes, OK. Just a client dragging their heels a bit,' she says without really looking up at me. I don't pursue it. We're about to do our first trial film to see what mistakes I make and the way I'm feeling there's going to be quite a few. I'm used to an audience and dealing with customers but that's different; that's for work and this, well this is personal.

I haven't been to Shoreditch much before. It never really featured on anyone's radar when it was still a dead-end suburb, down at heel and cheap. Not like that now though and it very much feels like her turf. It's quite different to the weekday only streets of the City. I've never seen so many Hipsters in one place; they don't tend to venture to the City. A beard the length of these would not be seen, that's for sure.

Angelique tells me that most people don't start work here until 10am because it takes that long to tame the facial hair in the morning and I fire back that surely that can't be true of ALL the women and she laughs. There are murals everywhere that say things like 'let's adore and endure each other', whatever the hell that means. Mum would have a fit at this; not a suit or a nine to five job in sight. Plenty of small cafés and shops and graffiti all over them. I feel like the odd one out in my shirt, jumper, jeans, shaved face and suitcase full of props and I'd guess there aren't many people over mid-thirties either. I wonder where they go, old hipsters? Must be a county full of them somewhere; Wiltshire maybe? Not like I stick out, but I definitely don't blend in either and I don't feel entirely comfortable with that, even though no one's even looking my way. It still manages to feel buzzy even though it's a bit of a grey day.

We end up in someone's office down a side street in a done-up warehouse and it's a bit stark, all open plan, jungle plants and pretend Crittall windows. Angelique wanted plain white walls so we could be anywhere and this is near enough. They're white painted bricks – industrial chic, apparently - and Angelique moves some of the desk lamps to light us up. There are a couple of people working late and she introduces me to one of them but they don't seem fussed, like people doing magic and filming themselves is all in a day's work.

Just because there's a camera there, my nerves have gone through the roof. Angelique can control the camera remotely; it's on a bookcase about fifteen feet away so she can be my audience of one. I keep glancing at it, like it really is watching me, like I'm in a jewellers, casing the joint and the CCTV is blinking in the corner. It's quite a swanky office, like you see in furniture shop ads. Potted palms sit on long desks on trestle table legs that everyone sits round instead of having their own. It's all a bit shiny and poncy for my liking.

Evidently I'm not hiding my nerves too well because Angelique is telling me not to worry, we can edit it later if I make any mistakes and we can always start again so that takes the pressure off a bit. We've been practising a few things but she thinks we really need to see it to know where we can improve things.

'Can I ask you a personal question?' she says when we're sorting the props out on to a table ready to go. I don't see why not so she says 'Who's the girl in the photo with you? The one with the ice creams, in your flat? Was she your assistant as well?' I'm slightly taken aback by this and don't answer straight away. People aren't normally interested in my personal life. Not the people I know anyway.

The photo is of Boxing Day fifteen years ago when Jenny and I went to Clacton Pier to escape our families. We drove up the A12 through grey drizzly weather in her cold, rattly Renault and it took ages. It seemed everyone was out visiting or sales shopping or something. Not like now with people sales shopping on the internet on Christmas Day; there's something just wrong about that but at least the roads are clearer. We didn't reach Clacton until lunchtime but it didn't matter. It never did with Jenny. The ice creams weren't very nice, too sickly sweet but we ate them anyway. And chips. And tea out of polystyrene cups that tasted like it had been brewing since October.

    Sitting in the café on the end of the Pier we could have been anywhere in the world. It could have been one of those houses on stilts in the Maldives they always use in ads for exotic holidays. It was luxury just to be with her. I always had this feeling she was too good for me, that I was punching above my weight but if she thought that too, she didn't show it.

    The photograph was one we took huddled together against the drizzle on the pier. We thought you'd be able to see the sea behind us but it just came out grey. It didn't matter. We'd gone in to the penny arcade to warm up and I cashed in a fiver for tokens and small change. She was excited, like a little kid on the slot machines and the ones where there's a cascade of coins and you have to try and create an avalanche. We didn't but I didn't expect to. Everyone knows it's rigged. Angelique was still waiting for an answer.

    'She was my girlfriend. Jenny. She died nine years ago.'

    'Oh,' Angelique says, 'sorry.' She carries on looking at me; she's still listening and get the impression I can talk about it, that it won't bother her if I do. Most people just look away.

    'She was a hairdresser,' I continue, 'she used to cut my hair in the kitchen,' I say and I stroke the back of my head, as if it's just been cut and feels soft like it did when she'd finished. 'It was nice, when she did it. She just used to spray my head and use the clippers. She'd put some wax in to keep it in in place,' and I mime rubbing my hair with wax.

    I can still smell the wax if I close my eyes. It makes me think she's standing right behind me again, tucking a tea towel into my collar. It was the smell of her that I loved; so close I could smell her clothes, the washing powder she used. And when she bent down to do the bits over my ears I could smell her lipstick and coffee. She would blow sharply into my ears to get rid of the tiny hairs and every time it made me jump, even though I knew it was coming. We'd both smile at that.

Angelique begins to fiddle with the props, subtly letting me know I've been quiet for a while.

'Is there anything you want to ask me?' she says, 'only fair.' I think about this for a minute. There are lots of things I've wanted to ask but wasn't sure I could. It's as if she's reading my mind when she says gently 'It's OK, ask anything. Might as well be open with each other.'

I still feel a bit hesitant but I take a breath to speak then shake my head and just mutter:

'No, no, it's OK,' she laughs, 'just bloody ask me! Trust me, it won't be anything I haven't been asked before.'

'What's it like? Being you I mean,' I ask, diving straight in, 'I mean, being so -' I stumble, trying to find a word that won't be rude, that won't insult her. I find myself using my hands to try and show what I mean – like I'm describing the size of a large fish I've caught and I quickly cross my arms and tuck my hands under my armpits. I screw my face up and can feel myself redden. Luckily, she feels my pain and throws in 'blonde?' I don't trust myself to speak so I just nod gratefully. She's quiet for a while before she says:

'I used to resent it, being blonde - oh, and small of course. I'd do the whole 'why me' bit, but now I'm just like everyone else – there's always something. Women are always saying their bum's too big, boobs are too small, lips need plumping, pear shaped, apple shaped, heart shaped face. Well I just take the view that I'm dwarf shaped. That's it really. I'm not going to say it's been easy getting to this this point; there's been plenty of pain but you have to decide if it's going to get to you or not. Sometimes something happens and it just does and there's nothing you can do about it, just carry on with stuff.'

'Can't have been easy.'

'No, not really. Put it this way: once you've been stuffed into a school locker once you kind of just want to make sure it doesn't happen again. I did it myself after that - just climbed right in until they got bored of it - as a sort of disappearing trick. It doesn't hurt so much that way.'

'Physically?'

'At all.'

'Jesus.' I know it's pointless to ask why she didn't stand up to them; I did the same thing in my way. 'I got the same attention,' I volunteer, 'but more the head down the toilet at break time than stuffed in a locker. Wouldn't have fitted.' She smiles at this and we share the same weary air of resignation. 'You know,' I start again, 'I do remember one joke they used to say to me.'

'Which was?' she says, but I hesitate, suddenly feeling some of the shame and embarrassment I had felt all those years ago and not sure how she'll take it. 'Come on, you can't not tell me now,' she says, and I see genuine curiosity reflected in her smile. I know she won't judge me.

'Ok, but don't blame me for the language.' I take a deep breath and launch in to it. 'They used to say that if my Dad walked in to a brothel he'd still be the only cunt in there.'

'Well,' she says, looking taken aback as well as amused, 'you have to admire the originality. Do you think they knew what a brothel was?' and now it's my turn to chuckle. 'Why were they so down on your Dad?' she asks and instantly I'm back there, the 1980's and the daily feeling of dread as break times rolled round and I'd have to go out to the killing fields that were the playground and the sports fields.

'Dad was a union man at the Ford plant. There was a ton of unrest in the 80's and most of the kids had parents there in one way or another.'

'But wouldn't that make him someone they looked up to?' she asks. I look at her briefly. I can see I'm going to have to do some explaining. I clear my throat.

'Well, with jobs being threatened by overseas production, strikes every two minutes, unions being undermined and Dad the union man in the middle of it, trying to keep the peace, I came in for a fair bit of flack myself.' She doesn't say anything and I feel like

Broken Wand

I can carry on, like I want to. I haven't ever really put this in to words before and it feels strange to be telling it to someone who can't relate to it. 'He couldn't keep everyone happy and when they couldn't do anything about the pay cuts or the job losses and it affected their families, it filtered down to the kids and they made sure they took it out on me in turn. I suppose it was their way of getting their anger out when money dried up at home. A lot of their parents struggled to find work after that.'

'Sounds tough.'

'Yeah.' We sit quietly for a moment but it's a comfortable silence, each lost in different thoughts.

I think back to all the bullying at school, all the times I'd tried to please everyone with magic tricks because it might make them like me or at least get them off my back. It wasn't my fault Dad had to lay people off but my guilt by association was damning. So I did tricks - diversion tactics, if you like - anything to get them to see me as something or someone other than who I was. Eventually, word got round about the magic tricks but it didn't exactly make me popular. I'd be expected to perform like a monkey, on demand. I learnt to improvise then, work with whatever I had to hand. Rubbers, pens, rulers. Eventually, I kept a pack of cards on me at all times, so I had a fall back.

Sometimes the teachers would catch me with them; the most confiscated cards in history. I think they knew what was going on because they were always given back at the end of the day, a regular occurrence at the staff room door. They'd just be on top of the bookcase inside the door and they all knew to hand them over as soon as they saw it was me, no explanation needed, just a raised eyebrow. Sometimes they just carried on a conversation while they did it. Maybe Angelique and I are not so different.

I look at her now and I do one of those smiles that screws your mouth up and nod my head a couple of times because I understand. She smiles back and something is said without either of us speaking. Then she turns away and turns her attention back to the props. I don't want this feeling to end. I can't remember the last time I felt that I had a common bond with someone, if that's the right way to put it. She glances round and catches me still looking at her.

'Did you tell your parents?' I asked her.

'No,' she said, drawing the short word out, 'no point. She wasn't exactly the wrap you in cotton wool kind. Never was and isn't now.'

'Just Mum?'

'Yes. My father left early on so I've never known him.' She says this so casually that I'm taken off guard and make one of those downturned smiles people do to show sympathy because it's the best you can do at the time. 'She had to do the whole thing on her own so there wasn't a lot of room for sympathy. And I'm not expecting any now,' she adds, staring at me from under raised eyebrows before I can reply. I nod a couple of times to let her know I understand and after a couple of heartbeats she says abruptly 'Right then, you helping or what?' with a challenge in her eyes, indicating the props.

'No, I thought I'd let you do it all,' I reply, blank faced. She picks up a pad of post-it notes from the desk and lobs it at me.

17

I'm in my start position and Angelique gets up on a chair to make sure I can be seen in the camera.

'Ready?' she asks. I can see the anticipation in her eyes. She's genuinely fired up and takes a breath, clenching her hands tightly. I nod. She hits record on the camera remote and I step towards it, automatically going into magic show mode.

Despite trying to calm down I can hear myself thinking about the steps, the moves, the sleight of hand, wondering how it will come across on film. After all, you can't fool a camera; any footballer will tell you that. I feel like I'm going through the motions, because I am I suppose, and I expect it will take a few goes before it feels completely natural. I try to add a few of the usual flourishes, the mock astonishment when something disappears or reappears or changes into something else entirely. I can't tell if I'm enjoying it or not but I get through it.

Afterwards, Angelique attaches the camera to a monitor and we watch the film. I'm as nervous watching it as I was when we I was doing it. It's excruciating, seeing myself on screen like that. I look uptight, stiff, nervous. My smile looks forced. Well, it was forced. I see myself doing little flourishes again, like I used to do for Jenny. When she was watching a show I'd do all sorts of winks and sly smiles and flourishes, sort of like a secret touch in a packed lift. I enjoyed those shows so much more.

We watch the whole thing through again and Angelique starts suggesting where we might edit, points out a couple of things we need to change that the camera on its own doesn't pick up on.

'Not bad, as a first attempt,' she says. I wonder if she's just being kind. 'What do you think now it's over?'

'Glad. That it's over I mean. But yeah, it's a bit different with a camera isn't it. I mean, there's no one watching here to spark off but there could be thousands watching.' I go a bit hot under the collar at the thought. But it's what you wanted, I tell myself. 'We'll keep it so we can see how far we've come later on. You need to

Broken Wand

relax a bit more, but that will happen. That second trick could be made to work harder though, the one where you make the watch reappear. I think we could split that up so each time something happens they expect to see the watch but it doesn't reappear until much later. We can play with the audience that way.'

'Oh. I actually thought it worked OK there,' I offer. She just looks away and shrugs a bit. 'But if that's what you think then we can look at that,' I add.

'Well I'd like to work it up a bit more. I think it has potential to be a big end of act joke, keep them in their seats, at least, whoever's watch it is will be there at the end if no one else.' The idea grows on me straight away; it's nice to hear how much she's taken on and learnt from me. I feel a small twinge of – what – pride? Maybe.

Just then Joanna arrives to have a look at the film. She was supposed to be here earlier but she got stuck in some meeting. She leans down to kiss Angelique on the cheek, muttering something about getting stuck in the crowded corridors of power before turning to me with a curt 'hi'. She flops on to an office chair, leaning back and leaning her cheek on a thumb and forefinger, stopping just short of putting her feet up on the desk. She drops her bag on the floor and it flops open. I can see some papers in there with crests printed on them, titles that say something like - She leans down and pulls the bag together.

'Nothing you'd understand in there, Mike,' she says with an icy glance and turns back to the screen. 'Ready when you are.' She says to Angelique. After a pause, there I am, smiling in to the camera. I feel differently about it with her watching. It's like everything is magnified ten times over, an ant in a sunbeam. She doesn't say much, though she does tap her cheek with her finger once or twice. She picks up on some of the same things we did while she's watching it then stays quiet for a few seconds after it finishes. Then she turns to me and says:

'I take it you just rehearsed the tricks and not your performance?'

'Well, yes, that was part of it,' I stutter.

'Oh,' she says, 'well, a bit of work to do there then.' She raises her eyebrows and purses her lips.

'Well I,' I begin, but Angelique chips in.

'Ease up Joanna, he's doing fine,' she says, turning to smile at me. Joanna sees this and I'm aware of her eyes flitting from Angelique to me and back again. For a split second it's as if she's calculating something, assessing a minute shift in the direction of a breeze.

'You know what this show needs?' Joanna announces, leaning forwards, elbows on knees, hands clasped.

'Enlighten us,' says Angelique.

'It needs you, that's what,' she says directly to Angelique.

'Me? In what way? I mean, it's already got me.'

'No, I don't mean masterminding, I mean in it. As a sort of double act. Give it some personality, character, something interesting, a bit of a star turn.' She turns to look at me. 'No offence Mike, obviously.'

'None taken.' I say, more as a reflex than anything else because I'm pretty sure she just took me down.

'I just think,' she continues, 'that you need something to balance out the, well, Mike really. The tricks are good, well planned apart from the points we discussed but it needs something extra. I think you could be that person Angelique. You've got personality in buckets and charm when you want to use it, you're beautiful - all that stuff. Come on, admit it, you're interested.' She's looking at Angelique and there's a half smile on her lips. I can see Angelique chewing it over at rocket speed until she says:

'Mike?' asking me so much in just that word.

'I don't know, I've never worked in a double act before. What do you think?' I throw it back at her. They're just assuming I'll go with this, that I'll change everything in a blink. Despite this, I start to warm to the idea. I mean, she's all the things Joanna said and she's clever. And let's face it, it hasn't exactly gone stellar with just me doing it, now has it.

'Well I have learnt a lot at the rehearsals and I know the tricks. We'd need to adapt them for two of course and work on our delivery. But let me think about it,' Angelique says, 'there's more to consider than a time commitment here. I mean, there are ways to be noticed and ways not to want to be noticed. I think we both know a bit about that,' she says, looking at me with serious eyes.

'But sometimes,' I say, 'being seen means being counted if you do it on your own terms. And you wouldn't be on your own.' She stares at me as she chews her lip. Eventually she says:

'So you're saying you'd like to give it a go?'

'Yes, I think I would. Nothing ventured,' I reply. I can see Angelique is quite surprised at this and as usual I can't really tell what Joanna thinks. Even so, the more I think about it, the more it makes perfect sense to have Angelique in the act.

As I'm heading home on the Tube I look round and see things through slightly different eyes. I don't mind the usual stuffy air or the newspapers tucked down the seats or the drinks can that everyone notices but ignores as it rolls up and down the carriage when it slows down or speeds up again. I don't mind the intense brightness of the strip lighting and I don't even mind the grating white noise that's supposed to be an announcement.

Because soon it might not be the only thing I can rely on to be there every day. Soon I might have other things to think about, not just the delays and smells and sounds that assault me every day. I feel a feeling I haven't felt for ages, years. I can't put a name to it – optimism maybe? All I know is I'm looking forward to this carrying on, to seeing how far we can push it. Whatever else happens, it'll be an adventure. Despite the late hour, I feel quite awake. I'm actually looking forward to something and that's a bloody big deal to me.

18

Angelique opened the door to her flat and sighed, feeling the weight of a long week lift from her shoulders as she'd scooped letters off the floor and thrown them and her keys in to a small bowl on the hall table. She'd kicked her shoes off and walked slowly through to the lounge, dropping her bag by the coffee table and taking her laptop out from the shelf underneath it. Logging in, she opened the file containing the footage from the previous night's rehearsal, setting it up to play and pausing it on Mike's face looking expectantly straight at the camera. She'd stared at the screen for a few seconds, thinking nothing but feeling a small flutter of affection at the familiarity of Mike's face.

She'd smiled at him before going to the kitchen to pour herself a tumbler of wine from the almost empty bottle in the fridge door, then settled back down in front of the screen, savouring a sip of the wine.

'Right Mike,' she'd said, addressing the screen, as she'd hit the play button, 'let's have a proper look at you without Joanna sticking her oar in.'

While they were filming, Angelique had watched his performance on the phone's screen rather than watch Mike himself and she'd noticed a flick of his eyes towards the camera. She noticed this again and froze him at the second attempt; her brows knitting as she tried to work his thoughts out. She got the impression of a small child standing at the board in a classroom about to tackle a serious maths problem in front of everyone. She sensed that at that moment, Mike couldn't see past the camera, couldn't see her standing there behind it and it made him look like he was performing to no one at all.

Taking him off pause he sprang back into life, the expression gone in a blink. As she'd watched he tightened, a hunching of the muscles only just visible and he became more like he was when she first saw him, taking each step as it comes, each trick on its own, no fluidity, no connection. She'd thought back to what she had said afterwards; trying to be nice about it, it was, after all, his first time at this but she'd found it hard to feel the enthusiasm she'd hoped she would. A moment of doubt began to take root as she sipped her wine, hoping it would help to chase it away.

Doubt was one of the feelings she'd had in the instant between Joanna suggesting she join the act with Mike and having to give an answer; thoughts and emotions had jostled for position, well-trodden arguments in her mind all wanting to be considered at the same time. Her knee jerk reaction had been fear; an anxious knot that formed in her stomach as it always did when something was thrown at her that she was unsure of. She'd tried not to let it show on her face as she'd begun to rapidly work through her complex reaction.

As soon as she was at home, alone, and had the time, she had tried to deal with them in a more rational way. The words 'It's a question of dignity' cut through everything. She'd sat back on the sofa, closed her eyes and drifted back to her childhood home, standing in the kitchen with her coat still on, looking up at her mother.

'So can we go?' she had asked once she had finished breathlessly telling her mother about the circus that was parked on the outskirts of town. It had been the talk of her primary school that day and one of her classmates, who had been to see it the day before, told her about a dwarf they'd seen dressed up as a clown, there to make everyone laugh and have stuff thrown over him or, indeed, be thrown himself. The way they had spoken about him made it sound like fun and she was delighted to hear about someone like her who was, to her young eyes, famous. There was no one else like her at her primary school and while no one really mentioned it much, she knew she was different. The circus clown intrigued her.

'No, Angelique, we won't be going,' her mother had replied. Disappointment and longing had flooded her. She'd begged her mother to take her but she'd still refused, saying that it was not the kind of role model she needed. Her mother had taken great care to show her the kinds of women she thought would be good role models – scientists, historians, authors, explorers – all very inspirational but they weren't Little People. 'Because your mind is as big as theirs, even if nothing else is.' she would say by way of well-meant encouragement. 'It's a question of dignity,' she'd said, when Angelique pressed, ending the conversation and her hopes.

She opened her eyes and went to the shelves that line one of the walls in the lounge. She edged down the side of the sofa and took out a white storage box from the bottom shelf. She placed it on the table next to the laptop and took the lid off, lifting out a scrapbook, a big child's one with a cartoon giraffe on the cover, each of the pages a different colour.

She'd fondly inspected the dog eared corners and the creases in the cover and returned the giraffe's smile before smoothing the cover out, even though it didn't need it. She'd taken another sip of wine before she'd opened it reverentially as if it was on a velvet cushion at the Bodleian. Inside, each page had pictures and texts stuck to it and some of the paper was wrinkled where the glue had dried and shrunk it a bit. She traced a finger over the first heading, written by herself in young felt-tipped handwriting. 'Ptah, Creator of the Universe' was the first. He was the one she had discovered by chance in a book in the school library, photocopied and later stuck in to her scrapbook.

The librarian who had helped her with the photocopier asked what her project was about and Angelique had simply replied 'people like me'. The librarian had smiled and offered to search out any other Little People that she could add to the book and between them, the collection grew. Angelique began researching people like herself who had done interesting things, amazing things, things she could emulate or do even better than; tracking down stories and anecdotes and keeping them tucked away, finding time to study them when she could.

What she found, over time, gave her a sense of belonging, a sense of place. She discovered as the project grew that Little People had as much a place in history as anyone else walking down the street, not just the Little People who were kept for entertainment or companionship. That first discovery in her scrapbook, Ptah, was an Egyptian God who literally created the universe. Later on she had discovered details of a small statue that was in the Louvre of Ptah as a dwarf, proudly standing with priests around him. Next she discovered a 16th century Flemish born anatomist who changed many misconceptions about the human body; next a mathematical and electrical engineering genius who was friends with Einstein, then a one-time Chief Architect of Bavaria who wrote fifty-five books on interior design. One of her other early favourites was Jeffrey Hudson, a courtier of Charles I who, having fought in the civil war, joined the exiled Queen Henrietta Maria in France. While there, he won a duel of honour when he was insulted, for which he was expelled from France, captured by pirates and spent the next 25 years as a slave in north Africa before making his way home to England. The daring and romance of his story had captivated her, before she knew that court dwarf was a job title and Little People had a long history of being bought and sold on a whim around the world. She discovered the Spanish artist Velazquez who made many portraits of Little People in the 17th century that were beautiful and portrayed Little People with intelligence and dignity. These she adored and smiled again at the curly, decorative borders she had drawn around the pasted in photocopies.

    Leafing through the pages she read each person's story again, even though she could have recited them all by heart. Many of them had followed their own path; they had persevered and led their lives on their own terms. But at the back of the scrapbook was a picture she kept pasted in as a cautionary tale. On a school visit to the National Gallery, they had visited room 13 to look at some enormous paintings of Roman gods in action when stifled sniggering broke out behind her. She was at the front so she could see the paintings more easily though it didn't always help as she had to crane her neck to see them. She noticed, almost at the same time as the sniggerers that in the bottom right hand corner of one of the pictures, 'Apollo Killing the Cyclops', the border had been painted to look as if it had been lifted. There stood a dwarf, an older man, with no trousers on, his stockings rolled down his legs and his undershirt barely covering his lower body. His arms were crossed in front of him and she could see his hands were chained together and attached to a barred window behind the border. It was the look on his face that held her. He had been painted with a thin, benign smile with his head tilted slightly to one side, as if he was resigned to what was happening to him, but it must have been humiliating. Compared to the beauty and strength of Apollo, he looked ridiculous. She felt humiliated for him and moved on, her cheeks burning, trying to ignore the glances that came her way, some of sympathy, some of curiosity.

She later found out that that the dwarf was a retainer of Cardinal Pietro Aldobrandini, who ordered the artist to paint him like this as a punishment for impertinence but if this was how they treated him, she thought, he could have been forgiven for speaking out once in a while.

She considered them all again, as she had done many times before. For every person who had succeeded, another had been bought or sold as a gift; for every person who had been worshipped as a God, another had been publicly humiliated.

She sat back on the sofa and ran her hands through her hair, ruffling it as though doing so would help to shake her thoughts up. Mike had made some good points after Joanna had suggested her joining the act; he'd talked about controlling it, making it her own and she knew he understood her misgivings, her nervousness about being in the spotlight and in a strange way, him knowing that gave her confidence.

'Maybe,' she thought to herself, 'maybe if I'm doing this voluntarily, not out of necessity, doing it because I want to and I can control it then maybe joining the act would actually be a good thing. If I, we, leave people in no doubt that their intellect has been played with as well as their sense of wonder, create a double act that uses more than just magic tricks - centre the act around telling a story, reference other art forms, make the magic almost incidental, magical tales that come full circle, use video, use live social media during the act - there's a stream of possibilities that would leave people in no doubt that they've been out-thought.

Broken Wand

Intellectual dignity,' she decided, her furrowed brow clearing a little as she looked back at the screen, Mike frozen in his final bow. It was a fine line, but one she was prepared to tread.

'Well Mike,' she said out loud, 'looks like you got yourself a partner.'

Broken Wand

19

I'm still a bit bleary on Sunday morning when Dad phones.

'Michael? It's Dad.' My first thought is that they need me to pick something up on my way over for lunch. Cream for the pudding maybe.

'Hi Dad, I was just getting ready to leave,' I say, searching through my jacket pockets for my keys, the phone wedged between cheek and shoulder, 'everything alright?'

'It's your mother.' There's a tension in his voice that immediately clears my mind and I focus my attention on the phone, holding it to my ear with my hand now.

'What is it Dad? Where are you?'
I get to the hospital and go straight to A+E.

'My Mum's here,' I say at the desk, 'came in by ambulance, Mrs Ruth Forester.'

'Oh, are you Michael?' a voice asks and I turn to see a nurse. I nod. 'That's lucky, I've just come to let the desk know to expect you. I can take you to your Mum.'

'What's happened to her?' I ask. She looks up at me, as if uncertain whether to answer.

'She's had a mild heart attack,' she says gently, 'but she's stable now. Let me take you down there,' and she puts a hand lightly on my sleeve, so that I'll follow her. My legs don't want to move though and I'm staring at the nurse as though she's slapped me. Immediately I feel like the wind has been knocked out of me and my face feels clammy. But it's not Mum I'm thinking of; it's Jenny. Nine years ago, Jenny had been pretty upbeat after her emergency appendectomy; she was home two days later, calling the girls at the salon to make sure they had the clients covered, just felt a bit like she had a cold, put it down to the after effects of the operation. Then I had a call from Jenny's parents telling me she'd been rushed back in to hospital. I couldn't think the worst, I didn't even want to consider it but by the time I'd got there the sepsis had got out of control and caused a heart attack. I was too late.

Broken Wand

'Are you OK?' the nurse's voice breaks my thoughts and I run my tongue round my dry mouth, wiping a hand across my lips while forcing myself to focus on her.

'Yes, I think so, just a bit of a shock,' I bluster. She leads me on to a cubicle where I see Mum lying on a bed, her eyes closed.

'She's had some sedation,' the nurse says, 'so don't be surprised if she sleeps for a bit.' She's wired up to several machines from lines in her arms and has a thin tube coming out of her nose. Her face looks sunken and her skin is an ashy grey colour, her chin cushioned by folds of skin where it sinks onto her chest. She looks so small in the bed and it's so bright in here, the lights make me want to squint.

Dad is sitting in a chair by the bed but he hasn't noticed me yet as I'm still a little behind him. He's looking at Mum and his face has a drawn look that reminds of times when I was a kid and things were bad at the plant. I'd known to be extra careful at school when I saw that face and I felt the same cold clutch in my stomach as I would then. I put my hand lightly on his shoulder to get his attention.

'Michael,' he says as he turns and his face eases a little. 'It's - she's..' All he can do is look at her and point, his voice snagging on the emotion in his throat.

'Don't worry Dad, the nurse told me what happened.' We both look at her. Her eyes are still shut and it's hard to see if she's peaceful or not with all the machines and coverings. 'They said she's stable, so that's good,' I add, looking down at Dad; he tries to smile and it's more than I can handle right then. 'I'll get us some tea,' I say even though I don't want any; I just need to get somewhere I can breathe and I head off to find a machine.

When I find it I lean against it, one hand on the side of it, feeling how weak my legs still are. I know I've got to get it together for Dad though, he's worried enough about Mum. I take some deep breaths and focus on the task in hand.

When I get back, she's still asleep. Dad offers me the chair he's in but I hand him his tea and perch on the bottom corner of the bed, beyond her feet, so I can face him. The tea is still scalding hot

Broken Wand

so I just hold it, grateful for something to do with my hands.

'So, what happened?' I ask gently. Dad clears his throat, turning the cup round in his hands, rubbing his thumb over the corrugated cardboard of the cup holder they slid on to make them easier to hold.

'She was peeling vegetables for lunch and I was in the garden,' he begins, 'down at the end, hoeing between the roses. The weeds can be shocking there if you don't keep on top of them,' he adds. 'I just happened to glance round and I could see her through the window, leaning on the sink and gasping like a guppy, white as a sheet. By the time I got in there the pressure in her chest had started.' He swallowed again and took a sip of tea before carrying on. 'She put it down to indigestion at first but while I was getting her tablets out it spread to her neck and down her arm and then she had real trouble breathing.' He glanced up at me and I could see the struggle in his eyes as he relived this. 'I sat her down at the table and got her some water but she couldn't swallow it. That's when I called the ambulance; I didn't know what else to do.'

'Dad, you did the right thing, that's all you could do.' I reassure him, again putting a hand lightly on his shoulder. 'And look, she's here now and she's going to be fine. It was mild, the nurse said, so that's good news at least.' Dad nods slowly in agreement and turns back to look at her. We both sit in silence for a while, looking at Mum, sipping our tea.

'They say they're going to move her up to the cardiac ward soon; they say she's over the critical bit,' Dad says eventually and I can tell he's trying to reassure himself as well as me despite trying to hide his own concerns behind an unconvincing smile. I smile unconvincingly back, letting him know I understand.

'She's in the best place Dad; they're really good here.' I can feel both of us at that moment put all our trust in 'they'.

When she's moved up to the cardiac ward we're allowed to follow along. I feel a bit like a spare part and try desperately not to look around too much. Not the most private of places. Once she's installed and a curtain is pulled round we're given notice that visiting hours are almost over and we'll have to leave in fifteen minutes.

The next day I come to visit after work; she's awake but still looks incredibly tired.

'So how are you feeling?' I ask, perching on the bed again. 'Dad said you didn't sleep well when I spoke to him this morning.'

'No, I didn't really.' I can hear the fatigue in her voice. 'It's so hot and noisy and they carted someone off in the night. Didn't come back.' It's hard to read what she feels about this, she says it so matter of factly. I decide not to pursue it.

'So, what have they said today? Did you get some tests?'

'Yes, they did quite a few. No results yet but they seem to think I'm actually in pretty good shape, considering.' She doesn't seem to have the energy to do anything but report the facts; it even seems to be an effort to turn her head to look at me.

'Any idea how long you'll be here for yet?'

'If the tests all come back fine I could be out in two days,.' she says flatly.

'As soon as that,' I say but she just looks at me. I'm struggling to know what to say next. It seems too trivial to talk about work and I'm pretty sure she won't be interested in Angelique. I glance at the window a couple of beds away but the view isn't worth it; it's just more buildings opposite, I can't even tell what the weather's doing, just that it's grey.

'You don't have to stay, Michael,' she says, as if reading my thoughts. I feel like I ought to protest, that I should stay and sit with her, that I should say comforting things but what I really want is to get the fuck out of here. I can't stand it, the way it makes me feel, the way it reminds me.

'Right,' I say. 'I'll come tomorrow.'

'Don't worry,' she replies. 'you've got work, Dad will come. I'll see you when I'm home.' I stand by the bed and put my hand over hers. She doesn't move hers at all and I take mine away, smiling my goodbye as I leave as quickly as politeness will allow.

20

I arrange a late shift and go to visit Mum the day she gets home. She's sitting in an armchair in the living room when I arrive, tired from the journey home.

'Brought you these,' I say and proffer the bunch of flowers I picked up at the station.

'Lovely,' she says without reaching out for them. 'Dad knows where the vases are,' she adds and I go to the kitchen to find him. He looks up from the laundry he's folding and follows my gaze to all the bottles of pills on the side.

'She pretty much rattles,' he says in a low voice, glancing at the slightly open door to the living room. 'Look at this,' he adds, showing me the calendar where Mum has itemised her medication by days and amounts for the next couple of weeks until she's due another check-up. 'Did that as soon as she got home,' he adds, grabbing the kettle and filling it.

'Thought she's supposed to take it easy,' I say, sticking the flowers in the washing up bowl as soon as Dad's finished. I pour an inch of water into the bowl until I can find a vase.

'Well,' he begins, 'they said she should be as active as she feels she can be; they don't want her just sitting about but equally she shouldn't start training for a marathon just yet,' he raises his eyebrows. I know Dad won't try to tell her what to do but he will remind her what They said. She'll listen to They.

Dad makes the tea in mugs while I pick the pill pots up and read them, though I've no idea what I'm looking at. I carry the tea through to Mum. She doesn't even blink that I didn't bring a tray with the pot on it so I know she's distracted. She looks tired but she's twitchy at the same time, like there's something she's waiting for. I don't like seeing her like this. She's always just been Mum and dependable and yes, a bit of a worrier but also someone who just gets it done, sorts things out. It feels like something has shifted in the family because of this, it's someone else's turn to worry about the small stuff.

Broken Wand

Dad sits down in the other armchair and I perch on the sofa. Mum takes a sip of her tea and puts it on the small table beside her. It tips slightly as it misses the coaster and a few drops of tea escape over the edge of the mug. Dad's up and getting the dishcloth before I can even offer to.

'No harm done,' he says in a cheery voice that he clearly doesn't feel. It's suddenly clear to me that this is my first real inkling that she won't be there forever and it makes me uneasy. I'd known it of course but never really thought about when; it was always just "in the future". Is this the start of it? It's a sobering thought and seeing how much time might be left with her has suddenly become a real thing. It's not just some mythical future I'm heading for, it's a small amount of time. If anything, it makes me more determined not to spend it in a coffee shop, however sensible that might be.

'What can I do to help, Mum?' I ask, my mouth dry, already knowing the answer will probably be nothing, just clutch at straws and wait.

'I don't know myself yet,' she says, picking at an invisible crumb on her skirt, 'there's a lot to look in to. We'll figure it out when the time comes.' I feel like she's trying to fob me off, like I'm still a boy, like this is just something for the grown-ups to discuss.

'We have to talk about this,' comes out harder than I mean it to, pushed out by the emotions stacking up inside me.

'Michael,' Dad cuts in. Mum takes a deep breath.

'We don't know any more yet Michael,' she says slowly, 'so let's just get on with things until we do know, hey?' and she smiles a tired smile with a hint of finality to it.

'Yes,' I say, 'sure.'

When I leave, Dad follows me out to the driveway. He stands there quietly for a moment, looking across at the gardens opposite, hands thrust into his trouser pockets. From the road we would just look like father and son having a chat in the late spring sunshine.

'You alright son?' he asks but I'm not sure if he really wants know or whether he just wants to be reassured himself.

'I'm fine,' I begin but I can see he's not convinced. 'It's just, I

Broken Wand

mean, she eats OK, she goes out and about..' I go on, 'I don't see how this has happened.'

'Some people are just prone apparently,' he tells me with more resignation in his voice than I was expecting, 'but there are still things she can change and medicines to take.'

'Prone to .. ?'

'They're 99% sure it's Coronary Heart Disease.'

'Coronary Heart Disease,' I repeat, as if this will make it sink in any faster, 'what do you mean 99% sure?'

'Well that's what they said at the hospital,' he says, pointing vaguely up the road. 'All those tests she had come down to that, basically. I didn't want to tell you on the phone.' Dad's looking at me now and I see the fear in his eyes that he can't quite hide anymore. The fear and the pain.

'So when will they start treatment? Have they said?' I ask gently.

'She's going to see the cardiac specialists to talk it over in more detail and make a plan. It's not treatment as such, more a plan of action they said.'

'And when's that?'

'Next week, not long.' He tries to smile again but it doesn't quite make it past a twitch of the lips.

21

Carlos comes out the back to talk to me on a fairly routine Tuesday afternoon. I know he's there because I can see him out of the corner of my eye but he doesn't talk until I turn around from my computer. He just stands there, as usual, with his mouth slightly open, waiting.

When I ask what it is he tells me that someone has a complaint. I don't expect Carlos to be able to deal with things like that; he's loyal and amenable but I think he's only still here because he can just turn up, do what he's told and leave again. Which it suddenly occurs to me is exactly what I do and this irritates me no end.

'I'll be out in a sec, just got to ...' and I wave vaguely at the computer that doesn't need my attention. I'm trying to inject some managerial distance but it feels a bit pathetic. He nods and walks out, unimpressed. I take a deep breath and close my eyes for a brief second before making myself go out to the shop. With a jolt of recognition I see the same guy from a few months ago who asked for a refund. He recognises me too, I can see it. I don't remember the guy with him but they're from the same mould. Cocky.

'Can I help you?' I ask, pretending not to have recognised him.
'This coffee's disgusting. I want my money back.'
'How much have you drunk Sir?'
'What?'
'How much have you drunk?' I indicate the cup in his hand.
'What the fuck does that matter? It's shit.' He says this last part slowly and stares straight at me.

'Company policy is only to give refunds where the product has been tasted and brought back immediately. Otherwise we can assume the coffee was of an acceptable quality to drink.' I have no idea where this is coming from.

'There's this much left,' he says, as he tips the cup and pours the little that's left on the floor from shoulder height, staring at me all the while. It splashes close to other customers who are trying to ignore what is going on. A couple leave rather than have coffee poured over them. Fair enough.

'Just a minute Sir,' I say, and go behind the counter. I catch Cathy's eye as I do and she's giving me a sympathetic look. I wink and her expression instantly changes to one of curiosity but she doesn't miss a beat while making her customer's coffee, smiling and handing it over. My 'customer' is grinning now and shuffling about like a low rent boxer as he talks loudly to his mate about crap service and standards. He thinks he's won and I'm about to refund him but I re-appear with a mop and hold it out to him. It goes very quiet in the café.

'Clean it up.' I say. He's silent for a few seconds. 'I said clean it up.' He tries to swat the mop out of my hand but I hold on to it and present it again. 'You heard.'

'You're a bloody idiot if you think I'm doing your job!' he hurls at me.

'And you have no manners,' I say, holding his stare. I can see he's wavering, wondering whether to beat his chest a bit more. He opts for an exit with threats.

He turns round shouting obscenities and 'you haven't heard the last of this' and storms out with his friend scuttling behind him. I'm left holding a mop in a very quiet café. I slowly become aware that I'm holding my breath and my shoulders are up round my ears, gripping the mop like I'm throttling someone. I look around and people are going back to their coffees and sandwiches, avoiding eye contact. I relax my arms, the mop drops to my side and I go back behind the counter, buzzing from the encounter, adrenalin pumping.

'Carlos, clear that up would you,' I say quietly as I hand him the mop. He just looks at me with his mouth open. 'Thanks,' I add and he takes the mop. Cathy turns away from the counter and mouths a quick "what the fuck" at me as I go out the back and grab my fags before she turns back to the queue with a smile. People start to order again at the counter and the hum of conversation picks up. I actually begin to feel quite exhilarated. I have never stood up to anyone in my life before; I've always kept my head down, taken

Broken Wand

the path of least resistance. I draw deeply on my fag and then start to smile, then laugh and for a few seconds, I can't quite believe what I have just done. I wish the Grad trainee had been here to see it, I'd love to have seen the look on her face.

22

I'm buzzed in to the rehearsal building and make my way up to the office; Angelique is already there, hunched over her phone and scrolling. She doesn't notice me come in.

'That's quite a frown,' I say, indicating her phone, 'something up?'

'Oh, no, fine really,' she says, looking up and pushing her phone away from herself, 'just waiting for an email from my Mum,' she tells me with a forced smile.

'Everything alright?' I ask carefully while I put my stuff down and take my coat off, not wanting to pry but wanting to make sure she's OK. I suddenly feel protective towards her, even though I know she's more than capable looking out for herself, my new-found confidence with bullies making me suspicious on her behalf.

'Oh, yes, she's fine, it's nothing like that it's just that I dropped her an email asking if I could pick up my birth certificate after a girl at work was saying how much she'd had to spend getting a replica when she couldn't find hers.'

'Don't tell me she's lost it?' I ask.

'No idea - she hasn't replied at all, which really isn't like her.'

'Maybe the email got lost?'

'Maybe, but unlikely,' she says, smiling at me. 'I think this is going to be one of those mother-daughter tug of war situations. God knows why but there you go; that's mothers for you.'

'But it's your birth certificate,' I persist, 'you need it for ... stuff. Actually, what do you need them for?' I'm genuinely curious.

'Well Clarrie said she needed hers for her impending nuptials but other than that I'm not entirely sure. But like you say, it's mine, so I want it,' Angelique replies bluntly, jutting her chin out in pretend defiance and slapping both hands down beside her phone.

'Fair enough.'

'So,' she says, signalling the end of the subject by taking a laptop out of her bag and getting it ready on a desk, 'I had a think over the weekend and I want to show you some things I found, to kick us off now we're a double act. There's a fair bit we could learn from I think. OK?'

'In what way?'

'To inject a bit more personality in there. I know I can do that - I'm used to presenting at work - but we just need to start with getting you back in the swing of audience engagement. Then we can combine that with us doing the tricks together. That's where you'll be doing the teaching.' I suppose I should have expected her to have a thorough plan.

'OK,' I say, 'let's give it a whirl.' And if saying that doesn't give away how nervous I am, nothing will.

The first thing she does is show me clips of old magicians from decades ago, black and white film, that sort of thing. They're wearing black tie and white gloves and doing all the usual things - doves out of hats, birds disappearing in cages, sawing women in half, climbing into cupboards and disappearing themselves, walking back on stage with a flourish and a deep bow. It's nothing new. And then she shows me street buskers, clips of them all over the world, on street corners, in marketplaces doing the same old tricks - balls under cups, coins appearing from nowhere, lots of things getting pulled out of empty boxes and cylinders, linking metal rings, cutting rope to bits and restoring it to one piece, levitation, hot foil that turns to ash in a person's hand and I'm at a loss. Why are we looking at a load of old tricks? Is this all she's got? I begin to feel deflated, that maybe I've put my money on the wrong horse.

And then she shows me some clips of guys telling elaborate, bizarre stories with more surreal illusions than actual magic peppered in there. It's close up and weird. When the last one finishes I don't quite know how to react, how to cover my embarrassment. There's a bit of a silence before she asks me what I think.

'Well, it's just - those are all old, they've been done, I don't see how -'

'You're not looking at the right thing.'

'Sorry?'

'You're not looking at the right thing. It's not the tricks.'

Broken Wand

'Then what am I supposed -'

'Look, watch again.' We start to look at the clips again. I'm starting to feel a bit foolish now. I can feel the heat building in my face.

'I'm sorry,' I break in, 'I just don't see - what am I supposed to be looking at?'

'It's not the tricks. The tricks are standard, you can do those backwards. But look at the audiences, look at the crowds they're pulling in. What do you notice about them?' I can't work out if she's being condescending or not. I take a deep breath, puff my cheeks out and I watch again. Slowly it begins to dawn on me what she means.

Their faces, when you can see them, are rapt. They can't take their eyes off the magician or the tricks. But it's not just curiosity, it's total absorption. There's nothing else going on for them at that moment. I can't remember the last time I saw faces like that looking back at me at one of my gigs and I'm beginning to see what she's aiming at.

The guys in the street have a full audience, several people deep but what's great is that no one wanders off after each trick, people are craning over shoulders to see what's so interesting. But it's not the tricks that are keeping them there, it's the magicians, the illusionists, the performers who do that. That's the real skill on display, attracting these people in the first place and holding them there, keeping their attention so intently that they actually part with money voluntarily at the end. They're all doing the same kinds of tricks but they're all doing them in their own way; some with flair, some with a wink, with humour, with slapstick, some with charm, some with an air of mystery and some so matter of factly that they generate an air of cool around themselves.

Point taken. Pretty sure she can see from my face that I've got the message because she gives it a minute before she says:

'You and magic need a bit of couples counselling.' She looks at me so seriously that I can't help smiling. 'Glad you agree,' she says, smiling herself now. 'People who stay together for money are rarely happy in the long term. And you do seem to be a man who

Broken Wand

has been going through the motions for a while, you know, forgotten how it felt when you first met.' I scratch my chin and twiddle with the chair arm. 'People can spot a dead marriage a mile off,' she continues, 'and after a while they stop being fun at parties, just bicker and get drunk.' Now I can't help raising an eyebrow. 'OK, that last bit was a bit over the top but I think you see what I mean,' she says, 'we need to bring the connection back. You're not just delivering an act, you are the act.'

'I'm with you. Personality.'

'And connection. And then we can faff about with the show itself, the nuts and bolts,' she adds, flapping her hands, 'are you up for that?'

'Yes. Yes, I am. If you think it will work?'

'I believe it will.'

'That's agreed then.'

We spend the rest of the afternoon doing the show in bits and pieces, taking it trick by trick and seeing if I can be charming while Angelique becomes more and more blunt with her feedback.

'Smarmy. Too camp. Not camp enough. Too toothy. More drama. Lighten up! Too quick - tease me, leave me wanting more. Definitely no winking. Sorry, what was that? A bit Errol Flynn. Continuity - where's the continuity?!'

We take a break and I fetch some water for us both. I lean on the edge of the desk, rubbing my eyes.

'It was easier, when I was a kid,' I say. She waits for me to go on. 'There's always the cute kid factor when you're young, you don't really have to work that hard. And they know you, the people watching, so you're half way there.' She still doesn't say anything but she's looking thoughtful. Now she's staring at me.

'What?'

'I want to try something,' she says, thoughtfully.

'Oh good,' I deadpan. She side eyes me and carries on.

'Choose a trick that you could do with your eyes shut. A simple one.'

'Well, I could make something small and annoying disappear?' I say pointedly. She arches her eyebrows.

Broken Wand

'No, don't do that, you might want children one day.' Despite myself, I can't help but snort-laugh. I go to grab something small off a desk and but there isn't a lot to choose from except a few knick knacks. I spot a small black stone swan near a monitor so I pick that.

'Good. Stand in front of me, like before. Now close your eyes.'

'But how will I engage with you with my eyes shut?'

'Trust me.' I close my eyes tight like a little kid pretending to be asleep and grip the swan tighter in my hand. I just want to go home now. I'm tired and I don't need the cod psychology.

'OK. Picture this. You're in a small venue and it's classy, the latest interior design. Small round tables with silver tablecloths, velvet covered chairs, a proper stage but intimate. People are sipping cocktails, wearing frocks. You're the headline act. In fact you're the only act, they're here to see you. Understand?' I nod. 'Good. Now I want you to imagine an audience of your own choosing, from your childhood if necessary, anyone you want. A bit like a dream dinner party - who would be there?' I open my eyes narrowly and look at her.

'Do you want me to tell you?'

'Not if you don't want to. Then when they're all there, do the act for them. You can just pretend; easier than fumbling about for stuff with your eyes shut.' I can't see how this will change things, but whatever. I close my eyes again, and roll my shoulders a couple of times to relax a bit. I clear my throat and start to think. I see myself first. I'm in a clean cut new suit by some designer, looking good, even to the point of cufflinks. I'm taller. But when I look out from the stage, it's different. There aren't tables, there are rows of seats, like a theatre. It's tiny, five seats wide and three rows deep and just black all around; I can't see any walls and the stage is just an area in front. It's very close, a matter of feet. Right in the middle of course, is Jenny. For a few seconds I just watch her, like there's a one way window between us. She's settling in to her seat, folding her coat, putting it over the back of the chair. She's wearing a nice dress and her hair's tied back in a tight, high ponytail. She used to joke it was called an Essex facelift, not that she needed one. She crosses her legs and folds her hands in her lap, glancing around expectantly.

Next in is Grandad. He settles next to her and they say hello but they don't chat, they didn't know each other; he was long gone before I met Jenny. He's wearing his suit and it hangs off him baggily like it did just before he died. His face is thin but not drawn and in pain any more. He sits with his arms outstretched, a hand on each knee. Mum and Dad file in the other side of Jenny because I feel like they should be there and, because it's my audience, they have to want to be there and they are really proud; Mum has had her hair done; she pats it a few times and smiles at Dad.

Then there's Paul Daniels with Debbie McGee the other side of Grandad but this makes me really nervous so I put them in the row behind. They're holding hands and Debbie's laughing at something he's said. He's not as small as I thought he would be but he does have to lean sideways slightly to see round Jenny's high ponytail. I move them along a couple of seats so he doesn't have to. And then, like audiences do with a bird-like intuition, they all face the front and go quiet at the same time, expectant. But I don't feel nervous at all, in fact, I feel at home.

Suddenly they can see me, they're all able to look at me and smile and they clap a little bit as if I've just walked out on the stage. It's so nice that I can't help but smile back. I open my eyes and begin to put the little black swan through its paces, making it disappear, appearing again in Grandad's pocket; throwing it in the air then looking confused when it doesn't come down again, wrapping it in a tissue and giving it to Jenny to hold then Dad finding it underneath his chair, the tissue empty.

Then I imagine borrowing Dad's watch which was Grandad's originally but he doesn't seem to notice and I pretend to smash it up, making Dad gasp with horror and then astonishment when it's fine, Mum holding her face in her hands, wide eyed, until she knows all is well. I click my fingers and fire comes out of my index finger, setting fire to a card I've signed that burns up in a flash then reappears in Debbie McGee's shoe.

I do another card trick and Mum finds one that they watched

me cut to pieces whole in her handbag. I smile and joke and chat and charm and I'm having a great time. They're all laughing and clapping and it's wonderful. And at the end, I'm smiling at Jenny and she's smiling back as I take my bows. I hold her gaze. And when I focus it's Angelique returning my gaze with a look on her face I can't quite decipher. I haven't felt like this in ages. I can't find the words so I just smile and say 'Well?' She doesn't answer for a few seconds.

'I don't know who was there but they're lucky people to inspire that in you,' she says. I don't want this feeling ever to stop as she adds 'I think we can safely call that a breakthrough.'

23

Angelique made her way in to the lounge at her mother's house and noticed that the footstool had been placed in front of one of the armchairs for her so she would know where to sit. It was a chair with a hard seat pad, easier for her to get out of when the time came to leave. She was still feeling positive after the rehearsal and despite misgivings about having to steer Mike through it a bit, it was a good start. Linda came in with two mugs and placed one on the small side table next to Angelique, settling herself on the sofa and her mug on to another small side table and crossing her legs at the ankles.

The set up in the lounge had been the same since Angelique could remember; sofas and chairs all facing each other, a TV tucked away on the corner of the room, only to be watched when there was a specific programme they wanted to see and then put away again. Bookshelves full and neatly arranged alphabetically.

'I'm glad you've come Angelique,' Linda began, 'I have some news for you.' She spoke carefully as she straightened the edge of her cardigan, gathering herself together to continue.

'Not like you mother; I'm intrigued.' Linda glanced at her briefly before starting to recite what Angelique knew would be a well prepared speech.

'As you know, I've been attending an Italian evening class since last September.' Angelique bristled inwardly at the use of her teacher voice. 'Well, one of my co-students Paul and I have been meeting to practise our conversation and, well, we've been seeing each other socially for the last few months.'

Angelique stared at her mother, her eyes narrowing almost imperceptibly.

'What do you mean, seeing each other socially? Is it serious? Are you 'an item'?' she added, making apostrophe signs with her fingers.

'If you're going to be like that,' her mother said instantly, already paving the way not to have the conversation if she wanted to stop it. Angelique closed her eyes for a second before answering.

'No. I'm sorry. It's just you've never, you know, had someone that you 'see socially'.'

'No, I haven't,' her mother replied bluntly. 'I had you to look after and a job to do. And now you're a grown woman and I'm working part-time I can move on with my life.' She knew this was just Linda's way of putting the facts out there but she couldn't help resenting the tone.

'Mother, I'm 27. What have you been waiting for? Don't use me as an excuse.'

'I'm not. I never have. It was a commitment to you I made willingly. You know that,' she added, pointedly.

'So what have you told him about me?'

Linda hesitated at this, looking into her mug thoughtfully.

'I've told him I have a daughter,' was her careful response.

'And?'

'And that you're an Oxford graduate working in London.'

'Mm-hm. So when are you going to tell him the rest? Or are you going to wait until you're another year down the line to drop that on him?'

'I'm not waiting for anything, it just hasn't come up yet. What I have told him is how proud I am of you, that you have a good job, your own place.'

'What do you mean, it hasn't come up yet? What, are you waiting until you're watching a film with a dwarf in it so you can casually say 'oh, by the way, my daughter's one of those'?'

'Angelique, I know this is a surprise for you but do you think you could be a bit less confrontational? I'm allowed to have relationships.'

'But you never have and I wouldn't care if you did.'

'Oh. Well that's nice.'

'I didn't mean - I just meant that it's your business but it would be nice to know.'

'You know now. Do you tell me everything about your life the minute it happens?'

'It's not really about that,' Angelique responded, trying to deflect her mother's quite accurate point, 'it's about why you haven't told him everything about me.'

'But Angelique, I haven't told him because it didn't occur to me that it would be a sticking point. He's a nice man and you're a grown woman. I don't foresee a problem.'

'So when will I meet him?'

'Soon.' Angelique knew better than to try to push her mother to promise a date or a month.

'Fine,' Angelique replied, putting both hands out in front of her, 'I hope it works out for you.'

'Thank you, Angelique," Linda said, bringing that part of their conversation to a stilted end. 'I'll make us some lunch,' she added as she stood to clear the mugs away, choosing to ignore the possibility of sarcasm. Angelique watched her mother leave the room knowing there was no point in pursuing the subject; it would continue when her mother decided it was time, and not before.

24

The floodlights at the dog track are so bright it almost feels like daylight except for the pitch black oval of sky above the open air stadium. It's warm enough in the evenings now to stand outside and watch, gets you closer to the action, have a pint or two, probably pick up a curry on the way home, a few bets on a few races. I'm not a gambling man usually but things are starting to feel different now I've made a decision about the act and it's Friday night so I'm a bit more relaxed.

Maybe it's confidence, maybe it's recklessness, maybe it's the smell of impending summer on the air but I do feel like taking a chance. I win £25 and for the first time in ages I'm starting to feel like something might be changing.

I lean my elbows on the barrier and pick at the rim of my plastic pint glass. Looking around me I unexpectedly feel a vague sense of affection for the place, something more than it just being familiar. I've known it since I was a boy; Grandad used to bring me here on Saturday afternoons to catch up with his mates though he never used to place a bet; he'd tell me about the dangers of taking risks and where that could lead. They'd stand about with pints and fags and chat while the races went on. They used to say it was a bit more entertaining than the pub though that didn't stop them going there as well.

It's not quite the same now – all no smoking and plastic glasses, hot dogs instead of pies, no wooden benches (fire regs) – but there's still a sense of kindred spirits around the place, shadows of the past that still pull people in.

If I close my eyes and think hard enough, I can still smell the dampness on his coat when it rained, a heady mix of fag smoke, beer and anticipation. I'm enjoying it, just being here. Afterwards, we'd go home to our house and watch a bit of telly.

'Let's put the magic man on,' Grandad would say as he plonked himself down in an armchair with a bottle of beer. I'd go and switch the TV on and we'd watch the Paul Daniel's show; Grandad would laugh at some of the things he said to the audience though I didn't always understand.

We'd watch closely and I'd try and do the same tricks in the days that followed. It was nice, that time with Grandad. Mum and dad would be at the social club up at the Ford plant in Dagenham, where Dad worked. Mum used to moan that he was there all week and couldn't they go somewhere different. Sometimes they did but not often. Dad used to say he needed to keep in touch with the lads and not just see them at meetings. It was important, he said, for a foreman to let his men know he was still one of them. It was a dance he said, a tricky dance between workforce and bosses with too many steps. That was all he ever said about it and I wasn't too sure what he meant as a kid, though I do now. My thoughts are broken by a voice next to me and a tap on the arm.

'It is you. Mike, isn't it?' I turn and see a bloke about my age, vaguely familiar.

'It's Darren, Darren Waits. Remember?' The name triggers my memory and he slots in to place.

'Yeah, yeah, I remember. Rainham Youth Club, right? How you doing?'

'Yeah, pretty good as it goes. Doing alright mate.' I can't believe the change in him. He was a fat kid at youth club, glasses and a bit shy. Now he's slim, well dressed in a suit and clearly not so shy.

'Can't believe I've bumped in to you now though, quite a coincidence,' he says, as if I'm supposed to know what he's talking about.

'Is it? Why's that then?' I ask.

'Well, what with you being a bit of an internet star and all.' He's grinning at me now and looking slightly gawky, arms spread wide like I should get the joke immediately.

'Sorry, I ...'

'Oh my God, you haven't seen it, have you? Allow me to enlighten you.' I'm starting to feel uncomfortable now, he's clearly excited about this and grinning all over his face as he gets his phone out and starts swiping and typing.

'Oh, you're gonna love this!' he says and I get the feeling I'm not going to at all. And then I'm watching a slightly shaky film in a coffee shop and there's a man with a name badge on shouting at another guy in a suit to clean up the mess he's made while holding a mop out to him. Everyone around the man with the badge is watching him, including the staff and his face is red, angry, furious in fact. He's holding the mop out like it's some sort of ancient staff and glaring at the bloke in the suit. My blood runs cold and I swallow hard.

'How did you get that?' I ask. My mouth is drying out, my palms are sweaty.

'It's all over the internet mate. You're trending. I knew it was you, I bloody knew it and then I run in to you – what are the chances, eh?' He gives out a loud honk of laughter and clamps his hand to my shoulder.

'You're trending mate, you're bloody trending.' He says this like it's a good thing. He tells me it's been posted by LilliputRises, some sort of anti-capitalist group and labelled as 'Java Hut coffee, the revolution starts here!' A knot gradually tightens in my stomach and suddenly I'm not too interested in the dogs anymore. Darren claps me on the back again with a loud

'Amazing, mate, amazing!' and goes inside to the bar. I hope work don't find out about this. I wonder how trending I am, just how far and wide this has gone and I start to feel bit hot and I need to go home.

I have to walk through the bar to get outside and as I do there's a cheer from a group of blokes and I see Darren is there with his phone out and they've all turned to look at me, smiling and making solidarity signs with clenched fists. They've all seen it and they're laughing but I don't think they're doing it nastily. Are they? I can't tell.

I go out through reception and the girl behind the desk says goodnight and smiles and I wonder if she's seen it. I pass some guys coming in and I hold the door for them to pass and they say cheers and smile and I wonder if they've seen it. I stop at the kebab shop, even though I'm not that hungry yet, and I glance at everyone wondering if they've seen it. There's a group in the corner sitting at the formica table and they suddenly laugh. I look round but they aren't looking at me, just laughing at each other, hunched over their food. I half expect to see it on the TV in the corner which is when I know I need to calm down, I'm freaking myself out now.

I tell myself to get a grip, that no one is going to be bothered about it in ten minutes time, that these things come and go so quickly. The guy behind the counter plonks the wrapped kebab in front of me, breaking my thoughts and asks for the money. I pay and hug the kebab to me inside my jacket, its warmth is oddly comforting and I relax a bit walking home.

By the time I get there I eat it straight from the paper watching some chat show, two people I've heard of and one I haven't, all vying to be the most excited.

25

I'm only just in the door of the shop on Monday morning when the phone rings. It's head office. They must have checked my schedule because they knew when I'd arrive and they've arranged for Carlos to cover me at lunchtime so I can go in for a meeting. Even though I'm fairly sure why, I ask anyway only to be reassured it's nothing to worry about, just some time to go over a few things. But it clearly is because there's no way they'd leave the shop in the hands of an assistant manager at lunchtime usually.

I plod through the morning by processing some orders – paperwork dulls the brain but is needy enough to keep your attention – and am on time for the meeting but kept waiting in reception. Cathy's last words to me as I left the shop ring in my ears: 'Don't let them bully you Mike. Stand your ground; you did nothing wrong.' But as I recall from experience, doing nothing wrong doesn't stop the bullies.

The reception is large area with a couple of hard sofas that are difficult to sit comfortably in and a long shiny desk down one wall where the receptionists wear headsets. The whole thing probably has a bigger footprint than my entire flat. I'm engrossed in mapping out an imaginary floorplan to check this as a few people come through reception and glance my way, one even stopping for a quick chat with the receptionist; they both glance over at one point, barely disguising their smirks.

I wish I was wearing my magic show suit, the smartest thing I own, but instead I'm in my shop shirt with a waterproof coat over my arm. I look like a train spotter. I'm perched on the edge of the sofa and my coat is straining across my shoulders as I hunch forward, my elbows on my knees. Not quite the sophisticated managerial image I would have gone for but there you go. I feel exposed here. It's the way everyone looks at me like they all know. Well I suppose they do all know. I'm not used to being seen unless I'm doing a show. It feels strange, to go from invisible to highly visible all of a sudden, like I've taken off a cloak and presented

Broken Wand

myself as the prince of the party.

Something buzzes and a receptionist shows me in to a large room with a large table made up of smaller ones. Some sort of training room maybe. There's a plate of biscuits and some coffee and water to the side but as there are already three people sitting down waiting for me, I don't ask and they don't offer.

'Have a seat,' says the bloke in the middle. He's not unfriendly but he's not exactly warm either. 'I'm Peter, I'm the HR Director, this is Emma, HR manager and this is Siobhan, PR Manager,' he indicates to his left and right and they give quick, professional smiles. 'Mike,' he continues, 'we're obviously aware of a certain film clip on the internet which has gathered some attention and we just want to have a quick chat about that really, try to form an idea of what might have triggered your response to this customer.' He pauses for a second to look at his iPad; they must have just been watching it again. I open my mouth to speak but he holds a hand up to interrupt me and asks: 'Is there anything you'd like to share with us about your current role, Mike? Any concerns?' I must admit I'm confused by this question. All three of them are looking at me. The PR woman is particularly annoying; a fixed fake smile while she pretends she's interested when she so clearly isn't. I can tell her mind is on something else. At least the bloke from HR has the decency to look like he's going through the motions. I wish they'd just give me a bollocking and get it over with.

'Not sure what you mean,' I reply.

'I just mean is there anything you'd like us to know about?'

'With my job?'

'Yes.'

'No.' I hold his gaze. I'm not being arsey, I'm just not giving any ground.

'Well, in that case, can you explain your response to this .. situation? Do you think you could have handled it differently?' he asks. Emma cocks her head to one side to make it look like she's interested in my reply.

Yes, I think, I could have shoved that mop right up his backside and cleaned the floor with him.

'Um, yes. I suppose I could have. But I didn't, did I? I responded like any human would when faced with a total – with a customer like him.'

'There's no need for that kind of attitude, Mike,' he says, 'though I can see you're still upset.' Siobhan the PR woman crosses her legs and purses her lips, clearly holding no truck with emotional responses in work situations.

'I'm not upset,' I manage to reply calmly, 'I'm trying to explain that it's about a basic human response.' There's a pause in the room. I've certainly taken them off the box ticking list now.

'Sorry?' he says, and he actually checks his watch, which hacks me off more than anything else has so far.

'Human responses. I responded like a human would in the face of a bully. I have humanity.' That takes the smile off the PR woman's face. She's looking a bit more worried now. Making it real, a thing that involved two people not just their employee is not what they want. They want to be able to wrap it in corporate bubble wrap and make it go away.

'Look, Mike, no one is making a comment about you personally.' He's trying to take it back to the list, wanting to wrap the meeting up so he can get out of there; it is nearly lunchtime after all.

'Then what are you doing, Peter?' I look him straight in the eye. 'It was me, I did it and I am a person therefore you have to understand it was personal and you are reacting to me as a person so the comments are personal.'

'I think we're moving off the point here.'

'No I think we're just getting to it.' I was beginning to find my stride. I crossed my legs, folded my arms and ploughed on. 'If you take the humanity out of life, work, whatever, then you take out the core of what we are.' I felt my face flushing as I said this, realising I wasn't entirely sure what I was saying myself.

'Oh Jesus..' Peter rubbed his forehead, 'we just don't want you to do it again, OK? Can you just accept that?' He stretched a hand out towards me, palm upwards. He seemed tired, weary, like a talking suit. He didn't give a shit about the person involved, just how it was affecting their image, their profits.

And then Emma the HR Manager kicks in. She's in a sharp plum coloured suit, all crispness and ironed, hair swept back and lipstick that makes her mouth look like one of those plastic sets of lips you get in Christmas crackers.

'Mike,' she starts, 'we really appreciate all the hard work you've put in over the years. You're one of our longest serving branch managers,' she says this like it's a good thing, 'but we think maybe it would be beneficial for you to attend one of our current management induction courses to make sure you're totally up to speed with our brand messaging and the latest management specifications; our culture, the company personality if you like. Not compulsory but obviously, in the circumstances, we'd really appreciate it if you'd agree.' In other words, agree you daft shit; I just want to say I've done my bit so I can file you under 'sorted' and forget all about you cocking things up.

I thought about it. Me and a room full of keen young things on a management induction course, all looking to make a mark on the coffee world. Me, jaded as fuck watching the clock, them making copious notes, swallowing it down whole with the coffee provided. I can't do it anymore. I can't hate what I do this much and pretend I don't. Finally I say:

'No, I don't think I can. I think it might be best if ...' I hesitate. I think of my parents, what they would say if I gave up my steady job now. How they would fear for my future if I stepped away from this safe job. Would I even have a future? It would be impulsive and impulsive had created this mess in the first place. My ears began to burn. I looked down at my hands in my lap.

'Mike?' Peter was looking at me expectantly.

'Yes, OK. I'll do the course.'

'OK, great. Well we'll monitor the situation and let you know if anything changes but in the meantime, just don't do anything like make comments or retaliate in any way if you are asked about it. If you do, just let Siobhan know and she'll handle it.' Siobhan smiles briefly but doesn't deign to speak. 'We don't want this to drag on and I'm sure you don't either. Let us know if you need to talk anything through.' The other two are already picking up their stuff ready to leave. Peter was back to being Mr Efficient again, quickly scrolling on his iPad. 'We'll email the details of the next management training course, thank you for agreeing to participate.'

26

We've arranged a free show in a pub near Angelique to try out the new double act. Angelique thinks it's going to be best if we go in cold with it and review people's honest reactions so we haven't promoted it. It's in the conservatory which means it won't be dark for a while but it should be OK.

'You seem a bit distracted,' she says as we're checking the props over in the pubs conservatory. 'Everything OK? Not nervous are you?'

'Oh, no not really. Well yes, a bit,' I correct myself while running my hands round five metal rings, feeling for the tiny fractures in them that allow me to create the illusion of slipping them through Angelique. 'Actually, I was called in to HQ a couple of days ago. They weren't overly happy about the video clip of me.' I say and I tell her the details of the meeting.

'Wow, they sound delightful,' she says with raised eyebrows.

'Yeah, well, luckily they're just names on memos most of the time.'

'Shame you can't make them disappear,' she says with a smile, 'you could sort my Mum out at the same time.'

'Oh?'

'Turns out she's got a new boyfriend, had him for a year. Won't bore you with the details but needless to say he doesn't know about me yet,' she adds, smiling ruefully at me.

Before I can ask more the landlord comes in and asks if we're about ready as he'll go round the tables and let everyone know to come in and watch. It feels a bit odd just to be standing at the side waiting for people to file in. As they do, there's a hubbub of chat and scraping of chairs and tables while people sort the seating arrangements, drinks on trays getting handed out where people have got rounds in.

Once people have settled a bit, we go to the front of the conservatory and Angelique steps forward to introduce us. I notice heads moving to try and see her better; the disadvantage of not

Broken Wand

having a stage. She quickly says something about this and encourages people to move their chairs while we get to our start positions.

Normally, I would pick my moment and just start but having Angelique there makes it very different - timing, reactions, choreography - all have to be split second perfect for us to look seamless. I picture my perfect audience, just like we did at rehearsals and it occurs to me that one of them is next to me. She's become part of the act yes, but also the reason I'm still doing it. I want to do it for her.

Our big final trick is one we have been working on quite a bit and I feel a sense of excitement mixed with nerves as we go in to it. While Angelique is charming someone in to being a willing volunteer, I pick up a big cardboard box from the side of the room and place it on the table, centre stage. I reach inside and take out a large roll of parcel tape. Once our volunteer has had a round of applause I hand her the roll of tape and ask her to inspect it. She does, confirming it is just a roll of tape. I flip the large box over and ask her to test the already taped join at the bottom and again, she confirms it is taped up. I take a permanent marker from my jacket pocket and ask her to sign her name across the tape so it will be obvious if it has been broken or replaced. When she has, I turn the box back over so that Angelique can climb inside once I have helped her onto a chair and then onto the table. She ducks down with a flourish and her arms are the last to go in. She puts a hand out of the box and I put her phone in it, after which I fold the flaps over her head and ask the volunteer to tape her in and sign it again.

While she's doing this I tap on the box and Angelique taps back. Then when I've checked the seal one last time I throw a cloth over the box and ask for a question from the audience – anything at all – and I text it to Angelique. Once I've done that I whisk the cloth off the box and drop it on the floor behind the table, throwing my arms up in the air. The box is still sealed. I pretend to be embarrassed and announce I'd better take the tape off to make sure she's OK. As I do so, I ask the volunteer to help me and she gasps when she sees that the box is empty except for the phone. I tip it up to show the audience, spin it round to show them the bottom is still intact and they ooh and gasp and laugh. Just then my phone bleeps and there is an answer to the question: 'The Statue of Liberty is over 300ft tall' and behind the table Angelique throws the table cloth off herself and walks round to the front of the table, triumphant. We hold hands and take a small bow to a genuinely impressed round of applause.

It goes well, all things considered and several people come over to say thanks and good luck and as we're packing up, a young woman comes over to us and introduces herself.

'Hi, I'm Daisy,' she says, 'loved the act. Look, if you've got a spare five minutes, I was wondering if I might have a chat with you both? I'm a freelance reporter and I'd love to do a write up for the local paper if that's OK? Can't guarantee it'll get in but you never know. Wouldn't need to ask you much, just the basics and then review the act. OK?' she asks cheerily. I look over to Angelique who quickly agrees to the interview and we pull some chairs together. She takes our full names and asks how we met and how much we've done so far and it's all over pretty quickly. She takes a couple of quick photos on her phone. 'These should be good enough,' she says to Angelique, 'but if not I'll give you a buzz. Great, well thanks for your time and good luck.' We say our goodbyes and she leaves.

'Well that was interesting,' I say, 'didn't expect that to happen.'

'Like she said, just happened to be here with friends. Lucky for us though; bit of publicity won't hurt,' Angelique says. 'Buy a girl a quick drink?' she asks, 'thirsty as hell after that.'

27

I pop a can of coke open as I climb the steps to the Tube platform on Saturday morning, the odd kebab wrapper caught in the railings the only mementos of Friday night. I take a few good gulps, the fizz-rush making my eyes widen momentarily, then put it down on a metal mesh seat, taking the weekend magazine out of the local paper, hunching my shoulders as I do so against the early morning chill.

I don't mind Saturdays in the shop as much; it's quieter and I can catch up on paperwork but the early morning starts when everyone else is having a lie-in grates. It's not so bad at this time of year though; at least it's light when I leave the flat.

The electronic board tells me I've got four minutes to wait though it's fairly unreliable and could be anything up to ten minutes so and I turn my attention back to the magazine. It's not that demanding a read, a few interviews but mostly listings, that sort of thing. I'm flicking through it, trying to keep the corners flat against the breeze that whips along the platform and yawning while I wait for the Coke to kick in.

Then, in what takes a couple of disconcerting seconds to process, I see my own face looking back at me. Page 19. 'Romford magic act conjures up new show' runs the headline. My stomach turns icy and my mouth goes dry. I thought they said they'd let us know if they were going to use it. I'm looking at the words on the page but not really reading them; my eyes keep flicking back to the picture of me and Angelique. The train pulls in and I step on, sitting in the sideways seat by the door. I take a long swig of my Coke and I reopen the magazine, telling myself to calm down. I'm feeling a mix of excitement and fear. The picture isn't the greatest, I always come across a bit moon-faced in photos but Angelique looks OK. She's slightly in front of me, a big confident smile on her face. I read on, anxiously.

'There's magic in the air for a Romford couple who are making waves with their own particular kind of entertainment.

Mike Forester and Angelique Watson have gone back in time with their own brand of family magic – with a twist. Already established on online channel YouTube, the pair have recently begun to do live shows with more in the pipeline. In a world where magic has taken to the streets with the likes of Dynamo and Blaine setting the trend for fly on the wall magic involving ever more inventive ways to perform what's been dubbed 'miracle magic', Mike and Angelique hark back to the era of magic shows with a front man and a glamorous assistant – with one or two updates. An odd mix, it seems that Mike is the straight man, almost to the point of wooden delivery, while Angelique, who instantly draws attention due to her diminutive stature, is all charm and smiles as she plays to the audience and is definitely no simple glamorous assistant. This journalist can't help wondering if the magic would be as impressive without the quirky characters that deliver it. Would we be as interested if Angelique was 5ft 10' and vacuous? Mike has been a familiar face in Romford pubs over the years so maybe this is his last chance to cut it. Is being quirky enough? Overall, the show is entertaining and fun but I say, with a bit of polish, could do better. 6/10'

    I can't quite believe what I've just read. It was meant to be a review, not a bastard shredding. She's stitched us up, the bitch. I want to screw the paper up but I can't tear my eyes away. What's Angelique going to say?

    I want to leave the train, go straight to her, I want to see her now and it takes a deep breath and closing my eyes for a second not to do that at the next stop. My neck prickles and my stomach churns. My leg starts to jiggle. I have to go to work, I have to wait. I'll phone her later, give myself time to think. I look around the carriage.

    There aren't too many people at this early hour but it feels like it's packed. Everyone's just carrying on, not looking at anyone else, just glued to their tiny screens. I read the article four more times before I reach to my stop, the print gets smudged with the sweat on my hands and I call her as soon as I leave the train.

28

That evening, at Angelique's flat, the paper is on the coffee table between us and Joanna is there, checking out the online comments. The same piece was put on the paper's website and it has kicked off a bit of a shitstorm.

'Well I don't think it's too bad.' Angelique says and I can't quite believe what I'm hearing.

'The whole thing is an insult,' I fire back, 'how are we meant to show our faces after that?' Joanna chips in:

'No one's going to recognise you anyway Mike. You've got one of those faces. And besides, this could be really good for you.'

'Oh really? How exactly?' I can feel the disbelief in my voice; it's almost physical. Despite my outburst, she doesn't bother to look up from her laptop and takes her time answering.

'Looking at these comments online,' she begins, 'there's a big debate. You're certainly being noticed now. It's opened up a way bigger discussion than whether you can do magic or not. Either you're a total bastard who's exploiting Angelique or she's a boundary breaking bad ass and you're helping her. Either way, the attention is there. The hits from those YouTube clips you put up last week are up already.' I can feel myself heating up again. I don't want to be thought of as a total bastard; this is not the sort of attention I was looking for. How can this be good?

'It was bound to happen sooner or later Mike,' Angelique breaks in before I can reply, 'this journalist is on a local rag, looking to get herself noticed so she starts a debate by being a bitch and the reader numbers rocket. It's a tried and tested formula. She'll no doubt go on to have a glittering career closely observing celebrity cellulite and royal offspring. She's done us a favour, trust me.' I do trust her, but I don't follow the logic.

'And you don't mind?' I say, half statement, half question.

'Well, I suppose a bit. It's just going to take a bit of getting used to.'

'Not sure I'll get used to people being deliberately nasty.'

Broken Wand

'Not them, us. People will have to get used to us. To me. When they see we can do the magic and create a show worth watching, they'll see past the other stuff.' She's quite calm about it all but then she's the one who's used to being noticed anyway, wanted or otherwise.

'So what do we do now?' I ask Angelique and she draws a breath to speak but Joanna gets in ahead of her.

'We set up a web page,' says Joanna looking at Angelique before turning to me. That 'we' hangs in the air like a challenge and her eyes are daring me to object. Angelique is quiet, looking at me sideways as if waiting to see what I will do. I say nothing but let Joanna carry on. 'We'll put our own version of events on and all the necessary booking details, next gigs and all that. We make the most of it,' she continues. I know she's right and what she says makes total sense and I resent that it's her saying it but what can I do? I'm no help with that stuff. I don't answer, just look down at my hands and fold them together.

'Great,' says Angelique briskly, with a quick smile to me, 'I'll buy a domain and we'll get started. Nothing fancy and we can work on the live streaming later. Let's put a home page up there at least then we can link to social media channels, add some profiles. It's sooner than I would have liked, we could do with more content but we can back fill.' She smiles at me and I think it's supposed to be reassuring but seeing the slight smile on Joanna's face as Angelique comes over to sit by her to start work on the laptop makes me want to sulk.

They huddle over the laptop, speaking in tongues. I watch for a while, redundant. I always thought it must be a complicated job to set up a website, but apparently not if you know what you're doing.

'We're just going to call us Mike and Angelique. OK with you?' Angelique asks, 'no time to come up with anything fancy really. Only we're going to need to register it now so we can secure the domain and start building.' She looks at me expectantly.

'Yes, fine,' I say, as if I have a choice and I try to sound less sullen than I feel like. She just smiles quickly and turns her attention back to the laptop. I sit quietly, watching them. Joanna is blunt but she listens to Angelique who is all business-like now. I put the kettle on though I'm not sure they're even aware I've left the room.

Just a couple of hours later it's done. Apparently it's a quick fix and will take a while for things to register and go live but that can happen overnight. Grudgingly, I have to admit it looks good. The name is at the top in fancy lettering, there's pictures of us and the YouTube clips are on there. Gig details and contact details – all there. It seems we're on Twitter and Instagram as well so we can talk to the fanbase we are about to build. We're out there now; I'm out there now. And even though I've put myself in front of people for years, it feels strange to know that people can watch me - judge me - and I will have no idea they're doing it unless they 'like' me or leave a comment. I feel the urge to check straight away, to see if anyone has seen it yet and at the same time I don't want to know. It feels like I'm standing at the front of the class or doing the school show but the lights are off and I can't see the audience. I'm not at all sure I like the feeling.

'Now we just have to agree what we're going to say about the article as the first blog entry,' says Joanna, fully confident of her hold on this now, not even a smug smile. Then she slowly reels off a statement, Angelique typing as she speaks:

'Mike and Angelique were interested to see the comments made in the Romford Times article, which you can read here. While some of the comments were valid – we are polishing the act continually for instance – we simply do not feel that direct comment about us is necessary. By all means review our ability to perform magic and entertain – we welcome feedback – but negative speculation based on physical appearance is unhelpful in a wider context. But you can make your own minds up – check out our videos and let us know – we'd love to hear from you!' She stopped and Angelique read it back, as if admiring a painting.

'That covers it as far as it goes,' says Joanna, 'I think it says what we need it to without giving her any more satisfaction. We don't want to start an argument with her. It's a dignified response. Now we just need to go to the comments on the original article on their website, put our web link there and a link to our social media and we're done. Let's leave it at that and see what the comments say tomorrow.'

They both look over at me, pleased with their work and looking like they are waiting for me to say something.

'Great,' I manage, 'really great.'

29

I go round to Mum and Dad's to hear how Mum's hospital check-up went. The weather's nice so I get off the bus early to walk across the park, enjoying the feeling of the sun on my back and the opportunity to make the journey last longer. When I get there, Dad pops his head round the kitchen door to say hello and that he'll be in in a minute so I sit down in the chair opposite Mum. I'm just getting settled in the chair when she comes out with:

'Why didn't you tell us?' I'm taken by surprise and I feel like I'm about to be told off for something.

'Sorry?' I say, confused, 'Tell you what?' She leans over to the magazine rack beside her and pulls out a crinkled newspaper. It's the one with the interview in it, me and Angelique.

'Why didn't you tell us?' she says again, making it pretty clear she wants an answer.

'Tell you what?' I say again, playing for time.

'What do you think?' she says, exasperated, thrusting the paper towards me, folded to the photo of Angelique and me. I take it and fold it back the other way, chucking it on to the coffee table.

'It's just a review in the paper, you knew I was doing some shows. I don't see..'

'Don't, Michael. Why didn't you tell us about her? That she's, you know.' It takes me a second or two to process this. When I fully understand what she's saying I resist the impulse to snap back with "Because I knew you'd be uncomfortable, because what difference would it have made?" It's not Angelique she's objecting to, it's that I didn't tell her. And that's just another way to have a dig about the magic in general. But even for her, this is a bit over the top. I have to take a deep breath and close my eyes for a second, putting both hands out in front of me, palms down, trying to keep my own anger at bay.

'I didn't think to tell you because it's not a big deal to me.' And it isn't. I only see Angelique's size now when other people do and even then, it's more just sort of me noticing them noticing her.

Broken Wand

'Mum, she's really nice. And clever. I think you would -'

'Michael, I'm sure she's lovely. But you could have told us. It's bad enough you pursue this without being cagey.' I can see this has really riled her. And I can see I haven't done myself any favours by not just dropping it in to conversation earlier.

'First thing I know about it is Kath shoving that under my nose,' she says, pointing at the newspaper and now the penny is starting to drop. Mrs Peterson seeing it first will not have gone down well. 'Caught me off guard while I was gardening, comes down to the side gate when she doesn't get an answer, waving the paper at me over the top of the gate. Couldn't believe her luck when she cottoned on I hadn't seen it,' she says, twisting her mouth and vigorously scratching her arm through her cardigan.

'Should you be gardening?' I ask. 'I mean the weather's warming up and you don't want to overdo it.'

'That's not really the point Michael,' she says, curtly. I shrink into my chair a bit.

'As if that wasn't bad enough,' she goes on, picking up where she left off, 'then she produces her phone and shows me the film of you in the shop, waving a mop at some poor lad. 'It's trending' she says; I had to ask her what that meant. She didn't know either until her grandchildren showed Amanda and she's told her. Knows what it is now though well enough. "Thank heavens for grandchildren, keeping us in touch." ' she spits this last part out and I feel the sting of it. Amanda and her brood. I might have known. 'And then,' she announces, waving an arm in front of her, clearly not done yet, 'she starts telling me about how Amanda met Kirsty Allsop who apparently loved her home dyed wool and is going to buy some and give her a plug. Bloody show off.' I snigger at this and Mum looks at me sharply, wiping the smile off my face.

'Look Mum,' I begin, 'I'm sorry if you think I didn't tell you anything on purpose, it just never really came up. You're always so against anything to do with my ambitions in magic, it just starts rows so I don't bother.'

'Your Dad thinks it's a phase. He thinks you're still ten. Phases don't last this long Michael.'

Broken Wand

'It's not a phase. I just hit the rocks a bit after .. after Jenny but I'm sorting things out. Things are starting to happen.' I can hear myself and it sounds like I'm whining, like I really am ten again trying to justify practising magic instead of doing my homework.

'Things might be starting to happen Michael but that doesn't automatically mean they're the right things. When are you going to start a proper life? Find someone new, settle down, have kids. You'll be too old soon.' Before I can respond she gathers herself up and stands. 'I need to check on dinner,' she announces, leaving the room. She's obviously not interested in a discussion and I think I'll just let it blow over. She's had her say now, maybe she'll calm down over dinner. When she goes in to the kitchen, Dad comes out, carrying a basket of folded laundry which he puts on the floor in the hall to take upstairs later. He comes back in and perches on the edge of the sofa.

'Hope you're hungry. She's made a casserole. I did the veg for it though,' he says, smiling weakly.

'Look Dad, I know Angelique will have been a surprise to you but it's going well. I can't see that it's such a big deal.'

'Ah. She mentioned that then.'

'Just a bit. Totally over-reacted. I mean, I know she's not too well at the moment but I can't see why it's got her so rattled.'

'It wasn't so much that,' he says, glancing at the kitchen door, 'as Mrs Peterson shoving that under her nose,' he replies, knowingly nodding towards the newspaper.

'Yes, that did get mentioned.' We sit companionably for a few quiet moments before I say: 'Dad, you don't think that the magic, I mean the recent stuff, Angelique and that ...' I trail off, immediately wishing I hadn't started that sentence.

'No son, I don't think you doing more magic had anything to do with the heart attack,' he says, lowering his voice. 'It annoys her but it seems this heart thing has been brewing for a while.'

'Is that what they said?' I ask, 'at the hospital today?'

'Pretty much.' He sits down and leans towards me, lacing his fingers together and squeezing his hands a few times.

'Tough day, eh?' I say, remembering the awful ache of fear

Broken Wand

when Jenny was ill and suddenly feeling the urge to hug him.

'Yes, it was,' he says, 'I don't like hospitals. All those smells and the signs about stuff you could catch everywhere; people getting pushed about on trollies and then there were these people in the waiting room, all discussing wills and things like it's hilarious,' he breaks off, 'nothing funny about it,' he mutters to his hands, the muscles in his jaw working overtime.

'Set the table will you,' Mum says from the kitchen doorway and we both start guiltily, sharing one last sympathetic glance before we make our way to the table.

30

Angelique calls and it's nice that she does, it breaks up a tedious Wednesday evening. I can hear she's pleased about something; it sounds like there's a smile in her voice.

'I've had a phone call,' she begins.

'Oh?'

'It was a TV company.' I hit mute on the TV control and turn my full attention to her. 'They've seen the stuff on the YouTube channel and our website and want to talk about a documentary they're doing on modern magic.' She says it so calmly that I can't tell if she is even smiling. I feel my pulse pick up and a warm feeling creeps across my neck, pore by pore.

'Mike, you there?' she asks.

'Yes,' I say, 'right. Well that's good isn't it?' I say, rubbing at the tiny beads of sweat that have formed on my forehead.

'Bloody hell Mike, yes of course it's good!' she laughs, 'it's the best thing to happen in ages, is what it is,' she adds. 'Will you be able to take time off work to meet them?'

'Er, yes, sure, just need a few days notice, sort the staff schedules out,' I reply, not knowing if any of that will be possible. I make a mental note not to tell work why I need to be off after my last outing as a social media trend didn't exactly go down well. 'Who is it for? The documentary I mean.'

'They're a production company; she didn't mention who they're making it for. We can check when we meet her.'

I'm at a loss for words. Maybe things really are starting to happen. I dared to hope.

'Sure,' is all I can muster. Now it's in front of me, facing me, I'm almost afraid to look it in the eye. I feel like I'm in the school playground again, backed in to a corner. Nerves rather than excitement fill me but I can't let Angelique know this; she'll be depending on me. I clear my throat.

'This is fantastic Angelique; this could be the start of it. We'll be Saturday night regulars before we know it.' I say this but I don't

Broken Wand

feel like I mean it. I can't decide if I'm enjoying this news or not, I've dreamed about stuff like this for so long that now it's here I just feel a bit numb. Maybe it will kick in later.

'Well, let's wait and hear what the TV people have to say first. Don't want to get carried away,' she says, the voice of reason. I suppose she's just more used to this than me.

'No, sure, of course,' I say, trying to keep my voice on an even keel.

'Also, the woman who called mentioned an online chat show; she could arrange an appearance to give us a bit of a leg up, give them a bit more to go on when considering who to include in the documentary, so it sounds like we should do that too. I'll find out more and let you know when it is.'

31

After the call I sit staring at the phone for a bit, slightly stunned. I can't decide if excited is taking over from nerves or not. I start smiling as it sinks in, as the possibilities begin to make themselves clear. I stay on the sofa, looking round the room but seeing nothing, my mind daring to dream, visualising all sorts of imaginary interviews and TV appearances. I sit more upright on the sofa, crossing my legs and laying one arm along the back of it, turning slightly to face the empty armchair.

'Well, Graham, it's great to be here, thanks for having us,' I smile and do one of those small waves at the imaginary audience, dipping my head once in humble acknowledgement of their applause. Graham Norton smiles at me from the armchair and asks how it feels to be one of the UK's favourite magicians. 'Well,' I say, 'obviously, it feels amazing and it's thanks to our wonderful fans that we're sitting right here with you. It's been an amazing and exciting journey and we can't wait to start our tour of Las Vegas next month.' More rapturous applause from the audience, Graham encouraging them with an excited expression. I smile at my invisible audience again. Eventually my fantasies slow down, the studio lights fade and I slump into the sofa, head back, staring at the ceiling. It makes it so hard to think about work but it creeps in; getting on that train and doing the same journey again, opening up the shop, sitting in that cramped little cupboardy office. Never have I wanted so much to walk away from it. The dreams feel so close, I will have to force myself to go to work tomorrow. I feel lightheaded, a bit out of control. I wonder how much it would take for me to jack my job in; I'm going to struggle to wait. I picture myself telling my parents and wonder what they'd say though I know they would be horrified. It makes me doubt it myself but at the same time I know I have to do it soon. I take a deep breath and rub my eyes. I'm tired and I try to put it all to the back of my mind but I come back to it in the night again and again. This is mine for the taking if I play it right. If we play it right. I wondered if

Broken Wand

Angelique was doing this as well, picturing the excitement in her eyes. It made me smile to picture her thinking and smiling as well. I'm glad that I could do this for her, that she would be taking part in this as well. It almost feels like I am taking care of her and I like that feeling, it's something else I could get used to.

32

A couple of weeks later we're waiting to go on the chat show and I'm not feeling too comfortable. I thought there would be a room to wait in but really we're sort of in a corner of a stuffy corridor on a sofa. Angelique has pushed herself right back so she can relax against the back of the sofa, her feet just about reaching the edge of the seat. We're sitting more or less in silence watching behind the scenes stuff, listening to the audience being shown in and told what expect. We can't see them and it makes it worse, trying to picture what they're like. I breathe deeply and stare at my hands, clicking my thumbnails together.

'Actually, that rehearsal wasn't too bad,' Angelique says turning to me, as if she's only just thought of it, even though that was easily forty minutes ago.

'I suppose not,' I reply, 'but it was a bit rushed. Still haven't got much of a clue what the rest of the show will be like.'

'I watched a few online,' Angelique says and I kick myself for not thinking to do that myself. 'It's a quick format,' she says, as if I'd asked her, 'lots of banter and one liners, people on and off. I don't think the interview will be too strenuous.' A young woman appears with the coffee we'd been offered a while back. I can tell from the smell it's going to be bitter.

'Not long now,' she says brightly as she hands the coffee over, glancing at Angelique and smiling a bit too much. Angelique gets the odd glance from people trying not to look as they scurry past. Some of them have headsets on that make them look faintly ridiculous rather than as important as they clearly think they are. And they all carry iPads instead of clipboards, tapping away at them and speaking into their headsets earnestly. What they do must be saving lives somewhere because it all seems very urgent. Someone uses a head-mic to talk to someone 10 feet away.

'I wonder how important you have to be before you actually speak to someone face to face,' I say quietly. Angelique smiles. The watchword, it has been explained to us, is interaction – a fun vibe like a chat with mates apparently. Having briefly met the two guys that will be interviewing us at rehearsal, I can't imagine we would or ever will be mates. They seemed very self-assured at the rehearsal, constantly having their make-up touched up and never really spoke in full sentences. The studio crew fluttered round them with a sort of reverence, all trying to be more pally with them than each other. I'm not sure what I expected though. Jeremy Paxman? Angelique seems to be far more comfortable with it all. She's been around internet types for a while though and, she says, internet and TV are almost one and the same now. She's been very patient, showing me how it all works. I know what hits, trending and algorithms are and I know how to post and share stuff. It still feels weird to me to know that people are watching us online but we don't see them. It doesn't seem right, not with magic.

The young lady who brought the coffee reappears and says cheerily:

'We're ready for you now, it's this way,' and she over-smiles again. She flicks her hair off her shoulder and waves her iPad towards the gap in the wall where we're ushered on to the stage area. The focus is on the two guys, sitting behind a glass desk and gabbling away. My nerves have intensified and I've started to sweat under my jacket. God, don't let it show, I think. They'll eat me alive. It's not like the pubs where they've all had a drink and are up for a laugh; this is serious and we have to get it right. Looking at the audience I suddenly understand what a big deal this is but at the same time wondering if Paul Daniels ever had to wait in a corridor. Maybe, when he started out, I think. As people in the audience glance our way expectantly, the pressure intensifies, focuses in on me and it's not what I've always thought this would be like. I thought I'd be more confident, I know that much but the nerves are getting to me. They're introducing us.

'Now we've got something we haven't had before on ChatBox; a little bit of magic!' The audience ooohs, encouraged by someone in a headset waving their arms up and down. 'They've made a quite a splash on the internet with their new take on Saturday night old-school magic and they're here tonight to show us a few of their favourite tricks. Let's make some noise for Mike and Angelique!'

And then we're on and we start. Angelique is fine, she goes straight in to it but I can't seem to get over my nerves. I'm barely smiling and I know it. The audience are young, studenty and I'm not sure if they're laughing because they're in to it or because they're mocking it. I can tell they're not sure if they should be laughing at Angelique but then she says 'try and keep your eyes on me, I mean, I know he's glamorous but let's not objectify', catches one or two of them personally with her pale blue eyes and she's got them. They're enchanted and curious, over their Politically Correct awkwardness. Then I catch Angelique's eye and she's smiling at me. I smile back at her but it's only on my lips. I go through the act exactly as we planned and thankfully, it goes off without a hitch. Angelique is just the right side of hamming it up and they like her. It works better with her doing all the front stuff; tonight she is better at it than me and I'm glad she's there. They warm to us.

They're genuinely interested by the time we finish and the applause is real. I've had plenty of practise knowing when it's not. Someone else in a headset indicates we should go over to the sofa on the main set so we do. We take a seat and while we do someone is making the audience whoop and cheer loads more than they did. I find out later it's so they can put that at the end of our act instead. To make us look better. And to make them look like they found a really good act instead of a mediocre one. Probably. The two presenters take control and seem to find everything really interesting or hilarious.

They ask questions of Angelique that skirt round the obvious. They ask me if I've been into magic for long and I tell them it's been decades which is apparently, also hilarious and I crack them up. I wasn't aware I was that funny. Angelique they find adorable but quickly revise their approach when they twig she has a brain on her and doesn't react well to being patronised. And suddenly I find myself thinking that, well, actually she is adorable, and I'm looking at her, not them. Well it's more like watching her because she's talking and I want to hear what she says, not them. I'm not aware they've asked me a question until she turns to me expectantly. I look at the presenters and they look at me.

'It was your Grandad, wasn't it Mike, who got you started,' Angelique says and I silently bless her for the nudge.

'Yes,' I say, and I tell them the story, hoping I'm answering the question. I try to be quick and trite and glance at the audience to see if they're listening. I stop short of telling them about the Paul Daniels magic set as I'm not sure they'd have a clue who I was on about. The presenters don't pick up on anything I've said and they don't ask any more questions. It's not quite the rock and roll answer they were looking for. One of them quickly says:

'We're going to a break now, and after that you'll see a whole new side to Mike.' Now they've got my attention and a cold feeling snakes through my stomach. We're asked to stay where we are while they get the next bit ready. It only takes a minute as it's filmed as if it's live and edited later so the audience are counted down to give a huge round of applause again. '

'Welcome back!' the two shout gleefully. One of the presenters takes the lead and talks directly in to the camera.

'Now Mike and Angelique gave us a magical moment just before the break and we've got to know and love them in just a short time, haven't we people!' and he whips the audience up into a frenzy again. 'But we thought you might like to see Mike in a more, shall we say, heroic light, he adds with mock seriousness. 'Watch the screen folks ...' and he points with a mischievous smile to a huge TV that's been wheeled on between them and us during the break. There's a logo of the show with a countdown from 5 to 1 over it. My stomach sinks, I'm pretty sure I know what's coming and I feel my jaw go slack as the countdown heads to one. I lean forward and stare at my hands, pressed together between my knees. Sure enough, wobbly footage of the inside of the Java Hut with me, taking on the idiot wanting his money back. I'm asking how much of it he's drunk and they're bleeping out the swearing in his reply.

The two hosts are acting all mock shocked and the audience is reacting to them. But then something else happens. When he pours the coffee on the floor and looks smugly back to the camera, the audience boo. Someone shouts 'tosser'. I feel awkward but somehow pleased that this is their reaction. I'm still mortified though; I'm actually going red and the sweating is getting out of hand. I glance at Angelique but she is staring resolutely at the screen, expressionless, though I can't see her eyes. Oh God, she's going to hate me for this, for ruining this chance. Jesus, if I have ever regretted anything in my life, it has to be that video. And then I'm going back behind the counter and coming back with the mop and the audience love it. They're cheering and whooping and clapping. And it's for me. I glance at the audience and then down at my clasped, sweaty hands and I feel a faint smile tweak the corners of my mouth. The noise seems to go on forever though it wasn't more than ten seconds and I'm feeling so mixed up I don't know what's what. For once in my life I have done something other people genuinely like.

I glance sideways at Angelique and to my surprise, she's looking at me with something like affection. The pale blue eyes have softened a bit and she holds my glance for what again seems like ages but again, is only a matter of seconds. It's enough. In my sweaty nervous state that look calms me and the grimace on my face relaxes. I feel something soften in me too. I don't know what it is and I'm confused by it but I like it. In a split second while they're clapping and whooping I can't remember the last time I felt this way about something, about all of it and I can't help grinning like an idiot at the audience. Then just like that, it's over.

'So there you have him guys and gals, showing you how to deal with the bad guys. Thanks for coming on the show, Mike and of course Angelique!' More applause. Then we're ushered off the couch and back to the corridor where the suitcase of props have been deposited. An important person in a headset is telling us how great we were and thanking us for being so "up for it". They point out the exit and they're off, holding their little mouthpiece and speaking urgently to it, busy, busy. When we've gathered our stuff together and we're outside I take a deep breath. It's nice and cool here in the street, despite how warm the day has been or maybe it's just relief. There are people leaving pubs and others just making their way to wherever. It's all so normal; it feels like something has changed but I don't know what and I don't understand it. I don't want it to end just yet, I think, as I look at my watch.

'It's still quite early; do you fancy a drink?' I ask Angelique, even though 10 isn't that early. She glances up the road at the Tube station entrance and she makes a polite excuse. Then she says:

'It went well in there I thought. I'll make sure we send it far and wide when it's broadcast.' I feel a bit deflated that it's back to business but I can see that she's tired. I don't have an early start for work tomorrow, I'm in later, but she does.

'Yeah, it was good. It went well. I nearly had a heart attack when they showed that video though. I don't think I ever want to see that again.'

'Well, I wouldn't hold your breath. It's out there now; I doubt you'll shake it that easily. And anyway, just think of yourself as the new Robin Hood.' We smile at each other and she waves as she heads off. I give a small wave back.

'See you Friday then,' I call after her.

She walks quickly off towards the Tube and even though I could walk with her, I just stand there and watch until she's safely through the archway. I move off in the other direction, like I have somewhere to be, the suitcase of props feeling quite light tonight. For once I feel like I want to be seen, but no one looks my way as I amble along. I blend in, as usual, but tonight that's alright because I have made something happen, I have taken a big step. And that feels OK.

33

Angelique helped herself to one of the small macarons on the plate between her and Linda on the kitchen table. She'd brought them round as an impromptu gift to have with coffee and a chat, as she had explained when her mother opened the door to her. It was unusual to just drop round, they normally fixed an appointment but Angelique didn't want to have to wait and it was easier to be spontaneous with her in the summer holidays. They talked about daily news while they drank their coffee and Angelique waited to ask what she'd really come there for.

'Oh, by the way, did you get my email about my birth certificate?' she asked as casually as she could as Linda left the room to fill up their mugs, 'only you didn't reply.' She noticed a brief hesitation in her mother's step before she carried on to the kitchen.

'Your birth certificate?' she called over her shoulder.

'Yes. I emailed you a week or so ago. Thought you might have missed it.'

'Are you sure you need that?' Linda asked as she returned, stopping to lean against the door frame, wrapping her arms round herself.

'Well, not immediately but I will sooner or later.' Angelique replied, sensing there was more to her mother's hesitation. 'Is there a problem? Have you lost it?'

'No, it's here somewhere. Do you want it right now only I'd need to go and look for it,' she said with a wave of her hand and a glance over her shoulder. She didn't look round at Angelique immediately.

'You wouldn't need to look,' Angelique said firmly, 'you know where everything is in this place to the last speck of dust. What's the problem?' Angelique descended from her chair and stood to face her mother, putting her hands on her hips as she did so and drawing herself to her full height.

'There's no problem,' Linda replied without conviction.

'Then can I have it please?' Angelique said, trying not to let the frustration sound in her voice but knowing she wasn't quite succeeding.

'Look why don't you just give me a call when you need it? I don't want to go rifling through files now.'

'Because that's totally unnecessary,' Angelique spat back, no pretence now at containing her anger. 'Why don't you want me to have it?' she demanded.

The distance between them seemed to evaporate as her mother took a couple of steps in to the room.

'Alright,' she said, emphatically, looking down at Angelique. Without a word her mother disappeared back down the corridor and was gone for a few minutes. Angelique fidgeted with the corner of a newspaper that was on the table, unsure now of what she was doing. When her mother returned, she had a piece of paper in her hand, folded in half. She sat down and slid it across the table towards Angelique.

'Is this it?' Angelique asked, suddenly unwilling to look at it, unwilling to see what had made her mother so secretive.

'Yes, that's it. Look at it Angelique, it's time we talked.' Angelique tried to ignore the uneasy feeling she had growing in her stomach and her palms felt hot as she tentatively reached for it as if scared of an electric shock. She pulled the paper towards her with her fingertips, sliding it off the table's edge and holding it for a heartbeat before gently unfolding it, the paper making the tiniest of noises as it opened. She took the document in, reading her own name and that of her mother before realising that the space where her father's name should have been was blank. She read it all again before focussing on that small empty box on the paper trying to fathom it.

'I don't understand. Where's my father's name? I know he left but he should still be here, shouldn't he?'

'Angelique, I need to clarify something here.'

'Yes, I believe you do. You said my father left and that you had to bring me up yourself. You said he couldn't deal with the idea of being a father, that he was selfish, took off weeks after I was born.

Broken Wand

So what does this mean?'

She held the certificate up in front of her so Linda was forced to look at it, the empty box that she herself had left blank. She shifted uneasily in her seat.

'Are you going to tell me anything about him at all?' Angelique felt her cheeks grow hot and her throat began to feel tight with the strain of not letting her emotions overrun her.

'To be honest, I don't really know very much,' Linda said quietly, paying close attention to her hands on the table, rubbing one thumb with the other. Angelique had rarely, if ever, seen her mother like this. Her head hung down as if it had just had enough of the effort it took to stay so straight on her shoulders all the time; as if she had given in to the weight of this secret.

'You don't know anything about a man you had a child with?' asked Angelique, incredulous.

'It wasn't a decision we made together,' she gazed in earnest at Angelique, emotions battling to be seen in her eyes, her voice.

'Then how did it - I - happen?'

'He was a supply teacher, only at the school every so often. We only went out a few times before I left the school. We both knew I was leaving and it seemed to be a natural end to it. I didn't see a reason to complicate things when I found out as I had already moved to Essex and the new job and knew I could manage.'

'But what about me? What about what I might've wanted? All this time I thought he'd left. I thought he'd left you holding the baby like some irresponsible bastard. You had no right.'

'I did what thought was best at the time. It was never going to be a relationship that went anywhere, we both knew that. We parted amicably.'

'Oh, well that's alright then.'

'Angelique -' Linda tried to interrupt her but Angelique could no longer contain her anger and shock, red faced and tears welling up.

'Would you ever have told me?' she shouted, grabbing the birth certificate and holding it up beside her like the final piece of evidence in a murder trial.

'What would it have changed? Really?' Linda asked, almost

pleading now with Angelique to see sense, to see her side.

'How can you even ask that? I could have found him. Are you going to tell me who he is?'

'No.' Linda said with a hint of finality in her voice.

'Is that it?' Angelique asked, her arms outstretched.

'Some things are best left alone.' Linda replied.

'That was for me to decide.' Angelique cried, clutching the certificate to her chest, scrunching it up.

'No, it wasn't. We would have stayed together for the wrong reasons and I didn't want you to go off chasing him later on. What if he'd rejected you? It would have caused more problems than it solved.'

'So you told me he rejected both of us instead. How is that any better? You lied to me.'

'As I said, I did what I thought was right at the time. And it has been fine, you and me. We've managed, haven't we? It wasn't easy but it felt like you and me against the world, really. Nobody else could be part of that, not really. You were the focus of my time.' This was by far the most her mother had ever said about her upbringing. It had always been practical – appointments, schooling, extra tuition by her at home – a determination to succeed as a mother by making Angelique succeed as a child.

Angelique tried to compose herself, closed her eyes and took a few deep breaths before asking:

'So you're not going to apologise?'

'For what? Doing what I thought was best for you? No.' Angelique looked at Linda feeling suddenly incredibly tired, knowing she would not be able to stay much longer.

'Wow,' she said, shaking her head and smiling wryly. 'Even for you that's callous.'

'I'm sorry you feel that way Angelique but once you've had a chance to calm down and think about it I think you will understand.'

'I doubt that mother, I doubt it very much.' Her eyes were still stinging and her cheeks felt flushed. She needed to leave, to get away from Linda and try to think this through. Struggling to get her

Broken Wand

coat on quickly she ignored Linda's request for her to stay and left without looking back.

34

'So?' asked Joanna as she'd opened the door to Angelique, 'how was Sunday with your Mum? Reasonable or fire breathing?' Angelique dumped her bag on Joanna's hallway floor and walked into the living room.

'Wine?' Joanna asked after her.

'No thanks,' Angelique replied, rubbing the sides of her head, 'headache.'

'Oh, that bad.'

'I don't know yet; still processing. Maybe pour one out and I'll see how I go.' She'd settled into the sofa, tucking her legs under her and leaning her head back, eyes closed, while Joanna opened the wine in the kitchen. She'd come in with three tumblers, one with ice in it.

'Want some of the ice in yours? It's that sort of day.' Angelique shook her head by way of an answer, eyes still closed. Joanna flopped down on the armchair opposite. The flat was silent, not even a clock ticking. Sparse and white, uncluttered, just neatly piled books on the coffee table, one large piece of dark, abstract art over the sofa, a large swiss cheese plant dominating one corner of the room. With an effort, Angelique leant forward, picked up her wine and savoured it's cold comfort before saying:

'She's met someone.' She held her free hand up before letting it drop on to her lap as she spoke.

'That's not such a bad thing, is it? She might lighten up if she gets a bit of action.'

'Joanna, really?'

'No, I'm serious. This could be a good thing. Clearly she's mellowing emotionally if she's letting this guy – what's his name?'

'Paul.'

'Paul. If she's letting Paul in then you never know, walls may come down.'

'That's not really the issue. I think it would freak me out if she started being emotionally available. She didn't call him her boyfriend or anything, just her co-student that she's been seeing socially for a few months. No idea what level of emotion that entails.'

'So what is the issue then?'

'She hasn't asked me to meet him yet and she's already known him a year,' Angelique replied, trying not to sound like a whiney child but aware that she probably was. 'They're thinking about going to Florence for a weekend to practise their Italian,' she added. 'Florence! I've always wanted to go there.' Joanna stifled a smile at that before asking carefully:

'Has she told him about you at all?'

'She's given him the Who's Who version, the 'I'm proud of her achievements' version but nothing actually about me.' Angelique said, tilting her wine glass to make the wine slip round it clockwise.

'Look, I'm not taking sides but looking at it objectively, you're not the focus of his attention. She is,' Joanna said. Angelique thought about this for a moment, not taking her eyes off her glass.

'You remember Sophie? From Uni?' Angelique began, 'her Mum got divorced when she was a kid and wouldn't commit to other men until they'd met her children. If the kids didn't like him it was no go,' she said emphatically slicing her hand through the air. 'She's known him for a year Joanna, a whole year. How's that going to look when he does finally meet me?'

'But to be fair,' Joanna replied, 'it's not quite the same is it. I mean, Sophie was a little kid and any bloke was going to have to bring them up, be their new Dad. You're a grown up with your own flat and a good job.'

'So why haven't I met him yet? Why is she ashamed of me?' Angelique's voice was catching and she was struggling to keep her chin from creasing.

'She's not ashamed of you darling, she's very proud of you.'

'Of what I've achieved. Not of who I am though, as a person.' Joanna put her wine glass down, carefully squaring the coaster against the corner of the table. Joanna said, carefully:

'You don't know that.'

'She's lied to me all this time.'

Broken Wand

'Technically, not telling you isn't a lie,' Joanna clarified. Angelique stared at her until she quickly added: 'Yes, she's hard work and no, she's not exactly a cuddle a minute but she had to build walls too and build yours for you when you were a kid. That's a lot of wall. She's been on her own for a long time and is probably just being incredibly cautious. You know what she's like.' Joanna tilted her head and looked at Angelique expectantly. Angelique's eyebrows raised momentarily and she picked at a fingernail, pretending to be absorbed.

'Is there more to this?' asked Joanna eventually, 'because I have to say I think you're getting this a bit out of proportion.'

'Actually, there is something else,' Angelique replied, taking a deep breath. 'You know how Mum always told me that my Dad left just after I was born?'

'Yes; couldn't handle the responsibility, Mum had to do everything, hard as nails single working mum etc. etc.' Joanna said in a sing-song voice.

'Well,' Angelique began, taking another deep breath before she could continue, 'it transpires that he never knew about me to begin with.'

'What?' Joanna asked, her head tilted slightly, eyebrows furrowed as if she couldn't quite hear what Angelique had said.

'He didn't leave,' Angelique said bluntly, 'he never knew about me in the first place.' Joanna didn't say anything, giving this news time to solidify. 'It wasn't a relationship that was heading anywhere apparently and she'd got another job anyway so moved away without telling him.'

'Woah.'

'Exactly.' They sat in silence for a while, the air between them thick with their unsaid thoughts.

'How exactly did this come up?' Joanna asked.

'Saw my birth certificate. No father on it,' Angelique replied quietly.

'Oh. How have you never seen that before?'

'She's always handled everything like that but one of the girls at work needed hers for something and I just thought it was time I

Broken Wand

looked after all that stuff for myself.'

Joanna raised her wine glass to her mouth and asked over the top of it:

'So is she willing to tell you who he is?' before taking a large sip, eyes fixed on Angelique.

'No. She knows who he is but she's not saying. She doesn't see what it would change. I mean, you know, apart from everything.' A thought crystallised in Angelique's mind like frost on a window pane. 'He might have other children, maybe, like me.'

'Maybe,' Joanna stretched the word out softly. Angelique gasped for a breath and swallowed hard, wiping her eyes.

'Angelique?' said Joanna, gently, 'I thought you were overreacting to the boyfriend thing to be honest but this, this is a huge deal. Maybe she'll come round in the future and tell you about him - it's early days. And anyway, you can probably find him yourself, employment records at the school, your date of birth, work backwards. I'm sure we could dig him up.' Angelique sat motionless as tears began to fall.

'It was 27 years ago, he could be anywhere.' she blurted out between gasps. Joanna stood and moved to the sofa, sitting down and opening her arms. Angelique moved across and climbed onto her lap, leaning her head on Joanna's shoulder and closing her eyes, letting the sobs finally come. Joanna wrapped her arms around her, leaning her cheek on the top of Angelique's head, a small smile played around her mouth and gently, so gently, she began patting her arm.

35

Angelique relaxed into her seat on the 7.30 train to Oxford and watched the platform slide by as they left Paddington. She was looking forward to getting out of London for the weekend to catch up with some old university mates; lunch in a pub garden was on the cards; so much nicer than in London which was always more oppressive in the summer and she would be able to forget about her Dad and Linda's boyfriend for a while.

She drank a couple of mouthfuls of the espresso she had grabbed at the station and found herself unwinding the further from London the train got and the greener the view. They were only about 20 minutes outside of Oxford when the train stopped at a small station and a few of the remaining commuters left while a few locals got on.

She'd been minding her own business, reading her Kindle so hardly noticed when two young men boarded the train. Her end of the carriage was emptying as it was past rush hour and she glanced up, distracted from her reading by their forced, loud laughter. She could tell by the way the men were acting that they were either high or pissed. Jumpy, twitchy, egging each other on and swearing with the exaggerated laughing. One was hanging off the handrail, swinging a bit and glancing round the carriage to see who was noticing him; his track suit top rode up to reveal a pasty midriff. The other one was sitting spread-eagled on a seat for two, one leg tapping out a fast rhythm, slapping his knees and dipping his head in time to some inner music.

It seems she had happened to glance up at just the wrong moment. She caught the swinging man's eye and saw a flash of interest go through him. Looking quickly down at her Kindle again in an attempt to break the connection she decided to calculate whether it was worth leaving the train at the next opportunity or to hang on until Oxford. She glanced at her watch. 18 uncomfortable minutes to go. She settled on sticking it out and getting to Oxford where her friends would be waiting, taking the chance that the two men might leave at the next stop in any case. The man hanging on the handrail did a couple of pull ups before dropping to the floor and swaying along with the lurching train as he made his way towards her. She watched his progress in the windows from under her eyelashes, his reflection brightly lit against the darkening sky outside, swinging his arms and clapping his hands in front of him with each stride. And then he started.

'Check it out; an Oompa Loompa,' he called over his shoulder followed by a burst of manic laughter.

'What the fuck, man,' came the reply.

'No really, man, there is, check it out.' Angelique concentrated on her Kindle, getting ready to put it away. It wouldn't be the first time she'd had unwanted attention and it probably wouldn't be the last. They generally grew bored after the first few insults but best to be prepared. He was leaning over the back of the seats in front of her now, openly staring at her and waiting for her to look up. She decided just to acknowledge him in the hope he would then lose interest. She looked up and met his gaze, trying to keep her expression soft and vulnerable. She had learnt that pale blue eyes, blonde hair and a submissive nature often went a long way to softening even the nastiest of people. She saw a slight change in his expression then; he calmed down a fraction; he was expecting a challenge and to counter attack or for her to plead with him out of fear but he wasn't expecting her to be passive. She could tell he didn't know quite what to do. He looked back to his friend and gave another shrill giggle of a laughter before slumping down in the seat, out of view. And that probably would have been it had his friend not decided to join him.

'What the fuck you talking about, crazy fuck.' This one was different, colder. He didn't look as stupid, clearly the one with the brain somewhere and all the more dangerous because he was clearly out of control of it. He was curious, and she sensed he would take more of an interest. He had the air of a snake tasting the air with his tongue, deciding what his options were. He made his way slowly, gripping each seat back as he passed it to keep him upright.

Broken Wand

'Fuck, you weren't kidding,' he said in exaggeratedly slow tones now. 'It's a tiny little person thing. Not an Oompa Loompa though; it's a hobbit I reckon.'
By now they were both staring at her again, the idiot laughing at pretty much anything the snake said and the snake standing there, twitching and staring, thoughts flashing behind his dilated eyes. After a few seconds he said, quietly:
'Not much bigger than its own bag and you know where they should go.' He glanced at his mate and raised his eyebrows towards at the luggage rack overhead. They grinned at each other and Angelique knew in a split second what was coming. She screamed and lashed out as they grabbed her but they were strong and determined and catching the idiot on his neck with her foot only made him angry and more determined.
'Fucking little bitch,' changed the atmosphere in an instant and she knew there was no point fighting them now. They shoved her in to the rack, her head banging on the top of it, sending sparks through her left eye. She gripped the edge of the rack, fearing falling out of it more than being in it by now. The snake was still shoving her, trying to wedge her in, to make sure she was well and truly in there and the other one was glancing wildly round the carriage, giggling and twitching and making snapping noises with his fingers, clearly getting quite a kick out of this. Her shoulder was hurting, a sharp pain lancing across her chest as she tried to twist round.
The train was pulling in to a station and as it did so, there was shouting from somewhere further along the carriage and banging as someone punched the emergency button. The two of them stood by the doors laughing hysterically and slapping each other's hands, shouting at the other passengers now who stood back, afraid of being attacked themselves. They barged out of the doors as soon as they opened, sprinting off along the platform, shouting and gesturing at the train. A man appeared beside Angelique with a briefcase in one hand, white faced and open mouthed.
'God, I'm so sorry, I didn't see what was happening. Are you hurt? Can you – do you need help getting down?' He put his

briefcase on the seat and held his arms out vaguely to help her down, tentatively trying to see how to do it. He was talking fast.

Angelique couldn't speak, barely had room to breathe and heard herself just let out a low moan. She couldn't turn her body to face him so to complete her humiliation, she had to let him help her out like a child and lift her down, her arms round his neck. His mac she noticed, smelt like the seats. He must have kept it on to travel. By now, a few other passengers had gathered to see what was going on and a woman also held on to Angelique as the man carefully put her down onto the seat. Some of the other passengers held the doors open, looking for help on the platform. Angelique sat on the seat, eyes closed, holding her left shoulder which was still painful and began to feel a throbbing in her head, above her left eye. She must have hit it harder than she thought. She remembered something about adrenalin masking pain until later and that was why, she reasoned, her head was only hurting now.

She tried to open her eyes but the left one would only go so far, swelling had developed in her eyebrow. A station guard appeared and was talking to the man who had helped her, asking what had happened. He radioed the station entrance to try and have the two guys stopped but the snake and his mate were long gone, jumped the electric barriers and headed off at full sprint.

'Don't worry love,' he'd said, 'we'll have them on camera.' Angelique sat dumb on the seat, letting the man who'd come to her aid do the talking for her, hearing the details explained to the guard as though it was about someone else, like a report on the TV. The guard spoke on his radio for police to be called and an ambulance and she just let it all happen around her, not really sure who was talking to who, a headache worsening. She closed her eyes again. Someone asked her if she was still awake, a woman's voice, the same voice talking to her to keep her listening, keep her focussed. The pain in her shoulder became less sharp but throbbed instead and when the medics arrived they put it in a sling to keep it steady until they could x-ray it.

She felt tiredness flood through her but there were no

emotions, not even anger, just shock and an urge to curl up and sleep, block it out, pretend it never happened. Announcements were made, the train wouldn't be moving for a while. People groaned and craned their necks to try and see what had inconvenienced their evening as they left the train, staring in the window as they stood on the platform, waiting to be told what would be happening to sort out their travel plans.

    The police arrived and took a brief statement as she was being transferred to a stretcher, asking basic details, her name, address, where she was going, anyone they should contact. She didn't want them to contact anyone, least of all her mother. She had her eyes open now but was just seeing the roof of the platform as they wheeled her towards the exit, unaware of what was going on around her. The medics suggested to the police that due to shock they reconvene at the hospital after a full check-up and some rest. They gave her strong painkillers which started to work as they took her out to the ambulance, making her feel woozy though she was already too exhausted to care about the stares.

36

On Sunday morning I get a phone call from Angelique, telling me there's been an incident. That's it, just that there's been an incident on a train.

'Can you come?' she'd asked and when I heard the strain in her voice I knew I'd be straight there and I call for a taxi, sod the expense. When I arrive, I buzz the intercom and she lets me in to the building. It only takes a few seconds to find her ground floor flat but even so, she asks who it is from behind her front door and peeps through the letterbox to check. I bend down and smile and do a sort of wave. She opens the door and seems glad to see me but looks tired, her eyes seem dull and the left one has some swelling and an impressive bruise. I feel my stomach turn and my face fall at the sight of it and I stupidly ask if she's OK. She just nods and she seems smaller, deflated somehow.

She's rubbing her left elbow and I'm not sure if it's through nervousness or soreness but either way, it's not like her to be so quiet. She thanks me for coming as if she's just been reminded to and asks me if I want tea and I say yes. It's all we say to each other as I follow her in to the kitchen and watch her make the tea. She has a small set of steps she uses to do stuff on the normal size counters and she climbs up slowly, her usual energy has deserted her. I want to offer to make it for her but I don't think that would help. She just seems to be on autopilot.

When the tea is made she puts the pot on a tray with two mugs, hardly using her left arm and lets me carry it through to the lounge where we sit at opposite sides of the coffee table. I lean forward, elbows on my knees, trying to be relaxed to be but not feeling it at all. We still haven't spoken and I'm not sure if she's waiting for me to say something. We carry on sitting in silence for a while and drink our tea. She seems to be content just to have someone there, she's relaxed a little bit, folded her legs under her on the armchair and tucked a big cushion beneath her arm to lean on, staring at the table as she cradles her mug.

Broken Wand

For the life of me I don't know why but I decide to try and break the ice a bit by taking something out from behind her ear. I find my lighter in my jeans back pocket though she hardly notices and I lean across the coffee table, arm outstretched, just feeling the feathery touch of her hair on my hand as I do so and she flinches. I occurs to me too late that it's probably a bit of a stupid thing to do to someone who is clearly upset. I sheepishly say sorry, hold the lighter up by way of explanation and put it back in my pocket. Then, thankfully, a half-smile breaks across her face and she shakes her head, putting her hand to her forehead where I see another small bruise under her fringe.

'Oh, Mike,' she says, 'where would I be without you?' I look at my hands, smiling to myself and to my surprise feel a warmth I haven't felt since the early days with Jenny. For the first time in a while I'm able to think about her without too much pain. Perhaps that wound is beginning to heal, perhaps the void is filling, perhaps –

'Mike?' I look up and see the question in her eyes.
'Sorry?'
'Could you pour me some more tea?'
'Yes of course.' When she's had a sip or two she relaxes a bit more and finally begins to talk.

'Thanks for coming,' she says again, almost as if she's just thought of it.

'That's OK,' I reassure her, 'I'd hardly say no. Do you want to talk about it?'

She looks at me and her eyes are suddenly so full of sadness that all I can do is look back at her and hope she sees what I'm feeling. Then she closes her eyes briefly, takes a deep breath and starts to tell me what happened. I sit back in the chair, trying to seem more relaxed than I am.

I can't quite believe what I'm hearing and I swing from anger to frustration to sympathy and all the while try not to let any of it show while she's talking. I don't interrupt; I know I have to be practical, to listen and advise if she wants me to but it's as if I'm feeling every detail: the insults, the blows, the claustrophobic luggage rack, the humiliation and I wish I could take them from her, that her telling me would make it be my pain, not hers. In the end, when she stops talking and stares at the table, all I can trust myself to say is 'bastards.' She looks exhausted, emptied, and I wait for a minute for her to catch her breath.

'What about your friends, the ones you were meeting?' I ask eventually.

'I sent a text when I'd had a bit of rest, waiting to be seen at the hospital. Said I'd been delayed at work, wasn't feeling too well and I'd see them next time.'

'How did you get home?'

'They kept me in overnight, did x-rays but nothing broken, just bruises and this delightful black eye. The painkillers put me out like a light and I slept through the night, on and off. By lunchtime on Saturday afternoon I felt well enough to leave. Just bruised. So I did.'

'Why didn't you call? I'd have brought you home. You should have called.'

'No, I was feeling better by then, I could manage,' she says, with a wave of her hand, 'just wanted to get home.' We sit quietly for a while. She puts her head back and closes her eyes.

'Are you tired? Do you want me to go?' I ask, not really wanting to leave.

'No. Stay. I'm just resting my eyes.' She lightly touches her bruised eye. 'They said it should go down and be more colourful by the end of the week,' she says.

'So what happens now?' I ask, 'Have the police been back in touch?'

'They've arrested them. Well, they're pretty sure it's them.' I can't help but be thrown by how calmly she says this but I'm equally glad to hear they didn't succeed in running away like the cowards they are.

'What? Already?'

'Apparently they were known to the police so they knew where to look,' she says. 'The rules are that they have 24 hours to pull evidence together so they can charge them. Luckily my late arriving rescuer agreed to be a witness and give a statement and they think they'll have enough CCTV footage.'

'They think? What if it takes longer than that?' My blood is up now. I weirdly feel responsible, that I should somehow have been there and I wonder why she didn't call me sooner.

'If it takes longer they'll be out on bail. But the police are pretty sure they'll be able to proceed. They were probably too off their heads to know how much they gifted the police by doing the whole thing on camera.'

For the first time in this conversation she looks up at me. I can see she's getting emotional and struggling not to show it. She grabs tissues from the box on the arm of the sofa and covers her face as she crumples. I step round the coffee table to sit beside her, my arm round her shoulder and she softens, like taut elastic reducing, and folds in to me, crying. I find myself wishing I could un-make it, turn back the clock, take the pain away. I feel responsible, holding her, frustrated that it's the only thing I can do. After a while she quietens.

'Sorry,' she says eventually, sniffing and breathing out heavily, almost a sigh.

'Don't be ridiculous,' I reply, my voice croaky. I clear my throat.

'I knew when I told someone it would all come out. I just couldn't think who to tell. Sorry it's you.'

'Stop apologising. I'm glad you have. You have to let it all out sometimes.' I think what a hypocrite I am, that I never have told anyone how much losing Jenny affected me. Only in time did I feel a bit better, but never healed, never that. It's suddenly clear that in this moment of need Angelique came to me first, not Joanna, not her other friends, she came to me. And I feel something like a warm pride or maybe it's gratitude or maybe I just feel. I haven't for a long time, so it's hardly surprising I'm struggling to know what it is. Then it's as if something wakes us up and she gently pulls away, turning to face me. Her eyes are sparkly with crying and it makes the light blue almost white in places.

'The thing is – the thing is Mike, I'm not sure I want to carry on.'

I blink a few times, trying to understand.

Broken Wand

'With – us? The show I mean?'

'Yes,' she replies quietly.

'Why? Because of this?'

'I've been thinking this morning and I'm not sure it's the right thing, you know, put myself in the spotlight.'

'Is that why you called me? To tell me that?'

'No, no, I wanted to see you,' she says, 'I just needed to talk and I knew you wouldn't start over analysing.' She smiles weakly at me. 'Also,' she says with a sigh, 'the TV company rang to see if they could set up some test interviews this week but I'm really not going to be able to do that, not like this. The thought of the documentary is a bit overwhelming right now.'

'Yes, but that's just now. It's only been two days since you were assaulted – not even that. Give it time, get some sleep, you'll be back to yourself in no time. I promise.' She looks up at me and I can see she's not convinced. Quickly I try to think of other ways to make her see it would be a mistake to stop now. 'We can always put the interviews back a week. If you give up now, after all the hard work, those idiots will have won. Don't you see that?'

'Oh don't trot that one out Mike,' she says with a frown, 'I'm sick and tired of not letting them win. Do you know how much energy that takes? How hard it can be? Let the bastards win, I don't care.'

'I understand that,' I say and she looks up at me, doubtful, 'no, really, I do.' I try to emphasise my point. 'I was at that point when you came along. Not for the same reasons, obviously, but I was blaming everyone else for passing me by and you made me see I'd just sat back and let them. Practically waved them off. We've both made this work Angelique. I'm not giving up now and I don't think you should.' She looked down at the tissue in her hand and twisted it round until it was as small a point as she could make.

'Thanks Mike,' she says, 'I hear you but let me sleep on it, OK?'

'OK.' She puts the things from the table onto the tray they came in on and goes slowly to the kitchen, taking the tray herself now it's lighter. I sit there, looking round the room. I feel uneasy about this. I want what's best for Angelique but I don't want to lose this chance.

'So look,' I say as she comes back in and I get up. 'I'll call you tomorrow. You sure you'll be OK?'

'Yes, I'll be fine. Bath and an early night. Thanks for coming Mike, I really do appreciate it. It's good to have friends you can rely on.'

37

That evening, Angelique was slowly making her way round the flat in her pyjamas, turning lights off and feeling more ready for bed at every step. The front door buzzer cut rudely through the silence and she stopped with her hand inside a lamp shade, thumb about to flick the switch. She stood still, clenching her jaw and looking down the hallway to the door. It buzzed again, longer this time and then fingertips burrowed through the letterbox, holding the flap open and allowing Joanna's voice to carry down the hall.

'Angelique, it's me. I got your text, came as soon as I could. Are you up? I saw lights on.' Angelique's shoulders tensed, her eyes closed for a second, her head tilting backwards as she knew she wouldn't get away with pretending not to have heard. She padded down the hall and opened the door, forcing a weak smile.

'Joanna this is lovely but I'm fine, I said I'd call tomorrow. You really didn't need to.'

'Of course I did,' she replied, stepping past Angelique, 'don't be ridiculous. Have you called the police? I'll take you for a check-up of course, we'll go in the morning unless you want to go to A&E now?' she asked, walking briskly in to the lounge.

'No it's - the police know, they came when it happened. It's fine.'

'Jesus Angelique, it's not fine - look at your eye! What the hell happened?'

'It was Friday evening, on the train, just a couple of stupid lads smacked out of their heads. It's being dealt with.'

'Friday?' Joanna had look of rare confusion forming on her face. 'I don't get it. This happened on Friday and you call no one until today?'

'It was taken care of. They took me to the hospital, did some tests, I'm fine and I came home.'

'So you called your mum?'

'No. Why would you say that? Of course not.'

'The two mugs in the sink. Someone's been round today and

you've only texted me late this afternoon so..' Angelique glanced towards the kitchen, instantly regretting her decision to leave the mugs until the morning. Joanna watched her with the look of a parent who already knows what their child has done but just wants to see if they'll admit it.

'I called Mike. He came over.'

'And you can't look at me while you tell me that?'

'I'm a grown woman, Joanna, I can call who I like.' Joanna snorted at this and looked her up and down, just once. A few moments passed, enough time for the atmosphere to change between them, for Angelique to sense enough to be on her guard. She'd seen this before with Joanna over the years, the influence of a possessiveness that was triggered by things that Joanna sometimes mistook for disloyalty; friends not contacted again because they'd brought someone new to a bar where Joanna had organised a gathering, influencing decisions that were not hers to influence. Angelique steadied her thoughts and told herself to stay calm.

'He's not your Dad you know,' Joanna said lightly, throwing her bag on to the sofa and herself down after it.

'I'm sorry?'

'He's not your Dad. You can't replace your Dad with this cheap copy. You can't magic up a Dad,' she replied, waving both hands and making an ooh shape with her mouth.

'Joanna - please, don't be like this. That's not why I called him.'

'Like what?' There was a steel to Joanna's eyes now, pushing Angelique to go further.

'Like this: jealous.'

'Jealous! I'm not jealous, you stupid little girl, I'm looking out for you, I'm the only one who knows you well enough to do that.'

'Look, I rang Mike because I just wanted to talk it through without turning it into a huge thing. You always do this, Joanna, I can't deal with it tonight.'

'Oh, so you only come to me when it's Mummy issues now do you? Good to know,' she spat. Angelique felt, not for the first time, the force of the spite behind it. But this time, something felt different; for the first time she saw in Joanna a desperation, a childish need and her fear of being the object of that spite evaporated. She held Joanna's stare, seeing her falter slightly as her spite was deflected back at her.

'You know,' Angelique began slowly, 'Mike may not be my Dad, but you sure as hell aren't my mother.'

'Excuse me?' Joanna said, taken aback.

'You're not my mother Joanna, you're a friend and friends don't tell other friends who they can and can't see and they sure as hell don't call their friends stupid little girls.' She felt a surge of adrenalin rush through her as she said this, realising it had been a long time coming, that she was growing tired of Joanna's over protective, possessive type of friendship. Angelique stood watching Joanna, almost able to see the response forming. After a few heartbeats Joanna leant towards her and spoke quietly.

'Would you like people to know just how friendly you and I have been? I'm sure everyone would be interested in your experimental phase at Oxford. Christ, I expect some people would probably pay to watch us.'

'I'm not having this conversation Joanna, I'm exhausted and you're not thinking straight. And anyway, no one would judge me for something that happened so long ago.'

'Wouldn't they? We'll see shall we?'

'You wouldn't.' Angelique said, though she knew the answer before Joanna said it.

'Wouldn't I. Happy to put that to the test?'

Angelique knew without a shadow of a doubt that Joanna was perfectly capable of acting on her threat. She had seen her win student votes at Oxford, all those years before, simply by dismantling the opposition before the vote even took place. Even the politics professors had been slightly in awe of her quite meticulous take-downs.

'You really don't like him do you?' Angelique asked before she could stop herself.

'He doesn't fit,' Joanna replied firmly.

'He does to me.' Angelique countered. 'Can't you just let it go?'

'Maybe this time if you apologised for calling him and not me.' Joanna replied, cocking her head to one side, knowing she would get her apology.

'Ok, ok.' Angelique put her hands up in front of her before rubbing her forehead. 'Ok. I'm sorry I didn't call you sooner.' They looked at each other, Angelique trying to see the thoughts in Joanna's head, hoping her apology would hit home. Joanna was staring at Angelique's bruised eye now; curiosity seeming to take the edge off her temper.

'So does it hurt?' she asked, seemingly instantly satisfied with Angelique's back-down, her shift of mood quite disconcerting.

'Yes, well aches; I've got plenty of painkillers, I just need to rest really, get some sleep,' Angelique hinted. Joanna nodded her understanding.

'And you're sure the police know what they're doing?' she asked, 'only I know people, I could pull some strings.'

'No, really, it's fine but I'll let you know if I need any help, promise.'

'Right, I'll get going.' Joanna said, gathering up her bag, 'let you get to bed. Are you off tomorrow? I'll pop round after work, bring some food.'

'Yes, thanks Joanna, that would be lovely.' Angelique said, agreeing simply to end the visit as quickly as possible, as if she had a choice. Joanna leant down briefly to kiss the top of her head and as Angelique shut the door behind her she leant against it and breathed out, her shoulders slumping, running her fingers through her hair as if to dislodge the kiss Joanna had put there.

As she walked to the kitchen she reached for the paracetamol pack and berated herself for not standing up to Joanna more. She hadn't minded it so much in the past as that was just Joanna and it soon blew over but lately it had started to wear thin.

It had shocked her that Joanna would use something that had happened between them so long ago to stop her from being friends with Mike; why was she so threatened by him? Or was it simply that he was her friend? There was no telling with Joanna what had riled her but possessiveness was certainly part of it. She

Broken Wand

threw the two tablets in to her mouth, grimacing at the bitterness as she swallowed them with water.

38

Angelique and I arrive at the rehearsal office as early as we can to run through a few things but really to make sure we have time to make things ready for the TV crew turning up. We're about to do the interviews for the documentary and they've said they want us to do some of the act as well so they have something unique that isn't already on YouTube. We've set the props out ready to go and Angelique is touching up her make-up, checking that the last traces of her bruised eye are covered. It's been just over two weeks now and even though we've met to rehearse this last week, she's been pretty quiet about it.

'You look fine,' I say and she glances at me in the compact mirror she's holding up. I smile and I see her eyes crinkle in response. 'Shoulder OK?' I enquire, even though I know it's still a bit sore.

'It'll be OK,' she says without turning round. Just then the entry phone buzzer goes and I take a deep breath, pulling my jacket straight and giving Angelique a thumbs up. She shakes her head, pulling her fingers thorough her hair and stuffs the make-up bag quickly back into her handbag. I click to let the TV people in, holding the inner door open until they appear in the corridor in a flurry of equipment.

'Hi,' I say, 'I'm Mike.'

'Yes,' says a young woman in baggy trousers, trainers, t-shirt, denim jacket and expensive looking sunglasses pushed up on to her head, 'recognised you from the videos. I'm Juliette, senior researcher.' She sticks out a manicured hand and I take it for a firm handshake. She moves aside to let the others in and announces them as she does so. 'This is Tim - he does lights and cameras, this is Jake - he does sound and helps Tim and this is Nick, he'll be asking the questions.' Just as she finishes another man comes up the stairs. He's older than the rest, a light sweater tucked in to jeans, heavy framed glasses on his bald head. 'And this is John, he's on the senior production team so what he says goes.' She looks at

Broken Wand

him and smiles flirtatiously and he grins back before saying hi and shaking my hand. I'm still holding the door and also that I haven't said anything beyond 'hi I'm Mike' but before I'm able to say anything Juliette says loudly: 'And this must be Angelique! So good to meet you finally.' She walks purposefully over to Angelique and crouches onto one knee so they are face to face.

'Hi Angelique, I'm Juliette; we've spoken on the phone.'

'Ah yes, good to meet you too,' Angelique responds with a big smile.

'Let me introduce you to everybody,' Juliette says, swivelling round and flicking her hair over her shoulder as she does so. She goes through the list again and they each stop what they're doing to come and say hi. John settles in to a chair next to Angelique and Nick perches on the edge of a desk. I wander over and Angelique looks up.

'Ah, Mike,' Angelique looks up, 'can you see if the coffee machine is still on? Would you like coffee or..?' she asks Nick and John who both say coffee is fine. 'Maybe see if anybody else wants anything,' she adds, smiling at me.

'Sure.' I go over to the others to see what they might like. When I have the orders I make my way to the kitchenette and start assembling drinks. I watch Angelique, listening intently as Nick talks to her, waving his arms towards the others who are setting up.

'So, ready to start?' Nick asks as I hand out drinks.

'Sorry, what are we - what's first?' I ask him.

'Just going to film you setting up, rehearsing, going through the act then we'll sit you down for some interviews. OK?' he says, not really expecting an answer and he walks off to the crew to make sure they're setting things up how he wants them. I feel the intensity of the cameras and it's like the first time we filmed all over again; it's like a stare I can't return. As soon as we complete a few parts of the act I'm able to put my nerves on hold a bit and switch to auto pilot. I'm keeping an eye on Angelique and just occasionally I see her wince when she puts her arms in the air or turns her head in a certain way but I don't think anyone else would have noticed. She'd asked me not to say anything in front of them so I don't but every now and then I just smile a bit and raise an eyebrow to make sure she's coping and we muddle through it.

They sit us down in two chairs and Nick is opposite, smiling broadly to relax us. I feel like I'm at a job interview and he has to ask me to start again on my first answer as I look at the camera instead of at him, the one time I'm not supposed to. Angelique smiles at me encouragingly and it helps. She, of course, is her chatty, bubbly self with the interviews, the self that performs, answering everything in a considered way and with a smile. I liked watching her while she speaks; it's like she comes alive in a different way. She listens to the questions with her head tilted a bit, really concentrating. It's nice to think of her as my partner and I like that I know her in a way these people never will, despite all the questions, as a real person, as a friend.

'Great,' says Nick when the last questions have been asked, 'I think we've got everything we need. John?' he turns to the senior producer, looking for agreement.

'Yes, great, that was really good, thanks so much,' John replies, slipping his phone in to his back pocket. He shakes our hands while explaining that he's needed elsewhere but Juliette will be able to help with any questions while the crew pack up. He's already looking at his phone as he leaves. The sounds guy moves in to take off our microphones and Juliette comes over smiling broadly, crouching down in front of Angelique again.

'I think that went really well,' she says. 'If there's anything we think we've missed I'll be in touch but I'm sure we can use all of this. You know,' she says to Angelique, 'you have a really good presence, quite natural.'

'I do a lot of presenting at work; it does come in handy,' Angelique confirms. 'Different when it's me presenting me though and not just a strategy or campaign results.'

'I know what you mean; different kettle of fish being in front of the camera and not putting other people in front of it,' Juliette says and they smile like old friends having a drink. 'Not like doing your own Insta posts.' she adds. I'm about to chip in with my own thoughts on being in front of the camera when Juliette stands to leave. 'Well, love to chat but better help these guys out of the building,' she says, indicating the crew. 'Really nice to meet you; speak soon,' she says to Angelique, shaking her hand and adds a cheery 'Bye Mike,' as she shakes mine. We watch them leave and it's suddenly a lot quieter. Apart from the mugs which they had politely put on one of the desks, you'd be hard pushed to say anything had just happened.

39

I'm at Victoria coach station for a 7am departure, sitting in a waiting room that seems to have been made from one large piece of moulded plastic and I'm sure has smelled better.

It's brightening up outside and the pigeons are starting to take an interest in the people standing about eating food in takeaway wrappers. I'd told Angelique that if she wanted me to, I'd like to come and support her at the trial and she seemed quite glad when I offered.

It's taken two months for the trial to come round and it's in Oxford which is a bit of a bugger but I definitely want to be there for her. She went up yesterday and stayed with friends so I'll see her at the court. She suggested I stay in a B+B because there wasn't much room at her friends' and it would be easier than taking the train each day but I found a deal for the coach for a pittance. It's a long trip each way and an early start but I can't afford B+B's and I'll try to get some shut-eye on the coach in any case.

I'm wearing my magic suit again so I look smart and business-like for the courtroom. It looks good as new as I wore it a few weeks ago when we finally did the documentary interviews and it was a bit sweaty so I've had it dry cleaned. Not cheap but it needed it. I board the Oxford bus and inch down the aisle to a vacant double seat. I drop my bag on the seat by the window and I take my jacket off to at least give it a chance not to be crumpled up by sitting in it. I check there's nothing dirty left in the luggage rack above the seat and I lay the jacket carefully in it, smoothing it down to make sure it doesn't crumple. As I do so, an image of Angelique's small body replaces my jacket, blue eyes fixed on mine as I run my hand down her legs. I stop, mid smooth, flinching away as if the jacket is red hot. My own eyes widen as I try to lose the image, feeling my face redden. I look down at my bag on the seat and wipe my hand across my mouth.

'When you're ready mate,' a voice says loudly and I start,

Broken Wand

surprised by its closeness, instantly feeling guilt and shame flood me. A skinny young man with a beard in baggy clothes is smiling at me encouragingly, his bag held in front of him, resting it on his knees.

'Sorry, yes, miles away,' I mutter as I awkwardly stoop and sit at the same time, busying myself with stashing my bag under the chair in front until he's past. I glance across the aisle but the young woman there has got her headphones in, slouched against the window, chewing gum slowly in a world of her own. I spread out as much as I can to try and fill the space up, not looking at anyone else who walks down the aisle. I end up with the seat to myself, at least spared the misery of small talk. I rest my chin on my hand and my forehead against the window and shut my eyes, pushing the feelings that had overtaken me as far down in my mind as I can.

Broken Wand

40

A couple of hours and a bit of unwanted traffic jam parking on the M40 later and I'm at the zebra crossing opposite the law courts, waiting for the lights to change. It takes ages so I have time to inspect it. The courts themselves are a basic, ugly building, low and boxy, a product of the 1960's. Made up of pebble dashed slabs like tombstones with rectangular inscrutable windows, it doesn't quite look as if life changing decisions are made inside it. More like an office block, processing cases like so many projects on spreadsheets.

There are a few people hanging around smoking and vaping on the wide steps that funnel you in towards large glass doors despite the low grey clouds that are threatening rain. A small child is running up and down the tacked on wheelchair ramp, its mother keeping one eye on it, expressionless, while she leans on the wall and smokes too. It strikes me how rare it is to see groups of smokers anywhere except outside a pub these days. It makes my fingers itch to join them as the lights change and I cross towards them. But I don't want to smell of cigarette smoke when I see Angelique because I told her I'm giving up. I walk as close as I can to one guy without being weird, just to get a hit of the smoke. But bizarrely, it hits me and I don't like it. In fact, it's quite an ugly smell. Maybe it was all I needed, a bit of time without it.

I walk in through the doors and straighten my tie. My bag is checked and I step through the airport style security frame, relieved nothing goes off and smiling broadly at the security guard who couldn't care less. I'm early and don't see Angelique so I make my way over to a refreshments counter tucked under the polished concrete stairs. There are posters up behind it that say "Tea revives you" and "wake up and smell the coffee!" in jaunty, old fashioned type. I have to wonder if they've put them there for a laugh. Fluorescent stars with prices on have been stuck to the side of the stairs and I see that the prices increase as the steps rise.

I order tea and it comes in a polystyrene cup with a thin

Broken Wand

wooden stirrer. Milk is in little pots with tear off plastic lids; the kind that tastes of caravans. I walk down a few steps to a corridor which doubles as a waiting room. A screen lists the various cases to be heard that day, each one allocated a number like a departures board of justice. There're a couple of TV people waiting in the corridor. The bloke with the camera seems bored. He's holding a cup of coffee and flicking through his phone; the other one is talking loudly on his phone and glancing from the screen to his watch. He stands up and hoists his trousers up by the belt, then sticks a leg out and puts one hand on his hip. As I watch he glances at me to check me out and make sure I've seen him. I ask a passing usher where the waiting room is and I'm shown in to the small, windowless room. Angelique is sitting at a table with four chairs at it and there's someone sitting with her who introduces herself as Paula, from the witness care staff. Angelique looks smart, in her suit, her hair nicely styled – long and down but clipped up at the sides, simple, professional looking. She's put a bit of make up on but I can tell she's nervous. Nerves make her withdraw, appear more like the size she really is. I've noticed that before, when we're waiting to do a show. She sort of folds inwards like she's pulled a cloak around herself, and then, when we go out on the stage, she opens up like a flower, following the applause and the spotlights like they're the sun. She seems so much taller then, like the seed of a stage presence is buried inside her, waiting to unfurl. She smiles as I sit down.

'Hey,' I say. 'How are you doing?'

'Alright, I think,' she says, unconvincingly. As I sit down her phone starts to buzz on the table. I see Joanna's name but she doesn't answer it.

'Isn't that Joanna?'

'Yes.' She says but she doesn't look up.

'Not going to answer?'

'No.'

'She probably just wants to say good luck,' I add, as the phone stops buzzing.

Joanna doesn't leave a voicemail and I don't want to push it;

Broken Wand

there's enough tension in the room. It's kind of awkward with Paula there and I glance over again and smile but she's oblivious, just sits there leafing through some papers, doesn't smile back. She must have done this a billion times, sat in small rooms waiting for people to be ushered here and there. I wonder when it stopped being personal for her.

'You nervous?' I ask Angelique, though I know the answer.

'Little bit. Just want it to be over with now.' She spreads her hands on the table, stretching her fingers out. I know she's been agonising about how to present herself when she's called as a witness: play the helpless female and cry, play the helpless female and not appear in court herself because she's too traumatised or go in bold and challenging. She reckoned this last one was the riskiest because it makes you less sympathetic but, she said, offset that against her size and condition and you're left with the plucky little aggrieved woman routine. It goes without saying she didn't want to play the weak and woeful woman card and there was no way she wasn't going to look the attackers in the eye so option three it was. 'Think I just need to gather my thoughts now Mike. Will you wait for me afterwards?' My cue to leave.

I find Angelique's court on the board and ask at the tea desk for directions to Court 3. They're efficient to the point of answering on automatic: it's upstairs, turn right, double doors ahead of you, second door on the right. I try a smile to lighten the mood, my mood at least, and it too is efficiently returned. I suppose it's not really the place for friendliness.

Going up the stairs reminds me of my old school, black metal railings and a deep wooden bannister running round the top. The stairwell echoes and the wood feels very smooth beneath my hands, worn down by decades of sweaty palms no doubt. Upstairs there's another corridor waiting room, wider this time but the same setup of rooms off it.

I go through the court 3 door and I'm shown to the public gallery. It feels a bit weird to be sitting here, for some reason I feel like I've done something wrong and I try to avoid making eye contact with anyone. My suit feels tight all of a sudden and I wish I hadn't worn it. And then more people start to come in to the court and take their seats, chatting as if they were just out for a coffee. I think about Angelique, waiting in that little room. I hope she isn't too nervous. I notice a couple of people with notebooks – reporters probably – looking a bit bored. I suppose it must be quite a bit of hanging about, doing stories at the courts, and then you're not guaranteed anything juicy. Local stuff, break-ins, thieving, drink driving.

My eye is caught by two men being escorted into a separate area that has glass panes all around it. Two young men in ill-fitting suits sit down with a guard either side of them. I feel my face twitch in instant anger as it can only be the snake and the idiot.

They look younger, smaller than I had expected, thinner maybe. Perhaps I was expecting big thugs but they are just lads trying to be bigger than they are. Their glances dart around the court from lowered faces; one keeps pulling at his too short sleeves as if by doing so they will lengthen to cover his bony wrists and the tattoo on his left arm, the other can't stop his left leg from twitching up and down, agitation getting the better of him. Not so funny now, is it, I feel like shouting.

A door opens at the side of the court and an usher comes in and says 'all rise'. A few official looking types walk in. They go through a small gate to the raised desk that faces everyone else and sit on the padded chairs that are waiting there. The chair in the middle is the biggest of the lot. The magistrate, presumably. They don't wear all the gear, gowns and that, but they look pretty smart nonetheless.

Everyone sits down again and the trial begins. Lawyers talk, witnesses talk the man from the train is very good, he seems to have some sort of photographic memory. It's nice to finally see him, I feel like I want to shake his hand. The police talk and evidence is submitted and it's all proceeding well until Angelique's asked to take the stand.

She comes in from the side of the court, makes her way to the witness box and steps up onto it. There's a chair there but it doesn't have a bar between the legs and there's no stool so it is a very undignified struggle for her to haul herself up on to the seat of it. An usher moves towards her but she motions for her to stay where she is. But when she sits on the chair she can barely see over the top of the box. The magistrate in the middle sees all this and concludes that a fuck up of the first order has just happened. You can tell by his face. One of the two accused idiots actually sniggers; the stupid one wearing the outsize suit. The magistrate does not take kindly to this.

'Silence!' he shouts, and he glares at him. The idiot just drops his head and covers his mouth with his hand, desperately trying not to laugh any more. The other one is wearing a smug face that makes you want to punch him. Arrogant git. I hope it adds a year or two to their sentence. I'm leaning forward in my seat and staring at them, working my hands together in a joint fist; the woman next to me, one of the scribblers, has noticed and is eyeing me a bit now. I sit back and put my hands flat on my thighs, looking ahead. I don't want to be recognised, the video on the internet still haunting the back of my mind, I don't want to embarrass Angelique. She seems to lose interest and carries on making notes.
Quickly, the Judge says:

'Could somebody please assist the witness..' and he trails off because he's not quite sure what to say next and he is looking straight at the usher. "Assist her to what?" I think. To grow a couple of feet in order to fit a standard witness box with a standard chair in it? By now there are murmurings from the court and more scribbling in notebooks and tapping on phones by the people around me. They're loving this.

The usher has an intense conversation through a half open door with someone in the corridor. By now the whole room is either staring at their hands in embarrassment or muttering under their breath. Angelique is sitting in the chair, I can just see the top of her head which is motionless. She's not making a fuss, not milking it. The usher has said something to her quietly and she's just nodded. A couple of seconds later and the door opens with a red-faced person handing over three large square cushions. The usher has the good grace to stand between Angelique and the courtroom

Broken Wand

while she climbs down, then places two of the cushions on the chair. But then Angelique has to accept her help in getting up on to the cushions. It's not very dignified, but she manages. And even though she knows all eyes are on her, she doesn't once look round the room, preferring to stare straight ahead at the magistrates desk. She pours herself some water from the carafe on the ledge and takes a sip. That's the only sign she's flustered. She doesn't like drinking water. But only I would know that so it's OK. The magistrate says:

'Miss Watson, please accept the court's apologies for the delay in seating you but I believe we are now ready to begin?' It was all he could say really. She nodded her agreement but didn't speak. He briskly moves on with things then; getting her sworn in, instructing the lawyers to carry on and begin their questioning.

She's asked by one of the prosecution lawyers if she recognises the idiots as her assailants, which she obviously does. She glances at them and says yes, firmly. She looks back at the lawyer and after that keeps her eyes firmly on him. He asks her to tell her version of events and she does so. Her voice stays steady throughout and she doesn't exaggerate or pause at any time. She must have practised this, going over it in her mind and not just for this moment. He asks her about the impact it had on her life in the days afterwards, how she feels now and if she is still getting medical care. She talks about her injuries, her week off work, the stress she still experiences. She is calm but not too confident.

When he is finished with her the defence lawyer is given the opportunity to question her but declines, probably realising it would do no good whatsoever. She gets down from the witness box and is shown out of the courtroom. It doesn't take long for the Magistrate to begin his sentencing:

'I believe this to be one of the most cowardly, despicable assaults I have ever had to judge. Not only have you not shown any remorse, you continue to find humour in this situation which I find reprehensible to say the least. My only regret is that I am limited in my sentencing by legal parameters but I will not hesitate to go to full lengths those parameters allow.'

Broken Wand

To the idiot he says:

'While I appreciate that you were easily led in this matter and simply went along with events you at no point attempted to stop them. You joined in this assault freely. I am therefore sentencing you to a six month suspended prison term, and ordering your inclusion on a rehabilitation programme.' Next he addresses the snake: 'As the clear leader in this act you showed no empathy for your victim or indeed any remorse after the act. Your behaviour was reprehensible; a vicious, senseless, cowardly act of violence against someone clearly no match for you. Consequently, I sentence you to the maximum sentence available to me of six months in prison.'

As sentencing finishes, I want to stand up and cheer, punch the air, point at them and roar. I leave in the small crowd from the public gallery and wait outside in the corridor on a blue chair but I can't sit still. I pace around, looking out the window at the car park below. The corridor quickly empties, it's the end of the day more or less so no one hanging around. I feel light inside and want to laugh out loud. It's strange to think we're out the other side of this, that the whole stupid thing is finished. We can put it behind us now and carry on with life again. When she appears at the end of the corridor, she looks a bit more together. She smiles when she sees me.

'Thanks for waiting,' she says quietly and suddenly I see how much this has tired her. She may be relieved maybe but tired mostly. I smile back and for a second we just smile at each other.

'Great result,' I say but she just says 'mm' back. 'Shall we?' I say, gesturing towards the door. I'm keen to leave as we're catching the coach back to London together this evening. It's quiet walking through the court, just our shoes on the tiled floor making a sound. The security guard presses a button to release the main door but when we step outside, there's a small crowd waiting for us. A couple of TV crews and some journalists are there. I hadn't expected this and Angelique seems to miss a couple of beats as she stands there, but only for a second. They have waited halfway down the steps so they are more or less at eye height and when they see her in the doorway they shuffle in to position and focus cameras. I put myself in position right beside her, feeling protective and ready to step in. Like she needs me to. I shuffle backwards a bit. A TV journalist holds a microphone near to her and loudly asks:

'Miss Watson, How do you feel now justice has been done?' Angelique glances at the TV camera and then back at the journalist, taking a few seconds to gather herself while a photographer shouts at her so she'll look at him and the camera flashes. Then she turns to the reporter and says:

'There have been many times in my life where I have been the butt of jokes, teasing and downright nastiness and while I'd love to say it's water off a ducks' back, it isn't. It hurts, every last bit of it.' She pauses, but no one interrupts. 'But I cannot in all honesty say I have ever been subjected to anything quite as humiliating and soul destroying as this attack. What happened to me was shocking, hurtful and totally unjustified. Everyone has a breaking point and this was very nearly mine but I will have to accept the conclusion of this trial as an end point, pull myself together and move on. Again.'

'Do you think justice has been done?' comes the next shouted question. She looks at the reporter and waits a few beats, considering this.

'Whether incarceration helps these people or not remains to be seen though most evidence suggests it won't and that it won't deter others. None of the wider causes or effects of this attack have been addressed or answers found, all it proves is that they assaulted me. So to answer your question, I feel nothing at this outcome except sadness. I'm optimistic for my future because I have to be, I can be for me, but not for theirs. Thank you.' There is a bit of a buzz after that and almost immediately someone else shoves a recorder near her and asks:

'Are you angry about the lack of adequate seating for you in court?' This one she comes back at more quickly.

'Again, more frustrated than angry but it was dealt with and we moved on.' I can see she's had enough so I put my hand lightly on her shoulder, steering her away as the journalists move off down the steps.

41

We make our way to the bus station and luckily we can catch an earlier coach. It looks like it rained while we were in the court but the sun is trying to break through now, just in time to start setting. There's just ten minutes to grab a drink and something to eat on the journey. The coffee kiosk does pre-packed sandwiches so we buy one each and some crisps. I'm still buzzing and going back over things, re-living the moment the idiots were sentenced and smiling to myself but when I look down, I can see that Angelique is flagging and I suddenly feel like scooping her up and carrying her to the bus.

'Not long,' I say, 'you can sleep on the bus.' She doesn't look up at me. She's looking away over the concourse at some teenagers, sitting on and hanging off the railings. They're talking and laughing and the girls have their skirts rolled as short as they will go, the boys are flicking each other and swearing, glancing round to make sure the girls have seen them. Angelique seems lost in thought but I expect she's just thinking about the trial.

Our coach swings round in to the allotted bay so I gather everything up and we make our way over, boarding the coach and finding our seats. She's soon tucked in by the window, my jacket scrunched up as a pillow for her, looking out at the motorway. The light is fading quickly outside but I don't want to put the light on yet; I've tried reading the magazine but it's just full of ads; I'm still buzzing. She's been pretty quiet since we were at the bus station so I try to make conversation.

'I didn't know you had written a speech for afterwards.' I say. She takes a deep breath, sort of a sigh really, and talks to her reflection.

'I didn't, really. I mean it had been going round in my head for a while, wondering what I would say if people asked but I didn't think they would. I didn't plan to say anything really, it just happened.' Her voice sounds distant, like she's stepping in to the conversation from somewhere else.

'Should be interesting to see what's in the papers tomorrow,' I persist, ' we'll have to search up the telly news on the internet. There's Wi-Fi on the coach, shall I give it a go?'

'Don't worry, I'll watch it later on catch-up. To be honest I'm a bit wiped out. Mind if I doze off?' Her eyes are already half closed as she sinks further into my jacket.

'Of course, it's been a long day.' On an impulse I reach for her hand and give it a squeeze, finding myself looking in to her eyes as she turns her head in surprise. Perhaps it's the tiredness, perhaps it's the relief at the verdict, perhaps it's something else that's starting to feel familiar again, but whatever it is that's blinking in the strengthening light inside me I don't want to let go and I smile at her. But something shifts in her and she gently says:

'Thanks for being there today Mike, you've been a good friend,' as she slips her hand out from under mine, giving a small smile, turning her head to the window and closing her eyes. I'm not too sure what to make of this but I get a creeping sense that she's letting me know that it isn't any more than that to her. Or maybe she's not saying anything other than thanks and I'm just overthinking; it wouldn't be the first time.

Seeing her asleep makes me remember I've been up since five, and I instantly feel really tired as well. It's over and she won and I'm looking forward to things being normal again, whatever that is at the moment. Looking forward to our plans being back on track, I think as I drain my coffee cup. Looking forward to doing that with Angelique, I think to myself as I lean my chair back an inch. Just looking forward, I think, as I drift off with a small smile on my face.

42

I'm up early and look up some of the papers online. There's a big piece in an Oxford paper:

'We may not have been able to see the victim in the witness box but we did see justice in court number 3 today. Pete Joffrey of Blackbird Leys was given the maximum sentence for his assault on Angelique Watson which saw him callously manhandle her on to the luggage rack of an evening train from London to Oxford. Richard Whiley, also of Blackbird Leys, was given a six month suspended sentence for his part in the assault. Magistrate Michael Howey said it was one of the most cowardly and despicable cases he had ever had to judge. Meanwhile court officials were left red-faced over a seating blunder which left Ms. Watson unable to see over the witness box. Ms. Watson who suffers with dwarfism, was made to wait for several minutes while cushions were found to accommodate her. Commenting about the disability rights blunder on the courtroom steps after the sentencing Ms. Watson said she was: 'more frustrated than angry but it was dealt with and we moved on.''

She won't like 'suffers with' I think to myself, nor will she like 'disability rights'. But they do quote her whole speech and it sounds so official, what she says, even though I heard it myself. It's like seeing it in a newspaper makes it real, makes it proper. Not like when you just hear some bloke in the pub spouting on, someone actually thought this was worth putting in a paper. In the photograph, she looks strong, standing there on the steps. Behind her, I recognise my magic suit, up to the waist at least, where I get cut off. I look like I'm standing stiffly, like a bouncer, but I remember the feeling I had. I'm feeling it now while I read this. I'm proud I was there, I'm proud I was with her. I'm proud of my friend. My friend. I say it out loud like an idiot, alone in my flat, sitting at the kitchen table.

43

'Sorry I'm late!' Juliette announced as she burst through the café door with a flurry, bag hanging off the crook of her elbow, phone in hand, flicking her trendily dishevelled hair off her face with the other hand, 'got stuck on a phone call,' she added, rolling her eyes as she dumped her bag on the floor and flung her phone down on the table, pushing her oversized sunglasses up on the her head. 'What would you like?' she asked as she gazed up at the large blackboard behind the counter, 'the iced coffee is SO good here,' she said to the room in general. She turned back to Angelique who smiled and indicated the large earthenware mug in front of her.

'I'm sorted,' Angelique said, 'thanks though.' Juliette went to the counter and took her time to scan the glass covered cake stands full of various types of treats. Angelique noticed the impression Juliette made on the male staff; their eyes subtly followed her as she ordered. She seemed oblivious, too oblivious perhaps, as she made her way back and sat down opposite Angelique. Once the how are you's were out of the way Juliette came straight to the point.

'So Angelique,' she said, leaning on the table, 'dust settled after the court case yet?'

'No, not really, that's why I asked to see you actually.'

'Oh?'

'I'm getting a few calls asking me to comment on news issues and join discussions and I'm not too sure how to handle some of it. It's all a bit new but I really want to do it, I mean, if doing this raises awareness of issues facing people like me,' Angelique explained.

'I see,' Juliette said. 'Who are you getting these requests from?' she asked as she leant back to make room for the waiter to put her iced coffee carefully down in front of her, taking extra care with the tall glass. She flashed him a smile which he returned.

'A local TV news programme, a radio talk show, some podcasts and a newspaper,' Angelique reeled off. 'It's not exactly big time to be honest but I do think it would be a good opportunity to get some points over. What do you think?'

'It depends on the query I suppose and whether you want to build your own profile or not. I mean, you're an interesting, intelligent person with some socially relevant views so no wonder you're attracting a few approaches,' Juliette explained, suddenly more serious than she had been before. She stirred her coffee with an extra-long teaspoon and briefly smelled it. 'The stuff you did after the trial was good; the TV news clips of you on the steps were strong; like I've said before, you have a great delivery.' She let that hang for a second. 'But, that said, you don't want to become rent-a-quote either; no quicker way for journalists or researchers to become bored of you.' She paused for another moment and then, almost as an afterthought, said: 'Look, if you like, you can always run stuff like this past me. I mean, I know what they're looking for and can give you a few insights. I've been thinking about branching in to talent management anyway so it could benefit both of us.'

'Are you sure? I mean, this may be all that happens but it would be useful to bounce it off someone else.'

'Pretty sure you'd handle it but yeah, sure, I'd be happy to. I can maybe suggest some contacts as well, like the chat show.' Angelique smiled, relieved that she had found someone she could discuss this new aspect of her life with. 'There's one thing we would need to be sure about though,' Juliette continued. 'Would you be alright with going in to personal details?' Immediately Angelique became wary.

'Well there's personal and there's personal,' she replied, emphasising the second personal by moving her hands from one side of the table to the other and lowering her head slightly. 'Which sort of personal are we talking about here?'

'Would you be willing to talk about genetics, for instance?'

'In what way?' Angelique pressed, though she was secretly relieved that was all it was; genetics she could handle.

'An explanation of how you became you, what happens at a genetic level and the implications for you, that sort of thing. You'd need to have something pretty standard ready for when people ask; and they will, by the way.'

'I've no doubt you're right,' Angelique agreed. 'It's pretty straightforward actually. My parents weren't Little People and you don't need a history of it in your family for it to happen. Achondroplasia, which is what I have, is a random, spontaneous mutation of a gene, usually from the father but it can be either parent. It doesn't mean I'm going to pass it on to a child though it is possible. That's the nuts and bolts of it but there's plenty of background where the science is concerned.'

'Do you want kids?' The direct question took Angelique by surprise but she decided to tackle it head on.

'Funny; people don't often ask me that. But no, I don't, not yet anyway. I want to concentrate on my career for now.'

'Very sensible,' Juliette agreed, smiling, 'me too.' Juliette picked her coffee up and held it in front of her. 'A toast,' she said, nodding to Angelique's mug so she would pick it up, 'to a mutually beneficial professional relationship!'

44

A couple of weeks have passed since the trial and we've all got together to watch the documentary. Well, I say we've all got together, basically I've joined Angelique and a load of her friends to watch it. It feels like years ago that we did the interviews for this, so much has happened in between and it will soon be autumn. I feel a bit like an exhibit as I sit in an armchair in a corner of the room. I know they're all thinking 'so this is the bloke she's been hanging out with' but they're not quite curious enough yet to want to be stuck with me; too busy catching up with each other.

Of course, they've all seen the magic show films online and they've probably seen the film of me and the mop as well which means they already know a lot more about me than I do about them. In fact, it occurs to me that they pretty much know everything there is to know about me that's remotely interesting. Every now and then I glance round and catch one of them looking at me, but they just smile quickly and look away again. And then, stupidly, I catch Joanna's eye. I look quickly away but not before I see her take the elbow of the bloke she's standing with and steer him my way. I stand up but don't move away from the chair, desperate not to lose my place in the corner.

'Mike,' she says, 'let me introduce Benji. He's in organic wine, owns a small vineyard in Sussex.' I shake his hand and smile as we exchange greetings. He's a good few inches taller than me, handsome in a healthy, posh countryside kind of way and confident that I'll be impressed. 'Mike's in coffee, aren't you Mike,' Joanna says before I can say anything to him.

'Er, yes, you could say that,' I say and I smile at Benji again. There's a pause while I try to think of something else to say that won't make me sound like me and I'm about to ask what sort of wine Benji makes when Joanna says:

'Riveting. Let's find a drink Benji. I want you to meet someone with stacks of cash and a need to invest.' She glances back at me as she steers him away and he sort of waves with a couple of fingers

Broken Wand

as they turn leave. I sit back down and feel the heat of my collar against my neck; I'm feeling pretty anxious as it is without her trying to cut me down to size.

It's 7.15 in the evening and my stomach is turning over on itself and the wine. I haven't eaten since lunchtime and whether it's that or nerves my palms are sweating but I'm not going to leave this armchair again for love nor money. I couldn't eat anyway, even those mini bagels with cream cheese on the table I've been eyeing. Or the mini quiches. All Angelique bite sized. But the wine is going down OK; maybe it's Benji's. I gulped it and now I feel a bit light headed. Not sure I can trust myself to have another and I'd have to leave the chair so I decide to wait it out. I stare at the floor in front of me, willing the time to go faster. Clearly, I wouldn't know what to say to any of Angelique's friends anyway; they all look too clever. They're quite earnest and I watch a couple close to me; one of them looks really intently at the other while resting their chin on their hand and nodding a bit. What's that about? Just fucking have a chat, it's not Newsnight. I feel instantly guilty for thinking this, as though I'd said it out loud. And then, mercifully, Angelique comes over with a bottle of wine to see if I want any more. I couldn't be more pleased to see her.

'You OK?' she asks, 'want me to introduce you to anyone?'

'No, please don't,' I say, immediately terrified that she'll insist and I'll have to face another Benji. 'It'll be on in a minute anyway so I'll just wait. Bit nervous to tell you the truth. Are you?' I'm gabbling.

'Yes, very actually. I could do without the audience.' I'm relieved to hear that. 'Joanna's idea more than mine to be honest. Wants to show me off to her collection of people.'

'Don't you know them?'

'Not all of them. But they know all about me. Joanna likes to show off her PC credentials sometimes.' She adds with a conspiratorial smile that immediately puts me more at ease.

'I know how you feel. It's weird, knowing they know more about me than I do about them. I'm not used to it.'

'Well, if this programme does its stuff, you'd better start getting used to it,' she smiles. Before we can chat further, Joanna takes control.

'OK everyone, 7.25 – putting the TV on, settle down!' She steps between us, not looking at me and whisking Angelique off to the middle of the room where she has put a small armchair ready for her, leaving me well alone in the corner and I'm fine with that. My stomach churns.

Joanna waves to TV remote like a wand and the volume goes right up. People are settling cross legged on the floor in front of me and leaning against the legs of people on the sofa. We wait for the ads to finish and they introduce the programme. In the first bit there's a load of little clips, bits of interviews to come – Angelique is in there - and some old clips of Paul Daniels and variety hall stuff, Tommy Cooper alongside David Blaine and Americans with tigers, magicians making London Bridge and the Statue of Liberty disappear. The narrator says they're going to look at current magic and see how it stacks up. "Have we reached maximum male magic?" is the question the presenter asks to the camera. He's taking it very seriously. I twirl my glass and fiddle with the stem. It's greasy now and covered in fingerprints.

The programme skips from a brief look back at past magic shows to looking at the big, naff magic tricks in the 1980's – the age of the tigers and the sequin suits. Then they skip to now and it goes on to show some interviews and then, suddenly, Angelique is on the screen, silently going through one of our tricks, being her usual charming self to the camera while the voiceover says: 'Recently, there's been a new addition to the magic scene here in the UK. This is Angelique Watson. She's one half of the duo Mike and Angelique who have made a name for themselves online, using social media to build a profile and a big fanbase as well as doing live gigs in their local area. But the question is, is it her skill, her gender or her size that draws attention? Do an online search for famous female magicians and the pickings are thin. Search for dwarf magicians and you're going as far back as ancient Mayan mythology.' Then it cuts to Angelique and I sitting next to each other. It's the interview we did at the offices.

Broken Wand

'I didn't set out to be a magician,' she starts, 'I was working with Mike on a personal project and a friend suggested I join him on stage. I think the fact that I have a rare genetic combination resulting in a shortness of stature makes me doubly interesting to people; they're going to watch me anyway. But as far as being a woman is concerned, when I was little in age I didn't think being a woman would be an impediment – I just viewed people as people – but being little in size can be a problem and at the same time an attraction, a curiosity. I think people can handle me being a little person and entertaining them more than they could me being a woman in a male dominated industry. A recent review of our act wondered if I would make such an impact if I was six foot and big breasted. You have to wonder at the stupidity of that remark really but I can see where it came from.' She beams a smile at Nick the interviewer just before it cuts to the next piece. As it goes on there's a bit more of Angelique among other female magicians trying to make a name for themselves. It's clear they're quite taken with her but this wasn't the angle I was expecting; they obviously decided to change the theme of the programme later on when they couldn't find many more female magicians. There's a couple of bits where I'm in it but just as part of the act. At one point I'm sitting beside Angelique as she answers a question about performing live and then just as I'm about to chip in it goes to another bit. There's a couple of awkward shuffles and I stare at the screen, trying not to let my confusion show. They're talking about how current female magicians could be role models, not just glamorous assistants. They're highlighting women in history now who from anecdotal evidence were actually the brains behind the acts but who weren't taken seriously in their own right; women who were promoters and producers and wives but never the main act.

When it finishes, everyone is congratulating Angelique and it's all very lovely and then it's awkward. A few people come over and say congrats and how it was a really insightful documentary and it's pretty clear there's squirming going on. I wonder how - even if - I can claw back some dignity. I smile and nod and stay put in the chair. I've never felt more trapped in my life. They're all between me and the door on the far side of the room. Joanna is looking triumphant; almost physically puffed up. Bubbling with laughter every now and then while she discusses the programme with people.

She goes to sit on the arm of the sofa with Angelique next to her in her chair and I notice her put her hand very lightly in the small of Angelique's back; she may not even feel it. She looks over at me once, just long enough for her to make sure I've seen this while she gives a little smile of triumph. I wonder if she knew the direction the documentary would take, but how could she have known? I feel ridiculous thinking it. I look down at the people sitting on the floor in front of me, talking animatedly and agreeing with each other, saying things like 'I totally take your point'. I don't notice Angelique come over.

'Well that was interesting,' she says, leaning on the arm of the chair so we're face to face.

'Yes,' I say, looking down at my glass.

'I didn't know they were going to take that tack Mike,' she says, almost apologetically, 'it's not what they said they were going to do. You were in the same meeting. You heard them.' I close my eyes and I just don't want to hear any more. My head is beginning to swim and I need to eat. I put my glass down on the table next to me.

'I think I'll just head off. Work tomorrow.' I look at her and she doesn't argue. She can see I'm feeling pretty shit and just nods.

'See you tomorrow?' she asks. I give her a nod and a half smile but I really don't know. I edge past a few people and try not to catch their eye as I do so. Luckily the door is down a hallway so for all they know I could be going to the loo. I slip out.

Broken Wand

45

I can't sleep. I haven't eaten and my stomach is turning over on itself and the wine. I'm sitting up in bed at 3am, propped on pillows, staring at the wall opposite. The light is on because the dark means I can't see anything and then all I can do is hear thoughts. It won't stop. Every time I feel a bit tired I close my eyes and some new hideous thought pops in there and I jolt again with a knot in my stomach. I know now that there never was any interest in me in the documentary. They probably only talked to us both so they could interview Angelique. Christ; the awful realisation that I've given my all for what – an almost mention in a documentary. What the hell will I say to my parents? Oh Jesus, this will not help Mum. I can't tell them they were right, that I've fucked it all up. It'll crucify them. I wonder if they watched it? I bet the Peterson's did. I bet Mrs Petersons there right now, rubbing it in. And Angelique, what about her? She'll dump me as soon as she can. In the magic show sense, not the - what? Relationship? Is that what it is? I don't want to lose her. I can't lose someone else I feel so close to. I don't blame her for this and I know she'll do the right thing by me, she has principles. But I want to run as far away from all of this as I can, bury myself somewhere that doesn't have the internet. Or TV. Or Wi-Fi. Or any of that shit. I bend my legs up, put my elbows on my knees, head in my hands. What a fucking mess. What a fucking mess. Thank Christ Jenny's dead, at least she doesn't have to see this. I think even she would have given up on me by now. I don't want the morning to come but I want this night to be over.

Broken Wand

46

It's been two weeks and I'm looking forward to seeing her this evening, to telling her some of my ideas. I've put on a clean shirt but not a tie; don't want to overdo it. It's just a working drink. I'm at the pub first and make my way to the bar, ordering a pint that comes in a warm, streaky glass, fresh from the dishwasher. I haven't been here before and I look briefly at the creased, laminated menu that sits in a little wooden block on the bar but it's vaguely sticky and it puts me off. There's an actual fingerprint in some sort of brown sauce on the base that makes me wonder what the food would be like. I have visions of a meal that would arrive a bit wet where it has been stuck straight in the microwave from the freezer. Hot in the inside, cold on the edges.

I see Joanna arrive in the mirror behind the bar first and this instantly straightens my back. I don't turn round immediately as I have no idea what to say to her and as soon as I see her coming over to the bar I'm pretty sure that she smells me hesitate. I turn to face her and put on a bright smile she sees through immediately. She has this way of locking eyes with you, unblinking. Probably why she's good at her job; she has this was of slicing your brain like you're a ham at the deli counter in Sainsbury's. The coldest of pecks on the cheek later and I order her a vodka. She thanks me and strolls over to a high, round table with metal bar stools. It's not very comfortable but we perch anyway.

There's not a lot of chat, never is with Joanna but we manage both being 'fine, thanks'. I wonder how Angelique will cope with these bar stools; maybe we'll move when she arrives. I'm about to suggest this as the door opens and I glance round but it isn't her. I glance at my watch; not like her to be late.

'Maybe we should sit somewhere a bit more..' and I pat the seat of the bar stool by way of explanation while looking around at all the other empty tables.

'Oh, Angelique isn't coming, she's busy,' says Joanna. I blink a couple of times while this sinks in. So Joanna and I are having a drink. I wonder how quickly I can finish mine.

'Didn't want to leave you sitting here on your own so I thought I'd come anyway,' she says by way of explanation.

'Oh right, that's fine,' I stutter with a fake cheeriness. Maybe this is a plan of Angelique's, to make us get to know each other better, two important people in her life and all that. Unlike like her not to text me though. Come to think of it, it wasn't Angelique who sent me the text to start with. Joanna did. Something starts to wriggle around in my head, something uncomfortable. I don't think Angelique knows we're here and that sets all sorts of alarm bells ringing. Joanna sips her drink and places it carefully on the table, keeping her fingers round the glass.

'I thought we could have a little chat Mike. You know, chew the fat. Just the two of us,' she takes another sip of her vodka but never once takes her eyes off me. She licks her lips and it feels like a threat. I have no idea what to say. I shift on my uncomfortable stool and wait for her to begin. I'm starting to sense a set up. I look around, anywhere but at her. The pub isn't too full, it is a Tuesday after all. I pretend to be immediately interested in the other people in here and glance round at them, buying a few precious seconds to gather myself. There're a few lads talking at the bar wearing their first suits and pointy shoes, looking like trainee estate agents enjoying having some cash and the freedom to spend it. Someone plays a fruit machine that pumps out tinny versions of 1960's hits. There're a few more people in the dim nether regions of the pub but it's not exactly buzzing. I expect it makes its money on Fridays when the advertised happy hour and cheap cocktails kick in. I take a long drink and feel a bit steadier under Joanna's gaze.

'Ever performed here?' she asks.

'No, not here. Other pubs around but not here.' Small talk over, she takes a new tack.

'It's good news about the documentary, isn't it,' Joanna begins. I look at her with what must be a blank face. I try and read hers but nothing doing. The documentary has been out for a couple of weeks now, and we know it had good reviews. I'm forced to ask:

Broken Wand

'How do you mean?'

'The new one. The one she's doing now. With Juliette's company. Good news, isn't it,' she repeats, ramming home the fact that I clearly don't know what she's talking about. So now I'm racking my brains to see if I can remember Angelique telling me anything about another documentary. Surely she would have told me about it? Asked for my opinion? I mean, if we're going to do another one - and then the penny drops, as it is meant to. This doesn't involve me. I feel my stomach churn and my face fall. The moment Joanna has no doubt been waiting for.

'Oh', she says lightly, 'didn't she mention it?' I try and keep my reply light.

'No, not yet. Just haven't seen each other.'

'Right,' is all she says in reply and takes another sip from her vodka. I could leave it there. I could just leave it there but of course I don't. I take off my shirt and I start to whip myself.

'What documentary, Joanna?' I ask and she smiles a small smile.

'Well, I don't think they've gone public yet but it's a documentary about the history of people with dwarfism; all the way back in history and across the world. You know, cross cultural references and attitudes, that sort of thing. Quite a big deal really. This could really be the start of things for her.'

'What do you mean?'

'Well, it's been great what she's been doing, you know, the magic project, but since the assault and all the attention from that she's grasped how much more she is capable of. She's really only been dipping a toe in 'til now.' She lets that settle between us. I'm trying not to react but inside I'm squirming. She carries on. 'You know, I have to be honest with you Mike,' she spreads both her hands out in front of her, fingers wide. The open, honest politician look I've seen on TV. 'Angelique's driven; not someone to hang around. She likes to run with ideas until they begin to bore her or she feels she's not getting very far with it. Or until she's achieved what she wanted to from it, of course.' I'm taken aback by this.

'Look, I don't know what you're trying to say here Joanna but

Broken Wand

Angelique and I are friends so if that's all you have to say then -'

'Friends? Did she actually say that?' she cuts me off, 'Has she ever actually called you a friend?' she persists, eyes steely.

'Well, I..' I'm struggling to think of more than one or two actual instances of Angelique using the word friend to describe me apart from on the bus when she was, I see for certain now, keeping me in my place. My face reddens and I study my pint.

'Thought so,' Joanna says almost sympathetically, 'I think you might just be about to see Angelique a bit more clearly. This was never about you Mike. She's ambitious and she'll do whatever it takes. You were just a project to get freelance clients interested. Actually, I think joining the magic show was just another way to annoy her mother.'

'Joining the act was your idea, you pushed her to do it.'

'She just needed a nudge. She knew in five minutes what you've never worked out in your life – difference sells. And she's certainly different. You just happened to be there, a ready-made vehicle for her to take the wheel of. I have to say though that I didn't see it working out. I thought she'd have realised her mistake and jettisoned you ages ago. Just goes to show, you never can tell.'

'Why are you saying all this?' I've tensed so much my feet are on the floor now, almost standing at this ridiculous table. 'You've never liked me, I've known that from the first moment you looked down your nose at me but why now?'

'I'm trying to help you Mike. I've seen it all before.' And my eyes open wider in disbelief.

'And how, exactly, are you doing that?'

'Look, she's going to move on and you seem to think you'll be moving on with her. I'm trying to spare you the pain, or at least give you a heads up about it.'

'I don't believe you. I don't believe a fucking word you're saying.' I'm starting to get angry now because part of me doesn't want to believe this is true. But a bigger, more frightened part of me sees that it just might be. She finishes her vodka, licking her lips calmly again as if relishing the last drops. And then she leans in and for the first time there's real venom in her voice, the look in her eyes is hard, and her voice is quieter.

'I hope you have a plan B Mike, I really do. Because you're going to need it.' She slips off the stool and puts her jacket on almost in one motion. 'Bye Mike,' she says coldly and she struts out of the pub, leaving me sitting there feeling sick and confused. I can't believe Angelique could be that cold. I don't even know if it's true about the documentary, Joanna could just be trying to stir things up but somehow, I don't think so. Why would she? Angelique's her best friend after all.

I automatically decide another pint would help so go to the bar. If I look shaken up or angry, the barman doesn't notice. Or care. His phone is of far more interest it seems, even managing to type it one handed while pouring my pint, not spilling any. A pint must take the length of a text to pour. I suppose it will only be a matter of time before bars in pubs become one giant vending machine and we can do away with bored twenty somethings and the pretence of customer service completely. At least in this pub. Not that I would come here again.

I sit at a proper table, staring at my overpriced pint and fiddling with a beer mat, shredding a corner. There are a few more people in the pub now; after work drinkers, some who looked like they sit at the same bar stool every night, nodding at others who came in and them nodding back. Some start conversations about football, some just sit alone. Like me. Maybe I should start doing this, sitting in a pub with a slowly warming pint and watching the day ebb away from behind a warm fog. There are worse things to do. And then the questions start to make their way through my anger, the doubts that will niggle away at me all night. Why would Joanna say what she did if there was no truth in it? I want to dismiss it as jealous friend talk, like the girls at school used to do if someone got above themselves. This is different though, she's in a league of her own, Joanna. This wasn't some bitchy chit chat, she meant this. She has no reason to lie to me after all, other than not liking me very much but why do something that would hurt Angelique? She likes her. On the other hand, she knows her well. Very well. Jesus, I'll never get the hang of this stuff, it's so bloody complicated. I sigh

Broken Wand

and sit back in my chair, hands in my lap, wishing I hadn't dressed like a bank clerk. I look like the rest of them, alone and drinking, putting off the moment when I have to go home to an empty place. If this was what Joanna intended then she's been successful; I feel utterly shit, confused and alone. I want to speak to Angelique but booze and anger don't always make for a decent conversation. I'll wait until tomorrow.

47

Angelique calls me the following morning. She sounds chipper enough though I'm not sure why I thought she wouldn't. I think I just sort of hoped she would sound anxious or guilty or sad or something. She asks how I am and I ask her back and it is all very pleasant. She doesn't pick up on anything in my voice to begin with, too excited to tell me her news to really listen.

'So, something really great has happened and I'm desperate to tell you about it. I can't go in to too much detail but -'

'You're doing another documentary.' I interrupt, impatient to cut straight to it like ripping of a plaster.

'Yes, how did you..?' I can hear the surprise in her voice and I immediately feel like a shit.

'Lucky guess,' I say lamely, already regretting my petulance. 'Is it with the same people? Juliette's lot?' Even though I already feel ashamed for tripping her up, I'm still trying to. Despite it feeling deceitful I don't want to tell her about my little chat with Joanna last night or that I already know Juliette's involved.

'Yes, she called a couple of days ago. They liked what they saw in our documentary so she suggested it and they're putting some ideas together. It's not a done deal yet, they don't have an outlet, just ideas,' she adds, more normally now though there's still a question mark in her voice.

'So what's it about then?' I lighten my tone, trying to be less of a dick.

'Well, broadly speaking, it's a history of dwarfism and how Little People have been treated over time, whether things have changed or not. I can't really say much more.' I can hear in her voice she's a bit deflated. Christ, I feel such a jerk.

'It sounds great,' I say and I try to sound enthusiastic, 'It really does. You'll be great.'

'Is there something wrong Mike?'

'No, I'm fine.'

'Then what? I can tell something's wrong.' I'm beginning to

Broken Wand

wish I'd never started this because I can feel myself getting angry. Why can't she see how this would hurt me? I squeeze my eyes shut and fight the urge to swear at her, trying but failing to keep my cool.

'Are you going to dump me now? Is that it?' I blurt,

'Is this Angelique going off and doing her own thing? Because if it is you should just tell me.'

'Mike!' she says, and in my mind I can see the surprise in her eyes. 'Where is this coming from? I thought you'd be pleased for me. This doesn't change anything.'

'You've used me all along. You saw me in the pub and thought 'there's a bloke about to go under, he'll do. I'll step on him and keep going'. This was never about us, was it? Always about you only I was too stupid to see it, swept along by your promises of a career in magic.'

'Mike, I didn't. I never did that. I saw you and I liked what you did; old school, proper magic, the kind we had as kids. I didn't know I would be offered this, how could I? I can't predict the future, I can't predict what people are going to do.'

'I thought that was exactly what you did do; bloody market analysis and all that stuff about web trends – you do know, that's just it.'

'That's different,' she says, defensively.

'Oh really. Well that's convenient, isn't it. Only I don't believe it was a coincidence.' I'm trying to stop but I can't. I put my free hand on my head and run it backwards and forwards a few times, trying to make my thoughts calm down.

'Are you saying you don't trust me?' she asks and again I picture her face, her confusion, her eyes continuing the question.

'No, it's not that I don't trust you, I just...'

'Don't believe me?' she says and now I can hear a tremor in her voice, a tremor of barely concealed anger.

'No. Stop putting words in my mouth.' I know I should tell her why this has hit me hard, not just because of Joanna, but the real hitch. I dive in.

'Christ Angelique, I'm sorry. I just don't know what to do. I jacked my job in.'

'You what?'

'I jacked my job in.' I say again and a sense of relief deflates my pent up anger and it all comes out in a rush now. 'I thought because things were going so well I could take a chance, make the jump. Well actually, they sort of suggested I should leave. I was taking all this time off for rehearsals and those interviews for the documentary and they were getting fed up after all that other stuff.'

'Bloody hell, Mike. Things aren't going that well. What are you going to do for money?' Now she was sounding concerned.

'What do you mean? It's what you said, you said sometimes you just have to go for it.'

'I know I did but not in a real way, not in a pack your job in with nothing to go to way. We don't know where this is going yet, we don't have a direction.'

'But the documentary, the meetings -'

'Just meetings, Mike, just meetings and one little bit in a documentary.' I feel sick and my mouth is dry. Had I imagined this too? Had I got carried away by dreams?

'What did your parents say?'

'What did my – what?' I bluster. Why should it matter if I've told my parents? I'm forty years old. Does she think I'm some sort of grown up child? Is that why she thinks she can just use me? Before I can put any of this in to words she says:

'Haven't told them, have you?' I don't know what to say. She doesn't sound like she's being nasty but I don't know what to think anymore. I decide to go with the truth.

'I was going to but, well, my Mum's not well; she's got Coronary Heart Disease.' There's a slice between us for a few beats. 'She had a mild heart attack a little while back. It didn't feel right to tell them, they were worried enough.' I almost feel the tension in the conversation ease.

'So there is something wrong,' she says, quietly and I think, almost with relief. 'Christ, Mike. I'm so sorry.' She says, and I believe her. I almost feel bad for dumping that on her but at the

Broken Wand

same time, I'm relieved to have told someone. 'What have they said? Is it, I mean, will there be treatment?'

'She had a load of tests while she was in hospital; they gave her a load of meds to take, feet up for a bit but they want her up and about now, consultant's orders.'

'That soon? How long has this been going on?' she asks, surprise in her voice.

'About two months or so.'

'Two months?'

'About that, maybe a bit more.'

'I'm surprised you didn't tell me,' she says, sounding confused and disappointed at the same time.

'Well, you know, the trial and all that. Didn't want to add to everything. Seems we're both a bit rubbish at keeping each other up to date.' There's not an awful lot you can say after that so we just listen to the space on the phone. Eventually, I clear my throat and say:

'Better make sure we line some gigs up seeing as I need the money. At least I'll have some time to put some bookings in. And now I have literally nothing to lose.' I smile weakly at the phone, as if she could see me trying to put a brave face on things.

'Let's just see what happens shall we Mike?' she says, in a soft voice, not convincingly. 'But you might want to start looking for another job. A part-time one maybe, you know, just in case.'

My stomach feels as if it has a block of ice in it. I know she's right but it kills that it's coming from her.

Broken Wand

48

That weekend, Mum, Dad and I are having a pub lunch for Mum's birthday. The pub's nothing fancy, the type with a menu that never changes because the bulk frozen food delivery never does either. There's a string of plastic hops trailing along the fake beam over the bar and the amount of dust on them has actually made them grey on the top. Must be a decade old that dust, as old as this traditional pub in fact. Mum's trying to enjoy it but she's just made her second trip to the toilet.

'So how's she really doing?' I ask Dad once she's out of earshot. He thinks for a moment.

'She's OK. Putting a brave face on it until we see the consultant again next week, then we'll have a lot more answers from the latest tests. They might adjust her meds.'

'Well that's good. Sounds like they're keeping a close eye.'

'Yes, they are,' he says, 'can't fault them,' he adds, emphatically.

'She seems a bit quiet though?'

'She is,' Dad replies, rubbing the temple by his right eye. 'The other day I found her staring at the bathroom window, you know, the frosted one with the leaf pattern in it. She said she'd never noticed how funny the trees through it when the wind blew; made them go all wiggly.' He looks at me as though I might be able to explain that, but I just smile. I see Mum coming back over dad's shoulder so quickly change the subject.

'So Dad, retirement soon. That's going to be nice.'

'Yes, Mum's been down to the travel agents, haven't you love,' he says, catching on to my tone. 'Thinking about splashing out and going on a cruise.'

'If you're splashing out you're doing it wrong,' I say, deadpan. Dad chuckles but Mum doesn't react.

'Seriously though,' I carry on, 'you couldn't leave the café on the Isle of Wight ferry Mum, you sure a cruise is a good idea?'

'It's just a thought,' she says, offhandedly, and I suspect it's just

Broken Wand

a thought of Dad's to keep her occupied. She doesn't appear to be too excited by the idea. Dad stares down at his pint, unable to keep the despondency out of his eyes. Mum's diagnosis has made him more neurotic than usual. Watching her now over the lunch table she's just staring into space. She's miles away. I'm not sure she really enjoyed her food and no one's saying anything about the amount left on her plate. Dad drains his pint and asks if I want another which I badly do. There's a waitress but he goes to the bar, for something to do I expect. Even from here I can hear the fake cheeriness in his voice as he orders, not wanting to be too much trouble as usual. I'm so desperate to cheer everyone up I decide, for some inexplicable reason, to tell Mum my news. Anything but this silence.

'OK Mum?' I say, just to get her attention. She looks at me vaguely as if she doesn't understand the question and then she gives a quick 'Yes, Michael, fine,' smiles and shrugs her shoulders a bit before taking a sip from her lime and soda. Her face starts to settle again and before she can drift away I say:

'I have a bit of news actually. Didn't want to bother you with it when – you know.'

'Oh?' and her face brightens a little. 'What's that then?'
So I tell her.

'I've packed in my job.' I plaster a smile over my face in an effort to hide my tension. I can't bring myself to mention it was a suggested redundancy just yet, at least make out it's my own decision. Her expression doesn't change but something shifts in her eyes, as if she's re-focussing.

'Why, Michael? Have you found a new one? Or have you been promoted?'

'Well no but we're doing loads of really great stuff with the shows, we have some TV lined up and -'

'Are they paying you?'

'Well, no not as yet but we're confident that –'

'Oh Michael.' At this point my Dad's back. He puts the drinks down and sits down heavily, making out it's a huge effort to carry a couple of pints back to the table.

Broken Wand

'Didn't spill a drop!' he says, like he's expecting applause. It takes him a second to cotton on to the atmosphere and he glances from me to Mum and back again.

'Thanks,' I say and pick up my pint. I inspect it closely but I can feel Mum's acid stare boring holes in me and I look up at her, trying to silently tell her to drop it, that I made a mistake, I shouldn't have brought it up.

'Michael's given up his job because he thinks he's going to be a star by Tuesday,' she says, half turning her head towards Dad but keeping her eyes, now rock hard, on me. I've never seen her this way before, out and out disappointment written all over her face. I put my pint down, making sure it is perfectly central on the beer mat.

'Is this true son?' Dad asks. He's keeping his voice calm, but only just. I could lie again, I could make something up but I can't bring myself to do it.

'Look,' I begin, 'I know you don't agree with this but it's my dream. I really want this and things are starting to happen. I've wanted this since, well, since Grandad gave me the bug. Can't you see how important it is? And this is my chance.'

'Grandad?' Dad looks confused.

'Yes, Grandad. He gave me the wand he made as a prisoner of war – I still have it.' They are looking genuinely baffled now and I'm starting to feel uncomfortable. 'And the cards, with the hidden map. He told me all the stories, the shows in the camp and all that.' I'm starting to get flustered now, they aren't looking any more enlightened. I keep talking, telling them what he'd told me, hoping they'd remember. How could they not know this?

'Son, that's not what those things were,' Dad said. Now it was my turn to look bemused.

'What are you talking about? He had them, they were his, he showed them to me, gave them to me.'

'I'm not saying he didn't have them or they weren't his but they weren't issued to him in some prisoner of war camp. He bought them.'

'Bought them?'

Broken Wand

'Yes, off a man in a camp in Aldershot,' Dad's voice was softer now. 'He never really went much further than that. Flat footed, never saw action overseas. I don't know what he told you but I think you may have the wrong end of the stick son. If you're doing this magic business because of some stories he told you..'

'But he told me all about it. He told me.' I hear the note of disbelief in my voice.

'Bit of a dreamer your Grandad apparently, according to your Grandma, bless her. Feet never really were on the ground before the war, never mind after, flat or otherwise. I think he might have been telling you bedtime stories, not real ones. You're just confused, that's all.'

I slump back in my burgundy velour chair, feeling like I've just had all the breath pumped out of me. I stare at Dad. I want to shout at him, at them. I want to tell them how wrong they are, how stupidly, utterly, completely fucking wrong they are because Grandad's eyes shining as he told me all his stories and my complete fascination with him and those stories were the constant things in my life that kept me going. The only thing I ever really believed in.

As I look at them their faces do that sad smile people do when they want to say "never mind dear". Well I do mind. Maybe he didn't do it deliberately, maybe he just let me believe it because he could see how much it meant to me. Either way, the stupid old bastard lied to me. And even though this is the thought in my head, the thought that is now lodged like a maggot in the heart of an apple, I know I still love him. And in a strange way I'm glad he lied. It doesn't change anything because it makes it even more my own dream. I look at my parents and I with awful clarity see that I don't have the same love for them. Our small family was more a collection of people that managed to function together, a daily list of things to be done – wake up, eat breakfast, make packed lunch, go to school work, come home, eat tea, telly, bed, repeat. Jesus. You're supposed to look back on stuff like that and feel all nostalgic but I just remember how dull it all was. And I know this because I'm still doing it. And this just makes what I say next easier.

Broken Wand

'Well at least he had a bloody imagination; at least he inspired something in me.' I can feel my face redden as I say it though I try not to spit the words out. The smiles slide from their faces.

'Michael,' my mother says. And it's all she needs to say. I see them for what they really are; scared, bewildered people just trying to keep their heads above water. Not so different. Dad blinks at me a couple of times and Mum's eyes are looking moist. 'We did our best,' she says, tucking her chin in, 'we did our best for you. It's different when you're a grandparent, I'm told.' This last comment stings. An invisible Mrs Peterson hovers over the table. My shoulders slump and I press my fingers to my eyes.

'Look, I'm sorry but this is what I want.'

'But what about the flat? How will you pay the rent?'

'I've got a bit saved up; it'll cover it for a while.' The truth is it would last about six months if I didn't eat. 'I'll be fine, really.' I add, trying to sound convincing. 'Haven't felt so good about something since, well, ever. Can't you just say go for it, just this once?' Even as I'm saying this my heart is going cold. I'm starting to lose the complete belief I had when I jacked my job in. I'm beginning to doubt myself.

'It's a big ask, Michael, I hope you know what you're doing.'

'Of course I know what I'm doing. Do you think I would do that without thinking it through?' Even as I'm saying it, I know it's not true but I plough on. 'Mum, please, you just concentrate on getting better. I'll be fine. Trust me.' I take the rare step of reaching out to pat her hand and she tries to smile. She really does.

49

'I'll get straight to the point; I've been approached to make a documentary about the lives of people with Achondroplasia through history to see what's changed in terms of attitudes towards them and how they've combated negative stereotyping and exploitation.' It was the first time Angelique and Linda had sat down together since their last meeting and the atmosphere was still a little tense. Angelique had called to ask if she could come over that weekend to discuss something that would be better discussed face to face and her mother had simply accepted, slotting her in to her diary like a dentist's appointment. They were at either side of the kitchen table, Angelique warming her hands up round her mug.

'A documentary?' Linda replied, with one eyebrow raised, 'with whom?'

'I'm working with a senior TV researcher from Must Have TV. She's kind of a colleague slash agent and she has some good contacts, which will save me a bit of time. She thinks it's a good idea.'

'Hm. And how do you know she isn't exploiting you herself, just to make her own name with something controversial?'

'I'd be disappointed if she wasn't. No point having someone with no spine or ambition working for you.'
Angelique countered.

'I see,' her mother sat up straight and folded her hands in her lap, 'and you're sure you want to do it?' she had asked, trying to keep her voice light.

'Well yes, why wouldn't I?'

'Oh, I don't know: pride, dignity, self-respect maybe?'
Angelique had told herself she would stay calm and reasonable while talking to her mother and reminded herself of this now. She paused, just one or two seconds, before carrying on.

'Why would this project take those things away from me? The last documentary we were in didn't.'

Broken Wand

'You only appeared for a short time, thank goodness. Debasing yourself by doing tricks all over the internet. How is exposing yourself on television going to help change negative stereotyping? You'll just draw attention to the negative aspects. That's all people want to see. I really don't think you should do it.' Neither of them spoke, Angelique tapping the table with one finger, her mother sitting still in her chair. 'Is this because of the magic? Is that how they found you?' Angelique rubbed her eyebrow as if on auto pilot, a dull ache above her eye. She hadn't told her Mum about the assault yet and luckily she hadn't seen anything of the news about it as it was mainly in the Oxfordshire papers. She knew it was only a matter of time before she found out but for now, it was better she didn't. 'Angelique, I don't think this is a direction you should be going in. You have a good job, prospects, why would you jeopardise that?'

'I'm not going to jeopardise that Mum. This documentary will be as well as that, not instead of it. I can fit it all in as things stand.'

'You'll have to make a decision at some point if you want to pursue it. Unless you get bored of it first.' Angelique fought the urge to roll her eyes.

'Don't you see how this could change people's perception of us?' she replied, indicating herself emphatically with both hands, 'I might inspire people to see things – us – differently. I could move the conversation on.'

'By opening yourself to ridicule on TV?'

'No Mum, by showing that I have talent, by building on my achievements. Wouldn't you be proud of that?'
Linda looked intently at her, considering this point before eventually saying:

'I can't stop you, if it's what you want to do. But don't say I didn't ask you not to if it all backfires.'

'I won't Mum. I can look after my own life; you can stop directing it now.' She made sure she looked her mother straight in the eye when she said this.

'Well if it means you leave this idiotic magic business behind then I suppose that would be a silver lining.' Linda said, imagining she conceded a point.

'I haven't decided what to do about that yet.'

'Well you must see it's a dead end? I mean, just how far do you think you can take it? No one will take you seriously as a public commentator if you carry on with that.' Angelique paused for a moment, as if considering this, before continuing.

'There was one more thing.' Angelique says cautiously, putting her mug on the table and turning it slowly so the handle is parallel to the edge of the table. 'I'd like to interview you as part of it.' Angelique saw the moment those words registered with her mother, her expression changed almost imperceptibly but changed nonetheless.

'Me?'

'Yes.'

They stared at each other.

'Why?'

'Because you're my mother and it would be good to get the experiences of a parent as part of this. It's a side to the story not many people will know, the parenting.'

'No, absolutely not. I can't believe you would even ask.' Linda's cheeks flushed and she struggled to control the anger that broke her voice.

'Well I'm going to talk about you anyway, give the facts, the genetic ones. So you can either put your point of view across or not. Up to you.'

'That – that's blackmail.'

'No it isn't, Mum.' Angelique pushed her exasperation as far down inside herself as possible. 'I just want to make sure you have an equal say. You don't have to.'

'And have you ridicule me as well as yourself? Is that what you really want?'

'I wouldn't be ridiculing myself or you. We'd be showing everyone how big the fight can be and how we overcame all that. It would be about how you coped and how you dealt with everything; how you carried us both.' Angelique could see Linda was stumped by that, wondering if Angelique meant it, her doubts reflected in the light chewing of her lip. Angelique felt the anger rising inside her, the resentment of the last time they met crystallising. Seeing her mother have doubts, no matter how small, gave her an opening she couldn't resist.

'Well I think you owe it to me as you denied me a father.' she said, matter of factly. Linda looked stunned. 'And are continuing to do so by not telling me who he is,' she added, to make sure the knife twisted a little further.

'Angelique,' Linda replied, her voice hoarse, 'I hardly think that's fair.'

'Fair? You want to talk about fair?' Her mother shuffled on her chair under the impact of this, smoothing down hair that didn't need it.

'Angelique, I know you're angry with me and I apologise if you still feel that I made the wrong decision. I still don't think I did but I'm not blind, I can see how you might feel that way.'

'You apologise?'

'Yes. I do.'

'Thank you.'

'You understand that I still maintain my decision was correct?'

'Yes. But it's nice you know you might understand my reaction to that.' They looked at each other across the table and for a moment Angelique felt a mutual understanding pass between them. Something was settled and while it would never be forgotten, it was progress.

'So, the interview..?'

'No, never.'

'OK. Just thought I'd ask.'

50

'She's not going to do it,' Angelique told Juliette with an air of finality. They were meeting over coffee to discuss the progress of the documentary which was gathering momentum; it had made it past the ideas phase and was now being turned in to a full pitch. 'Well that's a shame,' Juliette responded, 'you don't seem surprised though?'

'Nor would you be if you knew my mother.' Angelique half smiled at Juliette. 'I would have been more surprised if she'd agreed to be honest.'

'Maybe try again a bit later on when we've got something to show her. Sometimes people just aren't sure what they're being asked to do,' Juliette persisted, 'It would be great for the documentary to have her.'

'Well, we could try but to be honest, things are a bit ropey between us at the mo. Family stuff,' Angelique replied, trying to cut the line of conversation off and regretting she had been so candid with Juliette.

'Oh. Sorry to hear that,' Juliette sympathised. 'It can be a bit tricky with parents; I usually revert to a teenager when I have to spend time with mine. Just all comes flooding back. Is she usually supportive?'

'Depends what it is. Always supportive in a practical sense, yes.' Angelique slipped back in to a more work-like voice and saw in Juliette's eyes that she was finally taking the hint.

'OK,' Juliette conceded. 'Well, there are ways round that. We can use photos of you and your family to illustrate the science bit, make it a bit more interesting. The medical, genetic side of it would be better coming from someone in a white coat anyway and we could easily find someone to talk about that. There are bound to be specialists attached to charities who would be only too happy to get involved and the exposure would do them good. We could probably get some parents that way as well.'

'I could ask for some photos I suppose. We just weren't that sort of family.'

'I'm starting to see that. I think we should have a complete mix of interviews anyway; a contemporary family with a young Little Person, a Little Person who's a lot older with their own family, a mixed size family - you know, some really diverse opinions. Maybe go overseas but that's a budget decision. But obviously, the thrust needs to be looking back at history and finding some really good examples, male and female of how people managed as well as how they manage today. It would be interesting to see if our interviewees know about any of them, if they're interested and what they think of them and how they were treated.' She was off on her own train of thought. 'There was a group of Little People wrestlers from America who had their tour cancelled because of a local protest about it here in England. They were quite happy to come and do their stuff but everyone else was angry on their behalf and that was that. I doubt it's the only example we can dig up.'

'Do we have to be provocative?' Angelique asked, interrupting Juliette.

'How do you mean?' Juliette seemed genuinely bemused by the question.

'Well, is there anything to be gained by deliberately poking the wasps nest? I thought the main focus was going to be on how people, Little People, have coped and gone on to do incredible things?'

'And it still is. Think of it as scene setting. We have to ask the questions first. Remember your essays at school? Show you've understood the question, explain your arguments, summarise. It's a bit like that. People have to understand why this needs to be talked about in order to get them to watch it.'

'So, are we going to mention my assault case?' Angelique asked, cautiously.

'I expect so. We can use footage of you on the courthouse steps. Powerful stuff. Sets you up as the perfect person to be presenting this.' Juliette's enthusiasm began to grow as she warmed to her theme, ideas developing even as she spoke them out loud. 'You know, this could be the start of something big for you; a new career in media. Maybe write for news sites, magazines, create podcasts, become a thought-leading commentator. Change minds. Isn't that exciting?' Angelique didn't feel as excited as she felt Juliette thought she should. It didn't sound like a solid career choice but, she reasoned, it could lead to new, different things. A parallel career. Easy to say but in reality, probably a nightmare juggling act.

'Don't look so sceptical,' Juliette said, leaning over and speaking conspiratorially. 'Despite what you may see all-around you, a media career doesn't have to mean a stint in the jungle or a tell-all about your love life,' she grinned and sat back, draining her coffee.

'No, I know that,' replied Angelique, relaxing a little, 'but I also know what it can be like out there, when you are noticed. It's not always pleasant.'

'No, I can only guess at that,' said Juliette, raising her hands in the air as if conceding the point, 'but in a way, isn't it even more important that we make this work?' Angelique thought for a moment.

'You're right, it is important. But let's just take this step by step OK? I need to be sure about each piece before we move on it. I know it's exciting - and I am excited - but I'm also aware I want to walk before I run.'

'We're working on this together, Angelique,' Juliette said earnestly now, 'if there's anything you're not comfortable with, or that I'm not, we sort it out.'

'And if we can't?'

'Then we make a decision. There's no contract here yet, but we both have reputations on the line here so we need to know this is watertight before it reaches that point.' Juliette looked at her watch and, startled by the late time, announced: 'Got to run; meeting at 3 back at the office.' She gathered herself together and left, waving goodbye to the waiters and flicking her hair over her shoulder as she went.

51

I've been pretty tense since Joanna had her little word a couple of weeks ago; a constant nagging feeling that I'm waiting for something bad to happen, that I'm going to get found out, on edge and snappy. I haven't slept well, waking up at four in the morning and churning things over then sleeping in half the morning, trying to avoid going out, food losing its appeal altogether.

I've forced myself to turn up for this Friday night gig but it's the last one I want to do. I keep trying to figure out how to turn this round but I'm not sure I can. I can't help thinking that this has all been so fast and I thought I wanted it but now, I'm not so sure. It all feels so fragile, so temporary. Maybe it's a whirlwind because of how slow my life has been up till now but I don't think so. I feel disembodied, like I'm in someone else's shoes, that I was never meant to reach this far in the first place. Let's face it, I wouldn't have if Angelique hadn't come along. She's been everything these last few months and now she's moving on. Just like Joanna said.

Not that Angelique seems to have noticed how I'm feeling. She's been busy with work and her new documentary. She only arrived here today in time to get the props ready so there wasn't a lot of time for chat after the initial hello's. I haven't seen too much of her - we've only had two rehearsals for this gig and I don't feel too ready - and I've missed her. I'm not feeling inspired and frankly I'm a bit sick of it all. There are one or two more gigs lined up but money is running out. I'm going to have to find a job, anything, so I have some money coming in and now I have doubts as well as debts. What if they were right all along - what if this is a total fantasy? Joanna is on a loop in my head: 'hope you've got a plan B Mike', pulsing through my blood. Bitch. I can't shut her up; it just goes on. Christ, if I could just sleep.

We're walking out on to the small stage and the spotlights are too bright; I can feel myself wince against them, feel them showing me up, making me the focus of everyone's attention, attention I don't want. I try to slip in to character, put my stage face on and

Broken Wand

smile, but I find I just can't. I can barely put one foot in front of the other; I haven't the energy to do this, to fight this and my stomach is in knots. I try to keep breathing. She's next to me, full beam smile on, engaging. And then I hear it; a wolf whistle. It's the first time that's happened. But instead of ignoring it she turns towards it, smiling broadly at whoever it was in the dimness beyond the white lights.

And then it hits me, the cold hard truth. She really doesn't care about me at all. All this time I've fallen for the sleight of hand, been carried along by the easy deception. Oh my God, what a fucking mug I've been. All this while, thinking it was the two of us, thinking this was my chance. Just then the lights change and start to strobe so we look like we're in an old black and white movie and I'm helping Angelique into a small coffin, up some small steps, and closing the lid. I'm on auto pilot, There's a weird buzzing in my ears, in my head and a pain behind my eyes from the flashing lights. I'm squinting even more and I can feel the heat of the lights making me sweat. I fumble the clips on the coffin and Angelique glances up at me, a slight question in her eyes. I don't react. Why should I? I pick up the chainsaw. And then the chattering in my head begins; other people's voices – Joanna, Mum, Dad, that stuck up bitch in HR, Joanna again, Joanna again, Joanna again and I can't shut them up, it's like a stuck record in my head, like a tape going round and round – they were right, they were all right and I was so very stupidly, blindly wrong. The dizziness creeps deeper into my head and all I can see is the floor in front of me. I feel like I'm being emptied, like I'm leaving myself to spill on the floor – the heat is suffocating, I'm sweating, I can't breathe, I'm trying to loosen my collar but I can't and instead I see Angelique. She's looking at me from the coffin, not sure what's going on. I can see her mouth moving as I take the chainsaw out from under the coffin where it's been hidden by a tablecloth and start it up but I can't hear her, I hear Joanna telling me the truth, telling me how stupid I've been; the fizzing in my head is like interference, never mind the sound of the chainsaw as it kicks in to life. Even my own pulse is deafening. I swing the chainsaw up over my head but it's heavy and it takes my arms too far back and I'm going to lose my balance so I bring it back over my head almost at arm's length in front of me, about two feet from Angelique. I'm leaning too far forwards and before I can stop it I fall forwards and slam the chainsaw in to the stage, sending small chips of it in all directions. I seem to see Angelique in slow motion, screwing up her eyes and turning her head away, blonde hair flying. The impact of the chainsaw hitting the stage has shocked me out of whatever state I was in and I stare at my hand as I let go of it, the dead man's switch cutting the engine out as I do. I feel my face fall and my energy, what there was of it, deserts me – my legs buckle and I stagger backwards, landing on my arse with a thud that reverberates through my body. I can't focus and I can't tell how long I've been there. I'm sitting on the stage in a mess of sweat and tears and I don't know why. I blink and look around me; Angelique's head turns towards me, terror in her eyes and I reach out to her but at that moment somebody simultaneously kicks the chainsaw away and pins my arms to my sides from behind. I hear a grunt, possibly mine, and see sparks as my arms are yanked behind me. They don't need to do that, my arms are like jelly, probably from the effort of swinging that chainsaw around and I can feel tears and sweat running down my face.

    My breath is coming in hiccups but at least my eyes are starting to focus again. Someone has taken the chainsaw and someone else is telling the audience to leave by the nearest exit, they're making their way out, ripples of low conversation reach me but I can't make any of it out. The house lights go on and the stage lights are switched off, weirdly cooling after their intense glare. I sit there, limp, my head hanging now in extreme tiredness, waiting to see what happens next. Angelique has managed to undo the catches and open the top of the coffin. I can see out of the corner of my eye she's being helped out and I'm conscious that someone behind me is talking to me, asking if I'm alright but I can't see them; my head is as heavy as a melon and I can't lift it. Angelique wants to know if I'm OK, she's trying to come over to me, I can hear her voice through the fizzing in my head. My ears are whooshing and I can feel my heart is still thudding. Am I dying, I wonder, is my heart exploding? I shake my head slowly, closing my eyes again. I try to say the word 'go' but all that seems to come out is a moan. I try again, and again. Then someone else is there and they're talking gently, a hand on my shoulder.

'I'm a trained first aider, Mike.' He knows my name. This confuses me until I remember we're the act. Of course he knows my name. 'Can you look at me? Just want to check your eyes.' I raise my head slowly and look at his face. He smiles, sympathetically, and looks from eye to eye. He nods at someone outside of my vision and my arms are let go. They slump to my sides and I slowly put what weight I can on them while I sit on the floor. The bloke gently picks up one of my hands and takes my pulse. I watch his face, he's looking away while he counts. 'OK, that's a bit fast but you've had a shock. Did you hurt yourself when you fell over?' I shake my head and wipe my face. 'I have to ask, have you had anything to drink this evening Mike? Or anything stronger?' he thinks I'm pissed, or high. Or both.

'No, no..' I tail off. I talk slowly, deliberately. 'I'm fine, really. I just ... came over a bit funny. I just want to go now. Go home.' I can hear how lame I sound.

'Why don't you just sit there for a minute, gather yourself together a bit. Can I fetch you some water?'

'Yes, please.' They bring a mug and I sip at the water. It does help. My breathing has slowed and the fizzing has almost gone. The manager is there now as well.

'Mike, would you like us to call an ambulance?' she asks, 'Get you checked over?' The thought of spending hours in an ambulance or worse still, A&E gives me the sobering kick I need.

'No, sorry, I'm fine. I just want to go home.' After some 'are you sure' and 'shall we call a cab' discussion I go backstage with the medic, who just wants to keep an eye on me, and the manager who probably just wants shot of me. Angelique isn't there. Her clothes and stuff are gone too.

'Has Angelique left?' I ask the Manager.

'Ah, yes, she has. She thought it was best. She took the, err,

Broken Wand

prop with her too.' I look at her for a few seconds until it hits me she means the chainsaw.

'Yes, of course. Good idea. Did she say anything?'

'No, sorry.'

I nod a few times and chew my lip.

'OK.' I say, turning to pick my bag and the props suitcase up before heading for the exit. Just before I leave I turn and say 'Sorry about the show. I hope the stage is OK.'

'Don't worry,' she replies, 'we're insured. Hope you feel better soon.' She's closing the door as she raises a hand in farewell. I leave, glad to be out in to the chilly dark night and glad that it's raining. It feels real on my face, mixing with the tears.

Broken Wand

52

It's been two weeks since 'the incident' and I haven't seen Angelique. I tried to call but she didn't answer and I didn't leave a message. She didn't call back though she must have known it was me. I don't think I blame her.
I probably just gave her and her agent all the reasons in the world to leave me behind.
I'm sitting in my flat staring at the wall opposite where the bookcase used to be. It's in my parents garage now where I'll be joining it tomorrow. Not in their garage, obviously, but in their house. I can't afford to keep the flat on now, not without a job. I'd already given a month's notice before the gig. I'm half-heartedly eating a curry, it's more like going through the motions than actually eating. Maybe it's the time of year, autumn always makes me feel like hibernating anyway; it's getting colder but I certainly don't feel cosy. My plates and cups and all the rest are packed so I'm eating straight from the foil dishes. At least I remembered to keep a spoon. It's a bit messy but I don't care. I couldn't really have a more messed up life so what the fuck, basically.
There're just a few bags in the hallway, that's the last of my stuff so I'm pretty much done. The suitcase is there, the one with the props in. I thought I'd get rid of it, give it to a charity shop but I still can't do it. Not even now I know it was all for nothing. It just feels like too much a part of me, too many things associated with it and I can't let that all go, not just yet.
I went to the doctors for a check-up; I've never felt like I did on that stage before and I don't want to again. It frightened me, the loss of control. Feeling like John Hurt in Alien – something about to burst out of me and nothing I can do about it. The doctor listened to my heart, he took my blood pressure. He asked a lot of questions about what's been going on and when I stopped talking he said 'well it sounds like you've had quite a bit on your plate lately.' No shit, was what I was thinking. He put it down to a panic attack. Stress. "The body's physical response to an overstretched

mind" was how he put it. He printed off a leaflet about it. He said there were places I could go to for help and phone numbers on the leaflet if I felt bad but as it was the first time, I don't qualify for any more help from the doctors yet, not even medicines. Lifestyle changes are what I need, according to the leaflet. Dietary changes. More exercise, less stress.

I'm moving back in with my parents so at least the food will be better but the stress is unlikely to subside. I need to start looking for a job, see what's around. I might go down to the job centre tomorrow, anything will do. I don't care if it's bloody shelf stacking as long as it pays. The more mind numbing the better I think. I just want to forget everything for a while, stop feeling like this, maybe I could start now.

I wander about the flat looking for my jacket and wallet and decide to go to the off license. I'm going to drink myself to oblivion, to another way of feeling, out of this tiny fucking flat and in to a new existence, one where I just float about like the blokes in the park. They haven't got a clue what day it is, let alone what they're really feeling. My hand is on the front door handle; I grip it and I freeze. I can't turn the handle and it's like there's a big bloody fight going on inside me – one side is all for getting hammered, the other side scared of what might happen if I do. I'm chewing my lip and staring at the handle. I screw my eyes up and I let go like it's on fire. I throw my jacket on the floor. I know what I really need to do. I know what I really need. Apart from the doctor I haven't spoken about this to anyone. Mum and Dad don't need to know, they just need to know they were right. They've managed not to be smug about it. But they've made it clear it's not for ever. Mum's been reading about forty year olds moving home and taking over – she's not having that.

I go to bed but I don't sleep. I lie staring at the ceiling. There's nothing in my head, no thoughts, no feelings, just numbness. An empty space where stuff used to be. Daily stuff, minute by minute stuff, things, lists, ideas, memories. But tonight I can't be any of that. I can't even cry.

Broken Wand

53

I must have fallen asleep at some point because I wake up the next morning and I feel strange, numb, calm maybe. I didn't dream. I go through the motions of splashing water on my face and brushing my teeth then shove the last few bits into a plastic bag. I call for a taxi and carry the boxes downstairs in two goes. I take one last look round the place. It feels different with nothing in it, almost like it never really was mine anyway, like I was just borrowing it off a mate. It's not like I had kids here or any of that stuff, nothing to really tie me to it.

I take a deep sort of shrug-breath and head for the door, picking the suitcase up as I go past it. I almost trot down the lino covered stairs and out the front of the block where the breeze reaches inside my open jacket and makes me shiver. I look around, squinting against the low morning sun and see that the few trees in the street have started to turn and have even lost a few leaves already. The taxi swings round the corner and pulls up.

'This stuff for the boot then?' asks the driver through the window.

'Yes, please mate,' I say and he pops the boot, grabbing one of the boxes in a business-like way and pushing it in as far as it will go. He comes back for another one. I know I should help him but I'm just standing there, holding the suitcase. Suddenly I know what I need to do. I ask him to hang on while I sort something out.

I go round the side of the building to the car park and across it to the bins. The dumpsters sit big and squat waiting to swallow whatever rubbish comes their way, not proud. I put the suitcase down and open it, taking out the stick my Grandad used as a wand. I grab it at both ends and slide my thumbs to the middle, pressing. For a split second I hesitate, eyes prickling and threatening to spill over but before that can happen I grit my teeth and press hard. It gives easily, brittle with age and the clean snap is satisfying. I breathe out in a rush, unaware until then I'd been holding it in, lungs like balloons, waiting to be struck down, but nothing

Broken Wand

happens. Just a bloke holding a broken stick in his hands. I wait for something to happen, wait to be struck down by some unknown force as I hold the pieces in my hands like broken bones. But nothing comes. I quickly shut the case and don't bother doing it up, standing quickly to open the lid of one of the bins before swinging the suitcase up and into it. It opens a bit and gets stuck so I shove it in until it lands on the bottom with a loud clang. One final glance at the bits of broken wand in my hand and in they go too, soundlessly landing on the suitcase. I drop the lid so it bangs, staring at it for a few seconds but before I can think too much the taxi horn sounds. I take a deep breath and turn away.

54

At 3am the kitchen is peaceful. Just me and a mug of tea. I don't put the light on as it's nice just to look out the window, elbows on the table, chin resting on my hands. The sky isn't quite pitch black, too much street lighting for that but it still shows a few stars. It's cold but I don't really mind it. I've been asleep but my thoughts woke me and going over things for hours on end seems to be par for the course at the moment. Better to just get up. Something catches my eye; a figure slowly appears in the window, getting bigger, robes wafting around it and I'm momentarily confused until it solidifies and becomes Mum, walking into the kitchen from the lounge behind me.

'Thought I heard the kettle,' she says.

'You made me jump for a minute there, creeping about. Can't sleep?'

'No. And the kettle on in the middle of the night is either a thirsty burglar or you. Thought I'd investigate.'

'Sorry, didn't think.'

She smiles at me and sits down, pulling her dressing gown around her against the chill of night. She sits looking at me for a little while until it feels just about uncomfortable.

'How are you doing?' she asks, 'I mean, really.' I can see from her eyes that she really does want to know, that she's not just asking in a bumped in to a friend in the street kind of way.

'Oh, you know,' I start, poking at the tea bag still in my mug with a teaspoon, 'good days, bad days.' She doesn't reply, giving me the space to carry on; waiting for me to do so. Maybe it's the time of night or maybe it's the feeling that life has stripped me down to just the most basic parts that makes me feel like there's no point pretending any more. 'Disappointed, to be staying here if I'm honest,' I continue. 'No offence, obviously. And just a bit of a failure.'

'You're not a failure Michael, you've had a setback, that's all,' she says kindly. After a pause she asks: 'Do you think you want your old job back?'

'I don't think so and I'm pretty sure they wouldn't have me.'

'Their loss.' Something about the way she makes eye contact when she says this encourages me to keep talking.

'I have tried to make you proud you know, you and Dad. I know I'm not as successful as some,' I add, indicating with my head the direction of the Peterson's house, 'but I have worked hard and tried to make something happen.' She looks at me again and I can see this has reached her in some way; her face is softening a bit. She takes one of my hands in both of hers.

'You,' she begins, 'have made me proud, Michael.'

'But I thought - I mean, you always said..' I have to stop speaking at that point or my childish gratitude will overwhelm me.

'I know what I said Michael, but since this heart attack I've had time to think and time to open my eyes about a few things.' The emotion in her voice is surprising, she's not normally one for bold statements. 'I'm glad you didn't end up at the car plant like your Dad, stuck for forty years.' She doesn't look at me when she says this and it stands out all the more in the night time silence that surrounds us. 'Don't misunderstand me,' she adds, I'm not complaining, he was by no means the only one to go straight in to the plant and we've had a good, steady life. It was just what you did back then round here. But you - you've had chances he didn't. It's not your fault Jenny isn't here anymore but it is time to start again, make the most of things.'

'I thought I was on track Mum, I really did. But maybe I was just treading water.'

'She means a lot to you, doesn't she.'

'Jenny?' I ask, confused.

'Angelique.'

'Yes, she's unique. It's not a relationship in that way but I don't think I've ever felt like I had a real friend before, not really. I certainly never did at school, not someone who gets me like she does.'

'Good friends like that are hard to come by,' she nods slowly. 'I know that little madam over the road didn't help matters at school.

I saw the way she was with you, with everyone. Always thought she was a cut above.'

'You mean Amanda?'

'Yes I do. Always fancied herself, that one.'

'I thought you were always a bit envious of them,' I suggest. Mum couldn't have looked more surprised.

'God no. Let me tell you about them,' She says, pulling her robe more tightly around herself. 'I used to date Ian, long before Kath moved in to the area. Within weeks she's flirting with everyone, seeing who she could snare. Turns out he was easily swayed and that was that. Off he went with her.'

'Ian,' I repeat back to her, 'I had no idea.' She just gives me a wry smile.

'Ian heard your Dad and I were getting married and he came to see me, saying he'd made a mistake, that she wasn't really the one for him but I sent him packing. When they moved in over the road it was a bit awkward but I don't think she's ever forgotten that.'

'She knew?'

'Yes, he tried to finish with her but, well, Amanda.' I let this sink in for a minute. No wonder she was always shoving Amanda in Mum's face.

'Does Dad know?'

'He knew we were going out before but not that Ian tried to win me back and I'd like it to stay that way.' She says, tapping the table to make her point.

'Of course.' We sit in silence and it feels comfortable, like the air between us is linking us together. She fiddles with the belt on her robe, winding it round her fingers, lost in thought for a moment. I look at her for a bit, thinking about all of this ancient history. Thinking about how I could have been a Peterson. 'Why are you telling me this now?' I ask.

'Because,' she begins, 'life, as you know with Jenny, can be short and also because I can't tell your Dad and I've kept it to myself all these years. It's a relief to be honest. But what I really want to know is, have you been in touch with Angelique?'

'No. I'm not sure she'd want me to after what happened.'

Broken Wand

'You don't know that. If she's as clever as you say, she'll know it wasn't something you did intentionally. Call her, before it's too late to. If she really is that good a friend, she'll come round.' She smiles and pats my hand again before gathering herself together, saying good night and padding back through the lounge as silently as she came.

Broken Wand

55

Sitting on a bench in the park a couple of days later I think about my chat with Mum. I'm certain now that going back to my old job won't happen. Because going back is not an option. I'm glad that all ended the way it did, it did me a favour. I'm out of all that shit now, I'm free of it, I can start to live the way I want to now, even if it is from scratch. I feel lighter, like my shoulders can ease up a bit and I seem to be seeing some of the woods, not just the trees. There's just one last thing I need to do.

I open my phone and there's Angelique's name at the top of my list of contacts. I scan round the park quickly, hoping something will distract me; the trees are shedding leaves quickly now and squirrels are running around with stuff in their mouths to stash for later. I look back down at my phone and I know I can't put this off any longer.

What I want to say is that I miss her a lot. So much that I think about her every day. I thought I'd forget, that I'd be ashamed and want to put her as far behind me as possible as well but I can't. She's the person I want to pick up the phone to, to talk things over with, to make sure she's alright, to make sure we're alright. I miss her. I miss seeing her and it's all my fault and it's shit. But she hasn't been in touch in over two weeks and I need to accept that she's gone.

Slowly I type out a message: 'I'm sorry. I hope you will forgive me. Good luck with everything, you deserve it.' I hover over the X button but I don't add one. I stare at it for a while and after what seems like an age I hit send on impulse, like when you have to just jump off the top diving board without thinking or you never would. I shove the phone in my pocket and slump against the back of the bench. A breeze has picked up and the cold air makes my eyes watery.

I sit there for a minute longer, letting it sink in. That's it, that's the last contact. It's starting to feel chilly sitting here now, the sun is on its way down. The park is emptying apart from a couple of after work dog walkers, huddled in coats and using those long plastic ball throwers so they don't have to get their hands covered in slobber. I walk along the path towards the café where the exit is and they're closing up too, shutters are going on, chairs being stacked inside. I shrug my jacket closer round me and as I do so I feel a buzz in my pocket. Probably Mum, telling me tea's ready. The joys of being back at home. Jesus.

    I take my phone out and read: "I'm sorry too. Can we meet? Understand if not but would like to see you. A." I stop in my tracks and read it again to be sure of what I'm seeing. I get a flush of heat up my neck and run my hand over my face, covering my mouth. A rush of adrenalin creates a smile on my face. "Christ" is all I can mutter.

    I'm still staring at the phone when a ball comes flying past with a spaniel in excited pursuit. It catches the ball off a bounce and does a perfect mid-air U-turn, loping back towards its master with a very smug look on its face, ready to do it all again. I smile broadly at it as it runs past me and makes eye contact, showing off. I don't know what to do – should I call her or text? Where should we meet? I've already agreed in my head to see her; it's what I want, she's what I want. Then a warning voice creeps in, telling me to play it cool, not to get over-excited, to wait and see what she wants first before I do anything. I tell it to fuck off. "Of course. Rainham Marshes? Nice café. Tomorrow at 11?" Tomorrow is Saturday so I know she'll be free. It seems like an age until she replies. I think she isn't going to and then. 'OK. See you there. X' and there it is, the X.

Broken Wand

56

I wake up so bloody early that it's still dark. For the briefest of moments I think and feel nothing and it's all calm; then the day's plans come flooding in and I am truly awake. I make a cup of tea in my boxers and t-shirt, hoping I won't disturb Mum. I start feeling nervous, all the "what ifs" piling in. What if she has second thoughts, what if she doesn't come, what if she just wants to have a go at me and worst of all, what if Joanna turns up instead? My worst nightmare.

Joanna had managed to burrow into my head in a way no other bully ever has. She was unexpected and now I expect her everywhere. I shake my head at this and tell myself not to be such an idiot. It was Angelique's phone, her text. She'd said she was sorry but I have to admit I'm not entirely sure what for. It was me that over-reacted. Me that had the panic attack. Me that screwed it all up. I catch myself in this thought and stand up to look out of the kitchen window.

It's gradually becoming morning; birds begin visiting the bird table half way down the lawn. The leaflet the doctor gave me said to try and avoid over thinking, to distract myself, stop beating myself up basically. Staring at the bird table isn't cutting it though so I leave my tea and go and stand under the shower, the warmth and feel of it easing me a bit. I feel a bit better afterwards and decide to iron a shirt, all the time wondering if it's overkill. I wear it anyway, under a jumper.

By ten to eleven I'm sitting on a bench near the Rainham Marshes visitor centre with my hands on my knees, shoulders hunched forward, staring out at the water and mud wondering if she will show. It's quite stark here but it's peaceful; there's room to breathe the sharp autumn air with its own peculiar salty mud smell but I'm so uptight I can barely think let alone remember to breathe. I check my watch again. Six minutes. I turn my attention to the marshes and think back to when I was a kid; you could hear the military doing shooting practise down here. That's what it was for years, before it became a nature reserve; a place to practise killing people. Now it's a bird sanctuary. Talk about a turnaround. It has a fancy visitor centre now and bird hides and viewing platforms. It sits on the edge of the Thames, forever busy with industry and huge ships dragging their loads through the murky water. Look one way and in the distance there's Canary Wharf, skyscrapers standing guard over the river, like a sort of modern day city gate; look the other way and the Dartford Bridge looms into the sky.

They're not the prettiest surroundings but I don't think nature's that fussy and at least it's not having the crap bombed out of it now. Some of the bigger kids at school used to dare each other to break in through the fences and dig about for old World War 2 ammo. I don't think they ever found any. Every now and then you hear about some old shells that pop up out of the mud but none of it's ever live. They haven't had to detonate anything for decades.

I'm still reminiscing when a voice at the end of the bench says:

'Do you come here often?' I turn, surprised, to face her and she's smiling. The breeze blows her hair across her face and she picks a strand of it out of her mouth. In my confusion I half stand, realise that's a stupid idea and sit down again, blushing as I do. 'Hi,' I manage and indicate the bench for her to sit down. I glance at my watch and say 'You're, er, on time.' I thought she might have been early but I'd obviously been daydreaming for longer than I thought.

'Yes, I am,' she smiles and I smile back, feeling a bit foolish. She sits next to me on the bench and settles herself. 'I haven't been here before,' she says and I tell her it hasn't been open that long, less than ten years. I start to prattle on about how it used to be a firing range for the military and the noise it used to make and the second world war and when I catch her watching me; I hold her gaze for a second or two and her eyes say more than I have in the last few minutes. I quiet down. We sit in silence for a while, just looking out at the estuary. The sun comes out in patches on the water as the clouds dodge in front of it. It looks breezy out there, on the water. It's covered in sheets of tiny ripples and swirls and

Broken Wand

there are tiny plopping noises as it shifts about in the shallower mud.

'How are you doing Mike?' she eventually asks and it's gentle, undemanding. I don't look at her but carry on staring at the water, my eyes screwed up against the glare. How am I doing?

'Yeah, OK. Considering.' And I hope that covers it but she asks: 'Considering what?' I take a deep breath.

'Well the fact that I had a massive panic attack on the stage and terrified you for one.'

'Is that what it was, a panic attack?' She doesn't dispute that I terrified her.

'Yes, that's what the doctor reckons. The first aid bloke at the club suggested I go, you know, get checked over. Seems I'm fine, bit overweight but you don't need to be a doctor to see that.'

'What was it about? The panic attack? You seemed fine before, bit quiet maybe but fine.'

'Oh, you know, that I don't have a job, I thought I might have to move back in with my parents, and now I am and I need a plan.'

'You'll find another job Mike, this isn't forever.'

'It felt like it then. Especially after what Joanna said.'

'Joanna?' She looks at me, curious now, not just caring. 'I know she told you about the documentary but we discussed that.'

'It wasn't just that. Look, I don't want to cause more problems.'

'There'll be a bigger problem if you don't tell me Mike.'

'She came to see me, that's all. She said some stuff, said she wanted to help me.' I stop talking, aware that I'm trying to gloss over it. She encourages me with a light touch on my arm and when I look at her I know I just want it all out in the open, I want her to know what a cow Joanna is but I want Angelique to deny what she told me as well. I tell her everything about the meeting in the pub. She's quiet for a while, looking straight ahead. I can't tell from her face what she's thinking. I don't know if quiet is a good sign or not; I've never seen her lose her temper, not properly. I stare out over the estuary; some birds take off noisily in a flock, arcing round in perfect unison on their way up river. I'm glad of something else to look at.

Broken Wand

'And you believed her?' Angelique asks. I shrug, uneasily, still not able to look at her. I try to justify my shrug.

'Well, she's...'

'Persuasive?'

'Intimidating. She's known you a long time Angelique. I didn't want to believe her, it confused me. And with everything else, Mum, my job, losing the flat, thinking I was losing you..'

'Why didn't you talk to me about it before; what she said?'

'I didn't know what to think; I certainly wasn't thinking straight. And then you rang about that documentary and I thought well, if that's true, then the other stuff must be. Like I said, I just lost it.' I turn to her. She just looks at me and I'm not sure what she's thinking. She says:

'Do you trust me?'

'Yes. Yes, I do. I don't think I ever didn't. I mean, even when I was, you know.'

'Waving a chainsaw around near my head? Yeah, I remember that.' She has an expression of mock intensity, a smile playing around her mouth. I smile back.

'Jesus, yeah, I really am sorry about that.'

'I know. But I think we'll steer away from heavy machinery from now on.' Her smile is like a magnet for the tension in me and I feel a little of the tightness seep from my shoulders. 'It makes sense what you say though. About Joanna. I should have known.' She looks at me intently. 'I called her, after it happened. She said she told you about the documentary but not the other stuff. I think I sort of guessed though, deep down; you never really see the whole iceberg with Joanna until it's too late. So when you texted me, I knew I had to see you. I felt responsible.'

'Joanna. She really doesn't give up, does she.'

'Hm,' she murmurs, 'I do believe I may have outgrown Joanna.' I can't quite believe I'm hearing this, but I'm glad I am. It makes me feel like the bond between us is reforming, like a frayed piece of rope re-twisting.

'You'll come through this Mike, I know you will,' she says, and the seriousness in her eyes floors me. 'I'd like to help you, if you'll let

Broken Wand

me. If I can.' Her reassurance means more to me than anything but I feel like I'd be a dead weight for her, that I'd just be a sympathy case until she doesn't have time for me anymore.

'You've got better things to be doing now, Angelique, an exciting career that's taking off; I'll just hold you back. I think maybe you should concentrate on that.'

'That's very sweet and self-sacrificing of you Mike,' she says, 'but don't talk such bollocks.' Hearing her swear always gets my attention, she does it so rarely. 'Maybe you should ask me what I want. What I've been doing the last couple of weeks and what I think about all this.'

'OK,' I say, jolted out of my self-pity. I can't help but smile as I ask: 'What have you been doing the last couple of weeks, Angelique?'

'Thinking about you mainly. Wondering how you are but giving you space that I didn't want to give you and not knowing if any of it is even my business but wanting it to be.' It all comes out in a rush. 'You know, seeing someone you care about melting down and wondering if there's anything you can do about it is exhausting,' she continues, 'you've exhausted me.' Here it comes, I think, this will be the push, the let-down. I'm staring out at the water again because I can't look at her and hear those words, it would be overload. She carries on. 'I can't think of anyone else I'd still be around for Mike.' I look at her, wondering if I've heard right. 'I'll admit I wanted to do something to prove to my Mum that there's more to life than proving how smart I am. I wanted to throw it in her face, especially after she told me about my Dad and her boyfriend. Joanna was right about that much I suppose. But it became clearer as we went on, you and I, that I was enjoying it, I liked to perform, to be centre stage. It wasn't until the assault I realised why; what I was enjoying was having a real, proper friend to share it with.' She stops talking and now it's her turn to look at the floor and I can see she's struggling. 'This might sound weird' she says, 'but I feel with you in my life there's more of me, like there's an overlap, some kind of shared space between us that makes me feel more me. Does that make sense?' She looks at me and I see a kind of wariness, as if she's afraid she's said more than she should.

'You mean like a sofa instead of two armchairs?' I say and at first she looks confused then she bursts out laughing and her face transforms.

'Yes,' she says through her laughter, 'exactly like that.' On impulse I reach over and take her hand. I can't say anything so she fills the gap. 'Mike, you were the first person I wanted to call after the assault. You're the reason I wanted to carry on with the magic. I like being with you, I like your company and for the life of me I can't think why. Which means it must be real, right?' I feel another rush of warmth go through me and I hope she feels it go through my hand in to hers because I want it to. I need it to.

'I thought I'd lost you,' is all I can muster in reply.

'Don't be daft. Just because other things came along didn't mean I was moving on from you. You're my friend, Mike. That means more to me than anything. I'd like to spend more time with you, not less.'

I know she means this but I also know I need to tell her the truth about how I'm feeling. That I really do want to give up magic. That I see now you can't recreate the past, you can't go back and resurrect it. That my reasons for doing it in the first place are dead and gone and that that's OK. I'm ready to move on and begin my life, not cling on to something I should have let go of a long time ago.

'I don't want to do it anymore Angelique. I don't want to do the magic anymore.'

'I know. I understand. And to be honest, nor do I.'

'You don't?'

'Nope. I'm looking forward to new things, grown up things, being a voice for other people like me so that we can try and make some changes.'

'Are you going to leave your job?'

'No, not yet. I think we both know that wouldn't be wise. But I'm thinking about putting my freelance plans in to action, consulting, so I can manage my time better. Charge twice as much for half the time.' She smiles.

'You're lucky.'

'How d'you mean?'

'I've got nothing Angelique, nothing at all. I messed everything up. I feel like I'm stuck.'

'No, you're not. You've got everything ahead of you. You've been given a second chance. How many people get that Mike? How many people have the chance to wipe the slate clean?'

'I'm staying at my parents' house. I'm forty years old and I'm living at home.'

'Only until you're back on your feet. You've had a lot of disappointments, a lot to deal with. But that's in the past now.' She's right, and I know I'll see that eventually but right now it all feels a bit too recent. 'Look, this might not be the right time but I've had an idea. Something we can work on together.' My heart sinks a bit.

'I don't know Angelique, I thought we'd just said we were over the whole entertainment thing.'

'It's nothing to do with magic or entertainment.' She says emphatically. Her voice becomes more confident and she leans towards me a little.

'There's a job going, near me, in this trendy little coffee shop. For a barista manager. It'd be perfect for you.' I have to admit I'm a little bit less than overwhelmed. It's not exactly a fresh start.

'I don't know, Angelique. I think maybe I'm done with coffee too.'

'But it will be great training for when you set up your own coffee shop that I'm going to help you with.' This I hadn't expected.

'My own coffee shop.' I say disbelievingly.

'Yes.' Her eyes are wide as she looks at me, expectantly. She has thrown a slightly curved ball.

'But I don't have any money and where would we..?'

'What about your redundancy money?'

'Ah, yes, well, that was a bit of a cock up as well.'

'Why? What happened?'

'Well it turns out you only get redundancy for the amount of time you've been in the current role, not the time you've been with the company and as I was only made manager two years ago, that's all I got.'

'Is that legal?' she says quickly. 'I'm sure that's not legal.'

'It is.' I say, wearily. 'It's in my contract. Which I only checked afterwards.'

'Jesus, they're good. Avoided having to fire you and only paying minimum redundancy.' There's a silence while she thinks and I stare out at the marshes. 'Have you been to the job centre?'

'Actually yes, that's something I have done. It wasn't too successful because I still have some savings and I'm not paying Mum and Dad so I don't qualify for any help. She was nice though, the lady. She wondered if I'd thought about retraining. Gave me a leaflet for the college in Southend, business management courses and all that. There are loans and grants. I might give it a go, could be useful.'

'Great! Work part time at the coffee shop, study in the evenings and afternoons you don't have a shift, we'll both save up and in a year we'll open a coffee shop.'

'You seem pretty confident about this.'

'Yes, I suppose I am. I see it as a sort of partnership; you managing the café day to day, me doing the branding and the marketing and making sure we're packed out and on trend.'

'But what about money?'

'Well, yes, there is that but we can both invest in it and we can always go to the bank. We'll have a whole year to figure it out together. What do you say?' I'm still hesitant. It does seem to be a reasonable plan and I would like to own my own business. And it needn't be anything like Java Hut. But I can't seem to summon up the energy right now. I want to keep Angelique in my life; she's become important to me, a kind of anchor. She's opened up parts of me I locked down a long time ago and I don't mind. She senses my hesitation.

'It makes sense Mike. We'll go to Shoreditch or Hackney where the bearded folk roost and give them fair trade, organic, roasted on site, with any kind of animal or plant based milk they want. The whole eco-mile.' She's getting animated now, I can hear the excitement in her voice. 'You know what you're doing Mike, you've done it for years and it would be yours. Ours. You can run it, manage it and be your own boss; do what you like in the evenings and the weekends - or whenever. I'll be like a sort of sleeping partner. I'll do all the marketing stuff and help as much as I can and invest what I can. We really could do this Mike.'

My mind is racing now. There's so much to take in, so much to consider. I'd need to line some staff up – Cathy from the Java Hut would be great and I know she'd love it; she's always had ideas about doing her own thing as well. I could give her a few shifts to start with and if she likes it, make her the manager. Maybe she could be some sort of partner in the long run. I've missed seeing her every day and this would be a good reason to get back in touch. Purely business of course. But I'd need to think about all of this, take some time, weigh up the pros and cons and see what the options are. I can't just dive straight in to something like this, make promises for a year's time I might not want to do then. Where would I live? Would I have an income? It sounded like quite a gamble. But we'd have a year to plan ...

'Yes.' I say, with a nod of my head.

'Seriously?'

'Yes.' I say again and I start to laugh, a huge great big release of a laugh that feels better than anything has for a while. 'Yes!' I say again, grinning at her like a kid and now she's laughing as well.

Broken Wand

57

We're warming up in the café in the visitor centre with tea and cake and neither of us has really said anything except to order, find a table and ask each other how our cake is. But it's a nice silence, the kind of silence that wraps around you like an extra blanket on the bed on a cold night. The café is busy, mostly families with young children who are far from being tired out by their rambles around the reserve, tucking in to sandwiches, crisps and bottles of juice. The noise isn't annoying though, it's nice to see them together, squabbling and laughing and making a mess.

'Oh, by the way, I've already thought of the name.' Angelique says, taking me by surprise, 'for the shop I mean.'

'Oh?'

'Mike's Magic Beans.' She spreads her hands wide in the shape of a rainbow, like she can already see it up in lights above the door. She's grinning and expecting an answer.

'Mike's – what?' She laughs and says 'Your face!' and I'm glad she's joking.

'OK, ground rules,' I say seriously. 'I'm granted full veto on the name.'

'Agreed.'

'And I'm involved in all the decisions and the day to day running of the place.'

'Agreed.'

'We have to make a huge profit in week one so I can find a place to live.'

'Um..'

'And no more secrets.'

'Agreed.'

'And I'd like you to come and meet my parents.'

'Oh – wasn't expecting that.'

'I just think it's time that they met you, seeing as we're going to be business partners as well as friends.' Now it's her turn to hesitate. 'No pressure, just an idea. I'll come and meet your Mum as well if

Broken Wand

you like; even things up a bit.' She doesn't reply to that, just smiles. 'I'll meet your parents,' she says, in a conciliatory tone, 'but you don't need to meet my Mum, not yet. You need training first.'
'Shall we go then?'
'What, to your parents?'
'Yes.'
'Now?'
'Is that OK?'
'Um, yes, I suppose so. Why not.'
In the car I think about whether to try and reassure her but then I think about the number of times I've underestimated her and decide not to. I glance over while we wait at lights and she smiles back. She's tucked the seatbelt under her arm so it doesn't cover her face. There must be a gadget you can buy to fix that, I think and make a mental note to look for one.

At Mum and Dad's we pull up the driveway. Angelique is furthest from the house and as I've parked a bit close to the garage, she comes round the back of the car to meet me. I let us in and as I do so, Mum appears in the doorway from the lounge.
'Oh it's you, thought I heard the -' she stops as she sees Angelique.
'Oh.' She looks at me with eyebrows raised.
'Mum,' I say, 'I'd like you to meet Angelique.' Mum's not quite sure how to react so sticks a hand out and just says:
'Nice to meet you.' Angelique takes her hand and says
'Likewise.' There's a bit of a pause until Mum gathers herself and invites us in to the lounge.
'Is Dad about?' I ask, almost redundantly as he was there when I left in his car this morning so not likely to have gone anywhere.
'Yes, he's in the garden, I'll call him.' Mum says, glad of an excuse to go for back up. Normally, she'd leave him pottering, knowing how much he valued his time in the garden at weekends after a week at work. While she goes outside I sit on the edge of an armchair and Angelique looks around. She sees a school photo of me displayed on the sideboard and walks over to it.
'It was the 80's.' I chip in before she can take the mick out of my haircut.

'It certainly was.' She looks at the other pictures and the china statuettes of shepherdesses and the ornate fruit bowl with its raised pattern of grapes round the edge.

'Impressive sideboard,' she says.

'Waste not, want not. Original 1950's.' I wonder what Mum's saying to Dad or if she says anything other than the bare bones, giving him no option but to come inside. I hear Mum come back into the kitchen before bustling through to the lounge while Dad is taking his outdoor shoes off in the utility room.

'Well this is a nice surprise,' she says, with a meaningful glance at me, 'do please have a seat,' she says to Angelique, more formal than she needs to be.

'You have a lovely home,' Angelique says to Mum, 'I really like your curtains.'

'Oh, yes, they're new actually. Thermal lined, it makes a real difference in the evenings.' She says this with a hint of pride and they smile at each other again. A splurge for Mum and Dad; they're hoping it will help keep the heating bills down.

'I'll put the kettle on shall I?' I say in a kind of 'isn't this fun' voice. As I leave the room I hear Angelique telling Mum how much she enjoyed Rainham Marshes and their voices continue as I make tea. Dad appears and I can see questions all over his face but he just nods and goes in to the lounge. I fill the teapot and decide to leave it to brew, following him in.

'Angelique was just telling us about her job' says Mum. 'It sounds fascinating.' I'm pretty sure Mum wouldn't have understood half of it but clearly Angelique was working her magic.

'Actually,' I begin, 'We've got a bit of news on that front.' I say, looking at Angelique for approval. She nods ever so slightly so I carry on.

'Oh?' Mum says and she tenses up, clearly not ready for another surprise. She's not saying anything just yet, not in front of a guest. Dad's already looking disappointed.

'I'm going to go to college for a year and do a business course. Then, if all goes according to plan, Angelique and I are going to open our own coffee shop.' They don't say anything. 'In East

London.' They still don't say anything and I can't work out if that's because they're too stunned or because they're waiting for me to add detail. But for the first time I don't feel like backing down. It matters what they think but not enough to change anything. I'm more sure of this than anything before. It feels like floodlights at the end of the player's tunnel at Wembley as they run out onto the pitch.

'Your own business, son?' asks Dad.

'Yes. It makes sense; I know how to run a café, I know the bits of the business side of it and I'm going to learn about the rest and Angelique knows all about marketing. Obviously we need to work through the finer details but we're really sure about this.'

'So no more magic?' Mum asks, trying to put it as gently as she can but still not able to keep the hope out of her voice.

'No Mum, no more magic.' She doesn't answer, just folds her hands in her lap and looks at me almost with gratitude. The emotion in her eyes is quite intense and for a second I think she's going to cry.

'Well I think that's a great idea,' says Dad. It takes a couple of seconds for this to filter through.

'You do?' I say, 'wait, do you mean the coffee shop or giving up magic?'

'Both as it goes. But the business mostly. Why don't you look at the details and let me know if we can help. You know I'm up for retirement early next year and there'll be some money. I'd like to help if I can.' I can't quite believe what I'm hearing.

'Are you sure?' I ask, 'I mean, that's for your retirement.'

'I won't be giving you all of it you daft sod, just what we can spare. But maybe it's time you did your own thing so, go for it.' I've never heard him say 'go for it' before and it sounds weird coming from him. He looks at Mum and I wonder if she's about to give him one of her 'we'll talk about this later' looks but she doesn't. Instead she looks at him with something like contentment on her face.

'I – that's really generous – thanks.' I manage to splutter. I look over at Mum and she smiles. I look at Angelique and she's smiling too.

Broken Wand

'Actually, your Dad and I have been talking and we're booking a holiday.'

'Oh?'

'Then we're thinking we might sell up and move to the coast somewhere, maybe the West Country, slow things down a bit once Dad's retired. Fresh start.' I'm taken aback by this and have so many questions but just then, over Mum's shoulder I see a familiar figure making her way down the drive opposite and across the road. She must have seen us arrive. To be honest, I'm surprised it's taken her this long. The doorbell rings and Mum goes to answer it. I stay quiet, just glance at Angelique and give a little smile. I can hear Mrs Peterson in the hallway.

'Just thought I'd pop over and drop this back,' she's saying, 'shall I pop it in the kitchen?' and she appears in the doorway, clutching a baking tin, mock surprised to see us sitting there. She looks at Angelique. 'Oh, I see you've got company,' she says, not offering to leave. We both smile at her. 'Hello Michael,' she says, taking a few steps in to the room, 'how are you?'

'I'm very well thank you Mrs Peterson.' She stands there, smiling inanely at me. 'And, how are you?' I ask.

'Oh yes, very well as well,' she gushes, still hovering. Mum is standing resolutely behind her. It must be taking every fibre of her being not to offer her a cup of tea. I decide to give her what she wants and not be rude.

'Mrs Peterson, this is my good friend and business partner, Angelique Watson.' I indicate her with an open hand, as if I need to point out the only other person in the room other than my Dad. Mrs Peterson is delighted to meet Angelique apparently and says so nice and loudly.

'Ah,' says Angelique, 'you must be the neighbour. Mike's told me about you.'

'All good I hope?' she says cheerily.

'Not all of it, but nice to meet you anyway,' she informs her and smiles her broadest smile, giving a cheesy sort of shoulder shrug as she does it. Mrs Peterson laughs as well but I can tell she's not really sure. I have to look down at my hands to hide my smirk. I feel like a teenager again, knowing I should be polite to my parents' friends but really not wanting to be. I decide to join in.

'Actually, we're just about to have tea.' I say and she smiles again and actually looks around like she might be about to take a seat. I can see the look on Mum's face so I add, 'so perhaps you can pop back later?'

'Oh, I see,' she says, looking a bit tight lipped at this. She glances at Mum who just smiles at her and she finally takes the hint. 'Right, well, nice to meet you,' she says to Angelique and breezily leaves the room, handing Mum the baking tin as she follows and shuts the door behind her. When Mum comes back in I think she's going to tell me off but in fact she just pauses by the door on the way to the kitchen and says 'thank you', looking at us each in turn, lingering on Angelique with an almost kind look on her face and half a smile before disappearing to fetch the tea. Even Dad's got a smile on his face.

Broken Wand

Broken Wand

Acknowledgements

With thanks to the following for their invaluable help and friendship: Gill Harvey and Jane Lee for editorial guidance, Helen Hawken, Mary Connolly and Justine Holman for their early reading and feedback; Anna Cottle, Chris Bowers and Mariateresa Boffo for late draft reading and feedback. Additional thanks to Stephen Grainger and Nick Barr for legal and policing advice.

And of course to Stephen, Freya and Bob the dog for steadying the ship and keeping me real.

Printed in Great Britain
by Amazon